THE MAGPIE KEY

CROW INVESTIGATIONS BOOK EIGHT

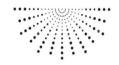

SARAH PAINTER

Published by Siskin Press Limited

Cover Design by Stuart Bache

For Dave. Always.

CHAPTER ONE

Tucked by the Regent's Canal, not far from the bustling hub of King's Cross Station, the sounds of London traffic were mixed with bird calls and the rustling of leaves. The canal water was still and black as oil and the sky had gone from orange to blazing red. Lydia couldn't tell if it was a spectacular sunset or her eyes playing tricks. She felt as if her chase across London, following Fleet to this place, had happened long ago. Her jangling nerves vied with an intense exhaustion and her eyes were gritty. The sense impressions from the man she had just realised was Fleet's father were strong and constantly changing, and her head was hurting from the effort of trying to parse them, while staying upright. It felt as if they had been facing this man, next to this shadowy waterway, for hours instead of minutes.

The man, on the other hand, was still smiling his bright white smile, casting a blinding light across her mind. Fleet moved to stand between her and his father, angling his body as if to hide her from view. 'I'm here. I'm ready.'

Ready for what? Dread cut through Lydia's jumbled thoughts and the bright light dimmed. 'Don't,' she said, reaching out to hold Fleet's sleeve. She wasn't sure what Fleet was planning, only that she didn't want him to do it.

Fleet's father reached a hand up under his hat and scratched his scalp. The curiously light eyes were assessing as he looked from Lydia to Fleet. 'This isn't the time, son,' he said, and turned to leave.

'I'm ready,' Fleet said again. There was a note of pleading in his voice that cut through Lydia. 'I'll come with you.'

Lydia tightened her grip on Fleet's sleeve. She knew that if he decided to move, it wouldn't stop him, but she wasn't going to let go voluntarily.

The other man was already stepping back onto the barge. 'All in good time.'

Fleet made a noise that wasn't a clear word. It was an animalistic noise of distress and every feather on Lydia's body lifted.

The man wasn't visible as the boat slid past them in the water. A sinister black shape against the dark canal. 'Come on.' Lydia was still gripping Fleet's sleeve and she tugged gently.

LYDIA WASN'T LETTING FLEET OUT OF HER SIGHT. He wasn't speaking, and his eyes were flat and empty as they walked back to collect their vehicles. At the last moment, Lydia decided to leave Aiden's car where it was. She walked with Fleet to where his car was parked in the multi-storey and got into the driving seat before he could object. 'I'm taking you home,' she said. What she didn't say was that she wasn't risking losing him if she went in a separate car. He looked physically healthy, but there was something terribly wrong. And he still wasn't speaking.

Fleet folded himself into the passenger seat and stared out of the window. Lydia navigated the traffic and felt the hum of adrenaline still coursing through her body. It was going to be one hell of a crash when she finally stopped. Once they crossed the boundary back into Camberwell, Lydia felt an easing of her tension. A subtle shift that was most welcome. Home.

Stopped at lights, she wondered if Fleet felt the same shift. Whether it would help him to open up. 'So, that was your dad,' she tried.

He didn't answer, didn't turn from the window.

The arc lights were on in the car park behind Fleet's building. Lydia parked underneath one and took a moment to text Aiden to let him know that his car was in a side street near to St Pancras.

Fleet didn't speak until they were inside his flat and, even then, it was a couple of short sentences. He was tired. He was going to bed.

Lydia brushed her teeth and changed into the sleep t-shirt she kept at the flat. By the time she joined Fleet in his bedroom, he was lying on his side facing away from her, his eyes closed.

She was sure he wasn't truly asleep, but it was a

pretty clear hint. There would be time to talk tomorrow, she decided. And fatigue was flooding her system as the adrenaline leaked away. The last thought she had before the darkness came, was to wonder why Fleet had been so keen to join his father. And why his father had changed his mind about taking him.

WHEN LYDIA WOKE UP THE NEXT MORNING, IT WAS still very early and she was alone in Fleet's bed. The shower was running and she stretched while she waited for him to return. When the water continued to run, she got up and pulled on her clothes, padding through to the kitchen to make coffee. She had been too tired and too freaked out the night before to notice, but something was abundantly clear this morning. The usually immaculate flat was a mess. Unwashed dishes littered the kitchen counter and there were piles of laundry and paperwork in the living area. It was probably a normal level of untidiness, but for Fleet it looked like a cry for help. She hadn't been spending as much time at Fleet's place recently and it had escaped her notice.

Lydia dialled Auntie's number while she waited for the coffee machine to do its thing. 'He's home. He's safe.'

Auntie thanked her, sounding even more formal than usual. Lydia put it down to her telephone manner, grateful that it had been a quick call. She wasn't doing anything wrong but felt uncomfortable at the thought of Fleet walking in and finding her updating Auntie on his whereabouts.

The Fleet that walked out of the bedroom five

minutes later was a pale imitation of the man she knew. His eyes were exhausted and the faint lines on his forehead seemed deeper than usual. He sat heavily onto the sofa and ran a hand over his head. 'I don't know what to say.'

Lydia passed him a mug of coffee and sat next to him with her own mug cradled in her hands. She curled her feet up underneath herself and kept her body facing his. Open. Calm. Ready to listen.

He sipped his coffee, made a face. 'That's strong.'

She waited. She could feel her tattoos moving on her skin, the power running through her blood and bone. All of it useless in this moment.

Still staring at his drink, Fleet said: 'I should apologise.'

Lydia wanted to tell him not to worry about it, but she kept quiet. She was determined to give him the space to speak, which was increasingly difficult as she wanted to ask a thousand questions. And the stress of the last few days was fraying her nerves. She felt the ache of unsaid words crushing her chest. The business with Daisy at Mikhail's house and the discovery that money had been transferred from Charlie's personal account, were momentous events that had been shadowed by her fear for Fleet. It felt strange that she hadn't been able to tell him, but his red-rimmed eyes and exhausted face kept her lips tightly compressed.

'I've not been doing so well.' Fleet couldn't look at her. He put his mug onto the low table in front of the sofa and leaned his head back on the cushions, staring at the opposite wall. 'I can't talk about it. I don't know how to talk about it.'

Lydia waited a while longer, sipping her coffee and feeling her synapses boot up. Eventually, when Fleet was clearly not going to start sharing, she decided on a different tactic. 'Let's get out of here. Go for a walk.'

He became instantly animated. 'I want to go to the heath.'

OVER THE LAST COUPLE OF WEEKS, FLEET HAD BEEN lying to Lydia. He had told her he was on a course for work in Coventry, but had been in London. When Lydia had tracked his car, it had been parked next to Hampstead Heath. When she had looked for him, the staff of a local pub recognised his picture. That Fleet had lied to her so fluently was still a bitter taste in her mouth. She knew he was in an altered state or, at the very least, going through an emotional crisis, but it still hurt. Now, he wanted to walk the heath with her. Auntie had told her that people came to the heath for two reasons – to lose themselves or to find themselves. Which was it for Fleet?

They parked in a residential street near the station at the southern end of the park. Fleet had visibly relaxed as soon as they had taken the first path into the heath. It had taken them up a gentle rise, along wide paths and past the deserted mixed bathing pond. Lydia had expected to see people splashing about as the air was already warm, but a sign informed her that it didn't open until seven.

The dawn sky over Hampstead Heath was streaked with pink and the air filled with the sharp scent of cut grass. Fleet held Lydia's hand as they walked together through the wide paths and cultivated parkland to one of the more open areas. Here, the grass grew long in places and was worn and scrubby in others. A stand of trees to their left creaked as if in a high wind, even though there wasn't so much as a breeze.

'It was here,' Fleet said, lifting his chin as if he was catching a scent.

Lydia inhaled, reaching out her senses. She got the usual impressions from Fleet, but nothing else. Then, a wisp of something unusual. She lifted her head and inhaled deeply. Cooking meat. Did someone have a disposable barbecue? Looking around, Lydia spied morning dog walkers, faces sleepy and clothing casual. Nothing out of the ordinary to see. It was definitely too early for barbecues, she realised. Still, there was the unmistakable smell of roasting meat. And, now that she stopped to pay attention, she thought she could hear music, very faintly. 'What was here?'

'The first place I saw him.'

Lydia knew she meant his father. She waited for Fleet to speak again, giving him time to gather his thoughts.

Instead, he started walking while he talked. He was leading her forward, up a gentle rise. 'You know I did a deal with Sinclair? She had heard that there was some-body new in the city. A whisper. CIs were talking about it in hushed voices and there had been an increase in Fox trouble.'

'The Family?' Lydia asked, checking that he hadn't just meant the urban animals which populated the whole of London.

He glanced down. 'I wasn't too concerned about that. Trouble for Paul Fox and his clan is fine with me, but it was affecting civilians. An increase in the number of missing person reports from the Whitechapel area. Uptick in street violence. Knife crime has been steadily increasing in the south for a few years, but we saw a surge in Whitechapel, the city, Limehouse, Hackney and even Islington.'

'Sinclair told me you weren't working for her, when you told me you were in Coventry.'

'I wasn't,' Fleet said sharply. 'I was doing my own job. I was using my service contact as a source.'

He sounded so much like his old self, the in-control copper, that Lydia wanted to cry. Instead, she tried to keep the conversation going. 'What led you here?'

Fleet had stopped moving and they stood, side by side, looking over the heath to the city skyline, under-pinned by a mass of mature trees and greenery. From this perspective they could have been deep in the coun-tryside, but Lydia felt like she could reach out and touch the buildings. She could see St Paul's and the Shard, could feel the busy streets and the crowded brickwork, the concrete and the hum of the traffic calling her back.

'I had a vision,' Fleet said eventually. 'I'd had a few dreams, but they were easier to ignore. But I couldn't with this one... I was wide awake. At work. In a meeting with three department heads and the chief superinten-dent. I don't know how long I zoned out for or what I said, but when I came back to myself... after... they were all looking at me like I'd sprouted a second head.'

'Feathers,' Lydia said, squeezing his hand in sympathy. 'That wasn't ideal.'

'No.' Fleet shook his head. 'Not really. I told them I hadn't slept and had a hangover. Luckily stress is high in the force, so they probably put it down to that.'

She expected a wry smile at that, but Fleet's face was blank. There was something fundamentally 'off' about his manner. It made Lydia want to run very fast, take flight, and punch something all at once. 'This increase in your visions. Do you think it's linked with your dad showing up?'

Fleet was gazing into the distance, looking at something that wasn't really there. His eyes snapped back to hers. 'You know they used to hold the Hampstead fair on the heath?'

'Yes,' Lydia said, surprised. 'I did a bit of research when you were missing.' *Visiting the heath and lying to me about it.* She didn't mention that she could smell the ghost of roasting meat. 'Coconut shies, shove ha'penny, skittles, all that.'

His face twisted. 'Sex, drugs, violence, more like.'

Okay. She waited. Fleet was still staring at the horizon, trance-like.

'He was here. It wasn't quiet like this. There were people everywhere I looked, a huge crowd. There was a dancing display. A bit like Morris dancing, but a load of the onlookers had joined in and it was chaos. Getting under each other's feet, bumping and cursing and falling over. Some of them had sticks and it was two steps from a brawl. Over that way,' he pointed, 'there was a hog roast and next to it, a man standing on a wooden box. He was wearing a black apron and he was selling a health tonic. An elixir of life, he called it. He had a wheeled cart which was painted all over with stars. It looked like a magician's prop, but he was doing a good trade.'

It sounded like a vivid dream. Except that she knew Fleet had visions. But his gift was usually for the future, not the past.

'It doesn't make sense,' Fleet said, looking around as if he expected to see the fair appear before his eyes.

'I smelled roasting meat,' Lydia said. 'Just now. I thought it was a barbecue but I don't see one. And it's far too early. Weird.'

He gave her a sideways look. 'Weird, like a supernatural thing?'

'Ghost roast. Yeah.' Lydia walked across the grass, inhaling deeply. Whatever she had sensed earlier, it wasn't there now. She thought about Fleet's vision and wondered if the spirits of Londoners past were crowded around her all the time and she only saw the select few on occasion, or whether Jason and the Fox and the woman at the bunker, were the only ones in existence. She preferred the latter idea. The thought that she was pressed from all sides by invisible spirits was unnerving.

She turned back to Fleet. He was crouched down, his hand on the grass. 'What is it?'

He straightened up, brushing his hands on his trousers. 'I don't know. How can I know?'

'Know what?'

Fleet held up a blade of grass that he had plucked, rolling it between his fingers. 'Whether this is real?'

'It's real,' Lydia said, stepping closer. She put her hands over his, willing him to take comfort from her confidence. She hadn't realised how bad it had become. Of course, he hadn't told her until now, so it wasn't exactly her fault, but the guilt stabbed her guts anyway. If she hadn't been so distracted, she might have noticed. Might have been able to help. Fleet had been struggling with his visions and she ought to have known. 'Can you pinpoint something that is different about your visions? Maybe that would help. Like, does time go weird or do things move strangely? Does it affect all of your senses at the same time? If you can work out what is missing in your visions, you'll have something concrete to look out for. A definite signal for what is a vision and what is reality.'

'I don't know. Some of them are like dreams. They just happen. Some feel like they are real and happening in the moment. Like I'm really there and I'm conscious. Able to make decisions and interact with them. Just like this,' he gestured between them. 'Just like we're standing here having this conversation.' His lips were compressed and a muscle in his jaw jumped. 'I think I'm dreaming and I'm waiting to wake up. Then I realise I'm sitting at my desk in work and it's been real the whole time. Or I'm driving my car but I haven't really been there. Not in my mind. And I don't know how long I've been in another place, or even how that works, how I haven't crashed into a pedestrian or a wall. I know I can't do that anymore; I know I need to tell work. I'm a liability. I feel like I can't stay in one place, like I'm being dragged around. Jumping in and out of scenes. I can't...' He closed his eyes, drawing in a long breath through his nose. 'I can't live like this. I can't do it.'

Hell Hawk. How had Fleet been functioning? 'I had no idea it was this bad.'

'Maybe it isn't,' he said abruptly. The words ripped from him as if they hurt. 'Maybe I'm just cracked.'

'No,' Lydia began.

His eyes were wide now. She could see his fear. 'I could be having a breakdown. I wouldn't be the first police to have a stress-induced mental-health crisis.'

'You're not ill,' Lydia said with certainty. 'This is real. It's not your mind playing tricks. You're stressed and that might be adding to the way you're feeling, but it's not the cause.'

He looked directly at her, his expression one of cautious hope. 'You really think that?'

'I know it.'

CHAPTER TWO

After walking around the heath for another hour, Lydia wondering when Fleet would have had enough of the green space but also not wanting to push him, they drove back to Camberwell. More silence in the car and Lydia wondered if she ought to turn around and start walking through the parkland again. They needed to eat though. Having seen the meagre pickings at Fleet's flat, she headed for The Fork.

Angel was back behind the counter and she grudgingly filled a plate with breakfast pastries for Lydia to take upstairs. 'I need that back,' she said, indicating the plate.

Lydia didn't even bother to give her a hard stare. She was just happy Angel was still willing to work in the cafe.

After she had made them both coffee and watched Fleet pick at a pastry, Lydia returned to her gentle questioning.

'You said he was there,' Lydia said. 'Who was there?'

'My dad.'

'That's good,' Lydia said, relieved. 'That means it was definitely a dream.'

'How so?'

Lydia didn't want to point out the obvious, but it seemed as if she would have to. 'The fair you saw was in, what, the eighteen hundreds? Nineteen hundreds? My history isn't great, but...'

'Yeah, it had a Victorian vibe, for sure,' Fleet said. 'But he was there, and it wasn't just a dream. I don't know what else to tell you.'

'Okay,' Lydia said. 'I believe you. He was there. Let's work out how.'

'Could have been astral projection,' Jason said.

Lydia jumped. She hadn't realised he was in the room.

Jason pushed at the sleeves of his suit jacket. 'Like, he might have projected himself into Fleet's dream.'

Lydia nodded. She had never heard of anybody doing that before, but that didn't mean it wasn't a real possibility.

Fleet was frowning.

'Jason's here,' Lydia said. 'Don't be alarmed.'

'I'm not,' Fleet said, glowering at the sofa.

Lydia decided not to tell him that Jason was leaning against the door frame. Well, towards the door frame, anyway. It looked odd as there was a clear inch of air between his body and the woodwork.

'I need to eat,' Fleet said. He glanced at the pastry he

had shredded to crumbs. 'I mean a meal. I can't remember when I last...' He trailed off, a deep frown creasing his forehead. 'Takeaway?'

'Sure,' Lydia said, still distracted by the problem.

Jason moved over to stand next to her and she felt the drift of cold air. It had ceased to bother her a long time ago and now was as comforting as Fleet's warmth. It was refreshing if anything. Especially on a day like this when the early morning sun was pouring in through the windows and heating the small flat. 'You okay?' Jason spoke quietly. Even though Fleet wouldn't hear him if he shouted. Probably.

'Fine,' Lydia replied absently.

'He looks upset.'

Lydia followed Jason's gaze to where Fleet was staring at his phone, scrolling through a menu and frowning as if he was taking a maths exam.

'I don't know if any of those places are going to be open yet,' Lydia said, realising that it was before ten in the morning. 'If you go down to the kitchen, Angel will warm up lasagne. Tell her I sent you.'

'You want some?' Fleet said, his eyes glazed.

'No, thanks.'

She waited for Fleet to leave and then indicated with her head that Jason should follow and headed to the roof terrace.

Outside, the sun was strong enough to make Lydia squint. The line of jackdaws on the railing flew up to the roof line and three crows arrived in their place. They perched, heads tilted, as if they had been invited to a meeting. Lydia greeted them politely and was only moderately surprised when Jason did the same.

'Fleet is having trouble with his visions. They're stronger. And more frequent.' She glanced through the window to check that Fleet hadn't returned. 'He says he doesn't even know what is real anymore. I don't know what to do to help him. I'm powering him up. Should I stay away?'

Jason hesitated before shaking his head. 'He wouldn't want that.'

Lydia felt a rush of relief. She didn't want that either. She still kept contact with her father to a minimum, just in case her presence powered him up and affected his mind the way it had in the past, before Smith used his healing power to bring him back to rationality. She didn't know if she would survive having to cut Fleet out of her life, too.

'I know what it's like to be unsure,' Jason said. 'When I used to disappear, sometimes I would come back and not be sure if I was back. Or if I was in a limbo state.'

'Did anything help?'

Jason shook his head. 'Nothing that will help Fleet. Getting stronger keeps me here. I don't disappear so I don't have to deal with the confusion. I'm sorry.'

Lydia patted his arm. 'That's okay. Thank you for listening.'

They stood in companionable silence for a few minutes. The birds on the terrace were grooming their feathers, ignoring the humans, and Lydia took several slow breaths.

Back inside the flat, Jason was still quiet. Lydia was about to ask him if he was all right, when he spoke.

'He needs an anchor.'

'What? Fleet?'

'Something that can keep him anchored in reality. A touchstone. You have your coin, right? That helps you to focus your power?'

It had done. These days, Lydia produced her coin for comfort and habit more than anything. Her control over her power had honed so that she could use it more easily and didn't feel the need for her coin in the same way. She still loved it, though. Still felt it as an extension of her body and a reminder of her true nature. 'You think Fleet needs a coin?'

'He needs something,' Jason said. 'It will be a constant, too. Something that can tell him whether he is in a vision or a dream or reality.'

Lydia didn't like the thought that Fleet was that uncertain. He had told her so, of course, but it felt different to have it described by a third person. And in such a matter-of-fact tone, too.

'Do you have one?'

Jason looked around. 'I have this place. It's my home and I know every part of it, every scratch on the walls, every creaky floorboard. I know the greasy patches coming through the fresh paintwork and the yellowing behind the white in the hallway. That's because the previous residents were heavy smokers, by the way. I know angles of every view from every window and the way the light changes in each of those views throughout the day in every season. I know this place so well and have catalogued every part of it so completely that I would know, in an instant, if I was in a poor facsimile. No illusion could ever withstand my scrutiny.'

Lydia nodded her understanding. On one hand, that kind of knowledge and certainty sounded nice. On the other, it reminded her that Jason was trapped in a cage. 'Do you wish you could leave?'

'No,' Jason said after a moment of thought. 'This is my home. And this is where I know I am real. It is the last place I held my love and the last place I drew breath.'

LATER, AFTER FLEET HAD EATEN A PLATE OF lasagne, Lydia had hoped it would be time for a proper talk. Instead, he had put his plate onto the floor next to the sofa and closed his eyes. He was shutting her out. Or he was so physically and mentally exhausted that he couldn't keep his eyes open. Hard to tell.

Her phone buzzed and she answered. Aiden had collected his car and wanted to know whether there was something else he should be doing. Lydia rubbed at her forehead, trying to ease the tension there, as she listened to his update. She knew she needed to tell him about Charlie and the way he had managed to interfere with the Family business and send orders to Daisy, even while locked away. But it wasn't a conversation to have on a mobile phone, and she was exhausted, pain pulsing behind her eyes. She made a mental note to have a sit-down with Aiden in the near future. Once she had dealt with the flight risk that was her boyfriend.

. . .

LYDIA SAT IN THE CHAIR BEHIND HER DESK AND watched Fleet dozing on the sofa. At least she thought he was dozing. His eyes were closed and his head tipped back against the cushions, but that might have been a ploy to avoid speaking.

They had slept, she had fed him, she had taken the gentle approach and walked around the heath. The anger and hurt weren't going to wait any longer. When she spoke, her voice was flat. 'You were going to go with him.'

Fleet's eyes opened and he met her gaze.

'Your dad,' Lydia said. 'You were going to get on that bloody boat and leave me.' She hadn't meant to say that last part. It had just popped out.

Fleet grimaced. 'Don't call him my dad. He's never been my dad. He's genetically my father, but that's it.'

Lydia nodded in acknowledgement. 'And yet, you were going to step onto that boat and sail away with him.'

'Is it still sailing when the boat doesn't have a sail? Should it be motoring?'

She wasn't in the mood to be playfully distracted. No matter how much Fleet clearly wanted to change the subject. 'That's something you can ask your dear old dad when the two of you fuck off into the sunset.'

Fleet flinched and Lydia felt like hell. She didn't apologise, though. Couldn't. Now that she knew Fleet was safe from immediate danger, the sense of betrayal had risen up like vomit. It was choking her throat.

'I wasn't going to...' He stopped, as if remembering that she had been there. That she had watched him and heard him. He swallowed hard. 'I don't know. It just seemed like the only option. A solution to all this.' He gestured to his head.

'Your solution to struggling with visions was to leave me and leave London with a man you do not know and who may very well mean you harm.'

'He said he could help me.'

'I bet he did.' Lydia couldn't believe how naïve Fleet was being, how unquestioning. It was unlike him and deeply frustrating. 'You know what your visions mean, don't you?'

Fleet's forehead creased. 'I know they are going to cost me my job. My life. My sanity.'

'Power,' Lydia said. 'They are a sign of power. And you know what Charlie was willing to do to get more power, to control those with power. What makes you think your father is any better than my uncle?'

'I don't think it's the same thing.' Fleet stood up and moved to the door, as if trying to signal the end of the conversation. 'You have actual powers, abilities. Maddie could control people's bodies, that's something people want. I don't know what the fuck is going on and whether anything is real. That's not power. That's a disability. You don't understand. He was going to help me. Look after me.'

Lydia was on her feet now, too. Fury pulsing through her body, multiple coins spinning around the room. 'What about me? I would look after you, if it comes to that. What about Auntie? Your true family? Did you think about us at all?'

Fleet didn't speak, the sound of the front door banging shut his only answer.

CHAPTER THREE

L ydia grabbed her keys and headed for the door, determined to follow Fleet. The panic was instant and all-consuming. She couldn't lose him again, she couldn't.

A cold hand on her arm stopped her before she reached the end of the hall. 'I've got to go after him,' she said, shaking free of Jason.

'Let him cool off,' Jason said. 'He's clearly embarrassed.'

'Embarrassed?' Lydia turned to face Jason, stunned into stopping moving. Fleet was extremely self-possessed, and one of the most mature and mentally robust people she had ever met.

'He's struggling,' Jason said. 'And he's not used to that. And he's doing it in front of you. He feels like he's let you down. He's ashamed.'

'How do you know that?'

Jason shrugged. 'It's how I'd feel.'

Lydia followed Jason back to the living room, still

fighting her desire to follow Fleet. 'What if he disappears again?'

'You can't watch him every moment.'

Jason went into the kitchen and she heard the fridge open and shut. 'I'm making you pancakes.'

Lydia wasn't hungry, but she trailed into the kitchen and snagged a cold bottle of beer. She wondered if Jason was right. Was Fleet embarrassed? Or was he running around the heath at this very moment, looking for his father, and not thinking about her at all? 'What is it about the heath?' She said out loud.

Jason was swirling batter in the pan and he didn't look around. 'He's had visions about it?'

'Yeah, stuff from the past, though, not premonitions. He said he saw his father at a Victorian fun fair.'

'Vivid dream?'

'Could be.' Lydia took a long swig of her beer. 'I smelled roasting meat when I was there, though, and heard some music. Old-fashioned music, maybe an organ.'

'Wait,' Jason waved the spatula, 'do you think he was seeing ghosts?'

'What Fleet described didn't sound like you. There was a whole crowd, and it sounded more like they were replaying a scene. Like a snippet from a film.'

Jason turned back to the pan so she couldn't see his expression. 'You don't think they are sentient?'

'No. I think they are just echoes. There must be something about that part of the heath. I looked it up. They held fairs there every year from the mid-eighteen-hundreds. All that pent-up excitement for a day off, all

24

the fights and romance that must have happened in that one place.'

'You could say the same about all of London. Why aren't you walking around seeing thousands of echoes every day?'

'I don't know,' Lydia said. She mentally crossed her fingers that didn't start to happen. It gave her a headache even to imagine it.

'Do you think I could see them? If I left the flat, I mean? There was that ghost at the bunker. And now you're saying there are hundreds on the heath...'

'Do you want to meet more people like you?'

Jason shrugged. 'It's just interesting to think about. Like, maybe it's all the same thing. Fleet's visions are future echoes and you and I see past echoes. Only not really echoes. Just everything that happens in the world is happening all at once, like there is no linear time. We're catching glimpses of what is really there and it's everything, all at once.'

Pain pulsed behind Lydia's eyes.

Jason flipped the pancake and got a plate down from a cupboard. 'Give Fleet time. He'll adjust.'

Lydia had told Fleet that he wasn't cracked, that he was perfectly sane, but what if this was Henry Crow all over again? Was her destiny to power up everyone close to her until they went insane?

LYDIA WAS NEVER QUITE SURE WHERE SHE STOOD with Paul Fox. But he had convinced Rafferty Hill to walk into a police station when she had asked for his

25

help, and she knew he would be keeping a tally. Fleet had mentioned 'Fox trouble' and increased violence in Whitechapel. The Foxes would be well aware of any trouble, but it would be a politically sensible move to visit Paul with the information. If she told him she had heard rumours concerning his Family, he might be more inclined to reciprocate with his own intel.

Paul Fox was sitting on a bench on the embankment. He stood up as Lydia approached and made an awkward move, as if he was going to lean in and kiss her cheek, and then stopped at the last moment. She hadn't seen him for weeks, but had mentally prepared herself for the hit of Fox magnetism. She let the impressions roll over her without resistance or panic. The flash of red fur, the warmth of an earth-packed den, and the pleasant stretch of muscles. Her stomach contracted with desire, and warm feelings spread over her body, making her skin tingle. She sat quickly and began speaking to cover her reaction. As usual, Paul was smiling slightly as if he knew exactly the effect he still had. Lydia had wondered whether her new tattoos would protect her from the Fox effect. Sadly, it seemed not.

'I have information you might be interested in.'

'So do I,' Paul said. 'But you go first.'

'First, I need to thank you for your help with Rafferty Hill.'

'That wasn't personal, I told you. Just keeping the peace.'

'I still appreciate it. Which is why I'm telling that I got a strong hit of Pearl from him.'

Paul tilted his head. 'From Rafferty? I didn't...' He

stopped himself. 'That's not surprising. Lots of performers have Pearl blood—'

'Not like this. I think he's really strong with Pearl mojo. He wasn't before, as far as I can tell, but when the Pearl King died...'

'The power passed on? Like an inheritance?'

'I think so. I don't know what it means. Rafferty is just an actor, and the Pearl Family are disbanded above-ground. Hopefully it's not going to be a problem, but I thought you should have a heads up.'

'Very kind.' Paul sounded neutral. 'Anything else?'

'I heard a rumour that there was trouble in Whitechapel.'

'Little Bird, are you worried about me?'

Lydia ignored that. 'And there's a stranger in town. He's not Family, but I got a hit of power from him.' She watched Paul carefully to see if he was surprised. He didn't visibly tense. Not so much as an eye flicker.

'Your turn,' Lydia said. She was watching him carefully, trying to assess if his calm was real or whether he was acting. It was entirely possible that Paul had already been in possession of the information. Foxes were tricky, and Paul was their leader. They had a history and an accord and, Lydia liked to think, a certain amount of mutual affection and respect, but that didn't mean she could let down her guard.

'I've heard rumours of a stranger,' he said musingly. 'You've met him, then?'

Lydia shrugged, indicating that she was done sharing. She wasn't going to tell Paul that the stranger was Fleet's father. Not until she knew what that bit of information meant. 'Are you going to tell me your news?'

'Twenty-three.'

'Sorry?'

Paul paused, studying Lydia's face as if he was wondering the same thing she had been wondering about him. Could she be trusted? Should he confide in her? 'There are twenty-three missing Foxes. They've just... vanished. Some left word with their families, friends, significant others. Others just disappeared. No warning, nothing.'

She frowned. 'The ones that left word. What did they say?'

'Nothing concrete. "Need to get out of London for a spell", that kind of thing. Vague.'

'Could it be coincidence? Just a group of people with different reasons for leaving London all heading off in the same few days?'

Paul looked at Lydia for a long time without speaking. Eventually she caved and said: 'Fine. Okay. Stupid question.'

'My brother. Jasper. I saw him last week and he didn't say a word. His missus hasn't seen him since Friday.'

There was no love lost between Lydia and Paul's siblings, but family was family and she felt for Paul. 'I'm sorry.'

He inclined his head, acknowledging her concession.

Lydia didn't know she was going to make the offer until the words were halfway out of her mouth. 'You want me to look for him?'

Paul's gaze warmed and Lydia felt it all the way from the top of her head to her toes. 'I appreciate that. But, no.' His smile was a phantom, but it was there. 'If Jasper doesn't want to be found, he won't be.'

There was another possibility. That he had been taken against his will, rather than disappearing of his own volition, but Lydia didn't want to be the one to voice that particular scenario. Paul wasn't stupid, and it would have crossed his mind already. There was no need to openly insult the head of the Fox Family unless she had to. Or wanted to. Instead, she focused on the most pressing point. 'You think the disappearances are linked to the new arrival?'

'That's my theory,' Paul said. 'I had heard lots of rumours. Lot of folk in the green spaces were unsettled. Nobody was saying anything coherent, though. Nothing concrete. I was starting to think it was just a story, a new urban legend. But now... My people don't leave London like this without good cause. Foxes go to earth. They stay in their dens.'

And the Foxes' dens were in Whitechapel. Lydia nodded her understanding.

'There is something else,' Paul said. 'It's a small thing.'

'I doubt that.'

His smile widened and Lydia mentally kicked herself. The man could make anything sound filthy. 'What is it?'

Paul took something from his jacket pocket and dropped it onto the bench between them. It was a small crow wing feather. Dark dusty grey, shading to black along one edge. 'Care to explain?'

Lydia tore her gaze from the feather. 'It's from a crow.'

'I know that, Little Bird,' Paul said. 'Touch it.'

Paul knew about her ability, so she told herself not to react. Paul seemed genuinely agitated, which was unusual. 'Where did you get this?'

'Is it one of yours?'

Lydia reached out a finger and gently brushed the barbs of the feather. The hit of Crow was faint, but unmistakable. A member of her family had handled it at some point in the not-too-distant past. Hell Hawk.

'Well?'

'Maybe,' Lydia said. 'It's hard to tell.'

'I found it on my pillow.'

An image of Paul Fox in bed rushed into her mind. Naked. Tangled in sheets. She swallowed hard.

'And you know where I live.'

'I do not,' Lydia said. Back when they were having an ill-conceived fling in her rebellious youth, they had spent private time in the dark corners of pubs and clubs.

'You know my bar.'

'If that's where you sleep, it's news to me.'

Paul studied her for a few minutes. 'You had better not be lying to me.'

'Why would I do this? If I wanted to annoy you, I'd just call.'

He nodded at the truth of this statement. 'So, somebody in your family is looking to make trouble. You need to get your den in order.'

CHAPTER FOUR

The secret intelligence service building used to be at 54 Broadway. The sign outside said the 'Minimax Fire Extinguisher Company', but it was the worst kept secret in London. You could ask any taxi driver to take you to MI5 and they would drive you straight there. These days, the outward face of the secret service wasn't even trying to hide. Their buildings were listed on Google maps and they had shiny websites and graduate training schemes. The truth, however, was that this was just as much of a front as the old fire-extinguisher company days. Everything real and vital about the service was hidden. And when it came to detention and research, this was very literal. There was a warren of tunnels and rooms stretching beneath the blocky building of MI6 next to the Thames, linking to MI5 and Whitehall. When people talked about the corridors of power, they weren't usually thinking about the conduits running beneath the streets. But they should have been.

Lydia had walked past the MI6 building and across

Vauxhall Bridge, the sight of the distinctive angular building and the knowledge of what it contained setting off her chain of thought. Nonetheless, she hadn't expected to see the familiar figure in the chiller aisle of the supermarket. It was like the woman had tuned into her inner thoughts and appeared like a genie.

Sinclair was wearing one of the woollen draperies of which she was so fond. The ones which made her look both comfortable and elegant, and could, it occurred to Lydia in that moment, hide an impressive array of weaponry. She was studying the dairy section with intense focus. A hand darted out and seized some Gouda. 'This is supposed to have caramel notes. I'm not entirely sure about it, myself, although the Norwegians do a brown cheese which is supposed to taste like savoury toffee, so I suppose there is precedent. I'm being prejudiced over the word as it seems to crop up everywhere now, have you noticed? Salted caramel this, salted caramel that. What's wrong with a bag of crisps and a bar of Dairy Milk?'

Lydia waited, not saying anything. Sinclair was using a technique to make herself appear unthreatening and distracted. Despite knowing this, Lydia could feel herself wanting to be dragged in. Sinclair was charismatic. She also didn't have a basket. 'This isn't a coincidence.'

'Naturally not,' Sinclair said. She raised an eyebrow. 'Oh, don't give me that look. You must know I keep tabs on you.'

If Lydia had thought about it, she would have assumed as much. And the stab of frustrated anger was the reason she didn't think about it. She forced herself to relax, breathing gently in through her nose and letting it out slowly. She picked up a package of garlic and herb soft cheese and put it into her basket. 'You best spit it out, I've got a packed day.'

Sinclair glanced into her basket. 'I don't recommend those bagels. Stuffed with preservatives. They have fresh ones at—'

'I'm really not in the mood for this,' Lydia interrupted. She was sick of secret-service agents who pretended to be your friend, and all the distracting small talk meant to lull and confuse.

'Very well,' Sinclair straightened up. 'Meet me outside in five minutes. Bench on this side of the river, next to the Millbank pier.'

Lydia moved past Sinclair, holding her basket out of the way. 'I won't, thanks.'

'It's in your best interests,' Sinclair said. 'It concerns your uncle.'

'Those two sentences are mutually exclusive,' Lydia said. She was proud that her voice didn't betray the way her heart rate had kicked up. The accountant, Jo, had told Lydia that money had moved between accounts and the only person with that access was Charlie. Either Charlie had broken free and Sinclair was trying to find out if Lydia knew anything about it, or she had no idea that Charlie had made connections to the outside world, which meant she wasn't doing a very good job of keeping him locked up. Neither was good.

Sinclair had stopped speaking while a man carrying his groceries awkwardly in his arms rather than using a basket selected a block of mature cheddar. Once he moved on, she took a step closer to Lydia and lowered her voice. 'We keep an eye on a number of key people. A disturbing number of these people have left London.'

'When you say key people...'

Sinclair gave her a quick, irritated glare. She clearly hated being forced to specify. 'There are certain people who are high up in their particular specialities. Mostly criminal. All rich and powerful. The kinds of people who feel the way the wind is blowing and have the contacts and resources to get out of the way before the hurricane hits. They're also the kind to work out how to make a profit on the shattered lives left behind.'

'You're angry.'

'Yes,' Sinclair said. 'And I'm tired. I've been doing this job for a very long time and we're still not winning. Not really.' She sighed. 'This really is a conversation for another location.'

Lydia ignored her. 'Who is "we"? The British government?'

'Whether or not you believe in this country and the rights and freedoms it represents, you must surely concede that there are a good many ordinary people who do not deserve to be killed or extorted or to live in fear.'

'You're the champion of the ordinary person?' Lydia didn't even try to hide her sarcasm.

Sinclair darted a look that was difficult for Lydia to read. 'Well, no. Perhaps I wouldn't go that far. But what do my personal motives matter? What do the service's motives matter? Surely we find ourselves aligned when the rats are deserting the ship we are both sailing?'

Lydia winced at the metaphor. She didn't want to think about boats of any kind.

Sinclair shook her head sorrowfully. 'I'm not your enemy.'

Well, she wasn't going to reply to that. A woman paused by the dairy cabinet and began flinging individual pots of crème caramel into her basket, and Lydia took the opportunity to walk away.

Lydia finished her shopping on autopilot. She wanted to abandon her basket and run from the building, but she forced herself to go through the checkout. She refused to look around for Sinclair. Knowing that she was being watched, she was determined to appear unfazed. Outside, the sun was shining in a bright blue sky and the flow of people on the pavement were wearing short sleeves and t-shirts. It was a normal weekday in the city and there was no reason for Lydia's throat to have closed up with panic. She forced herself to walk, not run. She headed away from the river, towards Victoria Station.

On the one hand, getting close to Sinclair would be a good idea. If there was a chance she could influence Charlie's future prospects, maybe even have contact with him and see if she could head off his interference, it could be worth it. On the other, she trusted Sinclair and the rest of the secret service as much as any sensible person trusted a shadowy government organisation with the power to issue kill orders.

Lydia wasn't paying full attention to her surroundings, so it took her by surprise when a magpie landed on the pavement in front of her feet. She stopped in time before kicking the bird. 'Feathers!'

The magpie had something in its beak. It dropped it on the ground between Lydia's feet before glaring at Lydia.

'Sorry,' Lydia said to the magpie, ignoring the man who had been forced to swerve around her on the pavement.

The magpie ruffled its feathers and angled its head, the glare somehow intensifying.

'Uh. Thank you?' Lydia tried.

Giving her the kind of look Lydia associated with her mother during her teenage years, the magpie took flight. Its wingtip caught Lydia's face as it passed her. A tiny, feathery slap. Rude.

The object on the pavement was a small, tarnished key. It lay in Lydia's hand, reproaching her with her lack of knowledge. It looked old and was made of a dull-looking metal. That was about all she had. It had a plain loop at one end and a simple head with just a couple of teeth. It was only an inch and a half long and looked like it belonged to an antique cabinet. Why the magpie had brought it to her was a mystery.

'Well, that's something you don't see every day.'

Sinclair. The woman was tenacious.

Lydia pocketed the key and turned to face Sinclair.

She was scowling. 'You made me follow you and I'm not wearing the right shoes.'

'I've got nothing to say to you.' They were at a wide stretch of paving. Rental bicycles were lined up on one side and a tall office building of mirrored glass was on the other. Lydia moved over toward the building so that she wasn't standing in the flow of pedestrian traffic and took out her phone.

'You look tense.' Sinclair was next to her, regarding her in the reflection of the glass.

'Being stalked by the secret service isn't exactly relaxing.'

Sinclair gave one of her trademark faint smiles. 'I need your help.'

'I believe you already owe me. For the Churchill War Rooms.'

'That account is settled,' Sinclair said. She took her own phone out and pretended to study it.

Looking at Sinclair reflected in the mirrored glass, she looked like a stylish mature woman, peering at her phone to read an email. Harmless.

'I hoped that would show you the benefits of working together on occasion. I have access to considerable resources.'

'Let me guess, it's a matter of national importance?'

'It might be. I can't say, yet. It's more a budgetary concern, at the moment.'

Lydia watched her own face in the window. She looked mildly bored, which was perfect. It might not be cool to practise expressions, but it clearly paid off. 'I don't really see...'

Sinclair broke in. 'The Service is spending a fair amount on keeping your uncle secure and comfortable.'

The image of a dark cell flashed into Lydia's mind. Manacles chained the wall, an emaciated prisoner and rats scurrying across the bare stone floor.

'We are getting some information and, thanks to your corroboration, I know that some of it, at least, is accurate. However,' Sinclair turned to face Lydia, 'I have a review coming up and I need to justify the continuing expense in front of a committee.'

'What does that mean?'

Sinclair held up her phone as if searching for a signal. She didn't look at Lydia, speaking to the sky instead. 'What do you advise? Should I maintain your uncle as an asset or cut my losses?'

'You're asking me?' Lydia didn't bother to hide the disbelief in her voice.

'As I explained to you before, I am not Gale. This is not my personal crusade. I am merely a cog in the machine and very keen to do my part.'

More false modesty bullshit. Classic Sinclair. Lydia forced herself to shrug. She didn't believe for a single second that this was a genuine question. She didn't know Sinclair's angle and, frankly, wasn't even sure she could be of use. 'He's not my problem anymore. You must do what you feel is best.'

'So it wouldn't be a problem for you if he is set free?'

Which told Lydia that, despite his meddling, Charlie was still currently locked up. 'Why are you asking for my opinion? What could I possibly say that would help you with your committee meeting? You have Charlie Crow. What else do you need to know?'

It was Sinclair's turn to look irritated. 'You and your bloody uncle. It would be easier to be rid of the lot of you.'

'But I'm one of those citizens you're so keen on protecting,' Lydia said, smiling sweetly.

Sinclair pursed her lips.

She knew one thing. She needed to speak to Charlie, to find out what she could about his plans, his capabilities. Not that he was likely to tell her without leverage, but maybe she could glean something. The downside was that it involved doing the one thing she really didn't want to do. See him.

CHAPTER FIVE

The public-facing part of MI6 could have been any corporate entity, if it wasn't for the abundant security that was clearly visible to anybody who knew enough to look. Lydia wasn't worried by the cameras that she knew were trained on every visitor, knowing that her Crow nature would cause any footage to be fuzzy. She was more concerned by the concealed weapons and highly trained fighters. Her senses were in overdrive, but she wasn't getting 'Family' from the smooth-faced man who had greeted her or the intense woman who was now leading her toward her meeting with Sinclair.

Speak of the devil, the woman was striding down the corridor ahead of them. Seeing Sinclair in her work environment sent a peculiar shiver through Lydia's body. There was power in a person's roost, and Sinclair was letting Lydia see hers. What Lydia didn't know was how this played into Sinclair's own agenda. Perhaps Sinclair had just got sick of running around the city to find Lydia, so she was hoping that this olive branch would buy her information in the future.

'I'll take things from here,' Sinclair said, nodding to Lydia's escorts. They melted away and Lydia was left with the impression that she was playing a role in a carefully planned act. Sinclair wanted her to see a curated version of the secret service for reasons Lydia could only guess at. She was under no illusions that she was going to be shown anything of real relevance or secrecy, and truly did not expect Sinclair to fulfil her promise and allow Lydia access to Charlie. Then, Sinclair blew that theory out of the water.

'You want to skip the tour and just get to your uncle, I assume.'

If Lydia had been drinking coffee, she would have spat it out in surprise. As it was, she swallowed some saliva the wrong way and spent a few minutes in undignified coughing.

Sinclair waited, a single eyebrow raised.

'You're being serious?'

'This way,' Sinclair began walking and Lydia kept pace.

They wound through identical corridors, lined with closed doors and the sort of hush that comes from excellent soundproofing, and descended several levels in a lift. Lydia didn't like going underground, didn't like to be so far from the wide open sky, and it hit her that if Charlie was still incarcerated, then he might not have felt fresh air for weeks. Maybe even months. Her shoulders itched with the need to spread her wings and she squeezed her coin to ease the feeling.

When the lift doors opened, it was clear they were in a very different part of the building. Two men in combat gear were guarding a metal door, which was locked with a biometric scanner. Sinclair pressed her fingers to the screen, and the door unlocked with an echoing thunk. Ignoring the guards, she gestured for Lydia to go ahead.

The inner chamber had another guard. This man was sitting with his feet up on a small table and his boots hit the floor the moment he clocked Sinclair. 'Ma'am.'

'How is he today?'

'Quiet,' the guard said. 'Calm.' His military training wasn't enough to stop him looking curiously at Lydia.

When the inner door was unlocked, Lydia realised that she had still been expecting this to be some kind of elaborate hoax. More play-acting from Sinclair for reasons unknown. To see how Lydia would react or to see if she wanted contact with Charlie, perhaps. When the blast of 'Crow' hit her senses, she rocked back slightly. In real terms, Charlie was nothing like as powerful as Maddie, but he was definitely the strongest Crow she had been near since she had jumped from the hospital roof with her deranged cousin.

Charlie Crow was sitting at a small table, a paperback in one hand and a pair of wire-framed glasses perched on his nose. He placed a bookmark between the pages before closing the book and placing it on the table. 'Hello, Lyds. You look well.'

There was no trace of the shark smile. Charlie's expression was mild, his gaze soft. Lydia tried very hard to swallow, but there was a lump in her throat. Charlie had tried to kill her once, but he had been her uncle for a long time before that. Her blood was singing, her feathers raised, and she could feel talons on a branch. The urge to roost. Family.

'Lydia was under the impression that you were no longer with us,' Sinclair said. 'I thought it best to disabuse her of that notion.'

Charlie paused a little too long before nodding. Lydia wondered what drugs they were using to keep him calm and how much they were affecting his cognitive ability.

'I'll leave you to it,' Sinclair said. 'You have five minutes.'

Lydia felt a spike of fear as Sinclair retreated behind the door. The cage was locked. She pushed aside that unhelpful thought, shoved her coin into her pocket and took the spare seat opposite Charlie.

'Do you have many visitors?'

A slow blink. 'No. That chair is new. They brought it today, I think. For you. They'll probably take it away when you go.'

'This place doesn't look too bad.' Lydia wished she could reach out and pluck the words out of the air. A cage was a cage was a cage. Never mind that Charlie had a double bed with plenty of pillows and a desk lamp for reading, and even a small kitchenette in the corner with a kettle. Lydia's mind snagged on that. A kettle could boil water. Which would make a handy weapon. They really had decided that Charlie wasn't an immediate threat.

He must have been watching her look around as he

said: 'I got the kitchen for good behaviour. There's a mini fridge and a microwave in the cupboard. They bring me plenty of food and give me choices, but there is something about making myself a drink. They say it's control and normality. Important for psychological reasons.' He shrugged. 'I just know I like it.'

His voice was scratchy at the edges. She wondered if that was from lack of use, or a planned affectation. He might be caged, but he was still dangerous. Of that, she was sure.

'How is my café?'

Lydia didn't say anything. She didn't have long and she knew that every word was being recorded, even if the video footage would be fuzzy. She tapped the table between them and, when Charlie's gaze was drawn to her hands, she turned her hand palm-side up. She had drawn a daisy in pen and a question mark. Not much of a code, but she hadn't wanted to risk him not understanding.

He stared at her palm for a long moment. When she could finally see into his eyes, they were flat and unresponsive. Again, Lydia wondered what drugs they were giving him. How present was Charlie? Or was this eerie calm a façade?

'I know it was you,' she said.

Nothing.

'You're never getting out of here. It doesn't matter how good your behaviour. I'm not fooled by this act.' She waved a hand to indicate Charlie. 'And they aren't, either.' She looked at one of the visible cameras. 'If you want more privileges, a better quality of life, bigger accommodation, you need to answer my questions.'

Then she saw it. A flicker on Charlie's face. The expression was so fleeting she almost missed it, but it was unmistakable. The real Charlie had emerged for a brief moment. Lydia sat back in her chair, allowing herself to smile. She kept her eyes locked with her uncle's and nodded. 'I don't know how you are doing it, but this is your friendly warning to stop.'

Charlie smiled his shark smile, and Lydia felt her skin prickle from her scalp to her toes. He didn't say anything, and, after a minute, she stood up. At the door to the cell, she knocked on the metal. A panel slid open and she saw the guard's face. 'I'm done.'

When Charlie spoke, his voice was clear and deep. No scratchiness, no hesitation. 'I'm coming for you.'

OUTSIDE THE CELL, LYDIA HELD OUT HER ARMS FOR a pat down. She assessed the guard as he worked. 'Is this your regular shift?'

'Yes, Ma'am?'

'How has he been?'

'He's no trouble. Now he's settled in.'

There was the taste of feathers on Lydia's tongue. She wanted to flip her coin, but was sure that Sinclair was hovering nearby. She didn't want to give her a show, didn't know how much of this visit was a trap for her and how much was a power play with Charlie. Her coin was in her hand, though, and she squeezed it as she asked her next question. 'You're the one passing messages for him, aren't you?'

The guard jolted. He began to shake his head and she squeezed her coin more tightly.

The shake became a jerky nod. Then his face drained of colour. 'I don't know what you are talking about.'

'Just making conversation,' Lydia said brightly as Sinclair walked through the main door.

'Are you ready to go?'

'Yes,' Lydia said, addressing Sinclair. She didn't look at the guard as they left, suddenly feeling a prickling of fear. She wanted out of this place with its stale air and locked doors.

On their way back to the surface, Sinclair kept quiet. Lydia hated to admit it, but she kind of missed the usual flow of small talk. She knew that Sinclair used it as a misdirection tactic, but the silence was unnerving.

It took everything in Lydia's power not to break into a run as they neared the exit. She handed her visitor pass back in at the front desk and turned to thank Sinclair for allowing her to see Charlie.

Sinclair had a strange, assessing expression. 'You see that he is quite safe.'

'I do.' Lydia inclined her head. 'You have no argument from the Crow Family with regard to his care.'

Sinclair smiled thinly. It didn't meet her eyes.

'One thing, though,' Lydia said. 'He doesn't need those glasses. Crows have excellent eyesight.'

. . .

Jason was waiting for Lydia when she got home. She did an automatic check of the surfaces, looking for hot chocolates, bowls of cereal, pancakes, or any other signs of distress. Jason might not have been capable of eating food, but he used preparing snacks as a form of stress control.

'Did you see him?'

Lydia nodded. 'I did.' Charlie had killed Jason, but that was a fact she had kept to herself. Having encouraged Lydia to look into his untimely death, Jason decided at the last moment that he didn't want to know the details. He had been worried that it would give him closure or some such thing and make him 'move on'. Lydia assumed he still felt the same way and would ask if he changed his mind. None of which meant that Jason was Charlie's biggest fan.

'So, he's alive.' Jason was standing in the doorway to the kitchen, his feet very slightly above the carpet. He seemed to realise the moment that Lydia noticed and he sank down an inch.

'Almost obscenely so,' she replied. 'He's got a mini fridge.'

Jason's eyes widened. 'He's not shackled to a wall in a dungeon, then. Shame.'

Charlie had tried to kill Lydia, and it seemed as if Jason was still holding a grudge. Lydia wondered how he would react to the news that Charlie had killed him and his new bride on their wedding day. 'He's play-acting,' she said. 'Pretending to be harmless.'

'What can he do from inside that place?'

'I'm pretty sure his guard has been passing information and orders outside. In return for money, I would assume. Unless Charlie has used some Crow whammy on him.'

'Are you going to confront Daisy? Or the rest of the family?'

'No.' Lydia threw herself into her desk chair. 'Maybe. I don't know what good it would do. I need to think.'

'I'll make some toast,' Jason moved into the kitchen. 'Unless you want pancakes?'

'I'm fine,' Lydia called back, knowing it wouldn't make any difference. Sure enough, she heard the sound of the fridge opening and the frying pan hitting the stove top.

Lydia was still trying to work out how she felt. She had suspected that Charlie was alive. It had seemed as if he had been passing on instructions, causing problems for the Crows, presumably to undermine her position as leader of the Family. But suspecting her uncle was alive, and looking into his flat shark eyes, were two very different things.

And then there was the question of Aunt Daisy and Uncle John. She didn't know if the latter had also been doing Charlie's bidding, but she had caught Aunt Daisy visiting the secret home of a known Crow employee, a man who had been following orders to leave threatening notes and spread fear and dissension. Aunt Daisy was her enemy, same as Charlie was her enemy, but she was still family. Charlie might have stepped so far over the line that she had cut him from her heart, but Daisy had not. As far as Lydia knew. And she could understand Daisy's fury. It was a mother's fury. Maybe it would burn itself out soon? Maybe Daisy would settle down and accept Lydia's position as the head of the family, given enough time and understanding?

Lydia didn't have enough experience in this area to know, but luckily she had an expert to hand. Emma picked up quickly. 'You okay?'

'I'm fine,' Lydia said, stung that Emma assumed it was an emergency. A reminder that she was overdue a visit to the cosy family home in Beckenham. And long overdue a boozy night of laughter with Emma.

'Are you coming home soon?'

'Not for a bit,' Lydia said. 'Things are hectic. Can I ask your opinion on something? It's about my aunt.'

'Daisy?'

'Yeah. She hates me.'

A short silence. 'What do you want to know?'

'If there's any hope, I guess. For us to get along. After... You know.'

Emma did know. Lydia had killed her cousin Maddie, Aunt Daisy's daughter, to keep her and her children safe. 'Hang on, I'm in Waitrose.'

There was a pause, with just the sound of breathing and the beeping of a checkout. A few moments later, Emma's voice was back. 'You know you did the right thing. I can never thank you enough for—'

Lydia broke in. 'Don't thank me. I didn't have a choice.'

'I don't think that's true and I'm still grateful. I'll

answer your question, though. If somebody hurt my babies. If somebody,' a hitch in her voice as if she couldn't bear to say the word out loud, 'killed my child.' Another pause, then Emma's voice, colder than Lydia had ever heard it. Cold and certain. 'I would burn the whole world to make them suffer.'

CHAPTER SIX

The next morning, Lydia woke up early thinking about Charlie. She felt as if he had been in her dreams, although she couldn't remember them now that she was awake. Still, his presence seemed to fill the room. The curtains were shut against the morning sunshine, but they were too thin to do the job properly and Lydia knew she wasn't going to get back to sleep.

Fleet was just waking up, so she went and made coffee. Jason was sitting on the sofa with his laptop, deep in concentration. He didn't even get up and take over making the drinks, so she knew he was fully absorbed in whatever he was doing.

In the kitchen, she tried to push thoughts of Charlie from her mind, but it didn't work. She had hoped that seeing him securely locked up would have allayed her fears, reduced the size of his threat in her mind, but it hadn't worked that way. Seeing him had brought up so many memories. And reminded her of his dangerous intensity. He wasn't going to stop coming for her, not until he was six feet under. By the time she had made two coffees, she knew what she had to do.

She passed Fleet a mug and sat on the end of the bed, cradling her own. 'I've got to deal with some Family business today,' Lydia said. 'Do you have any particular feelings I should know about?'

Fleet paused, his face going still while he looked inward for a moment. Then he shook his head. 'Nothing is leaping to mind.'

'Nothing about Daisy?' Lydia pressed.

'You're worried about her?'

'Her and John. I know Daisy has been doing stuff for Charlie.'

They hadn't had time to talk since Lydia had discovered Daisy at Mikhail's house and confirmed her suspicion that Daisy was running errands for Charlie. Fleet frowned as he processed the news. 'How is Charlie delivering orders to Daisy?'

'He has human guards. My guess is one of them has been corrupted. Charlie can be very persuasive. And I think Sinclair consistently underestimates him.' Lydia was relieved that Fleet was asking pertinent questions, although he still seemed vague and disconnected. He didn't ask how she knew about Charlie's prison arrangements, and she didn't tell him that she had been into MI6.

Fleet nodded his understanding. 'I haven't seen anything involving them.'

'Okay. Thanks.'

Fleet took a sip of his coffee.

Lydia was just feeling hurt that he wasn't asking

54

anything else about Daisy and Charlie, like how she knew about Daisy, and whether she was okay. She had never required his concern before and it made her feel weak and needy, but it seemed the further away he felt, the closer she wanted to cling.

'You can use your power on your aunt and uncle, right? Control their bodies?'

Was it her imagination, or did Fleet sound slightly resentful? Had he felt her attempt at the canal? That was yet another thing they hadn't talked about properly. 'I could,' she began cautiously, 'but it's not something I want to make into a habit. Especially not with family.'

'Family, huh?' Fleet said. 'What about your partner?'

Feathers. 'I was scared for you,' Lydia said carefully. 'I was trying to protect you.'

He handed Lydia his coffee mug and threw the covers off, getting out of bed. 'I can't talk to you when you're like this.'

'Like what?' Lydia was genuinely bewildered. She usually knew when she was being a dick.

He waved his hands. 'Queen of the world.'

'That's hardly fair...' Lydia began, but Fleet had stalked out of the room. The bathroom door banged shut and, a moment later, the shower began to run.

Fleet had always been so even-tempered. Now, he seemed on edge all the time. They had been awake together for less than five minutes and they had argued. She knew he was tense about his father and struggling with his visions, but she didn't know how to help. She knew one thing for certain: she didn't feel like the queen of anything.

. . .

LYDIA WENT TO FIND JASON, HOPING FOR A sympathetic ear. He was standing in the alley that ran behind The Fork. He jumped when Lydia opened the door and found him there. 'I'm pretty sure you're supposed to be the scary one,' she said, patting his arm. Her own troubles were momentarily forgotten in the peculiarity of his expression. 'What's up?'

He turned slowly. 'Sorry. What?'

'What are you doing out here?' Lydia looked up and down the deserted alley. Something rustled in the pile of bin bags behind the metal bin. Just the wind, Lydia decided. Definitely not a rat.

'I was just...' He trailed off.

'Testing yourself?' The last time they had left The Fork together, Jason had made it to the end of the alley before becoming translucent and incorporeal enough to hitch a lift in Lydia's body. A side effect of being powered up by living with a human battery.

'No. Not exactly.'

Jason was still looking away from Lydia, down the alley. 'I thought I heard something. That's all.'

Lydia waited. Jason was shimmering slightly in the bright noonday sun, but she couldn't tell if it was the effect of seeing him outside or whether he was upset.

'There,' he paused. 'Did you hear that?'

'No. What is it?'

'It sounds like a kid. Little girl, I think, but it's hard to tell. Could just as easily be a boy.'

'Someone like you?' Lydia was proud of herself for using tact and not asking 'someone dead'.

'Yeah. Maybe. They keep going in and out. Like a radio station going out of tune. I can't stay locked on...' He stopped speaking, head tilted like he was listening intently. 'There. Again. Did you hear that?'

Lydia closed her eyes and listened. She could hear the traffic and, in the distance, a siren. The birds hanging out on the roof of The Fork were chattering and calling, the sound familiar and comforting as the hum of conversation, but nothing else. She opened her eyes. 'I'm not getting it. Sorry. Do you think you've found an echo?'

Jason shuddered, his whole body rippling. And then he disappeared.

It had been a while since he had done that and Lydia stared at the patch of air where he had been a moment earlier, just in case he blinked back again. He didn't.

When Lydia had first met Jason, he had often vanished. It was as if his hold on this world wasn't very strong and could be broken with the lightest touch. Over time, with Lydia powering up his physicality and his consciousness, he had become more and more solid, more firmly rooted in the land of the living. To Jason's great relief he had stopped disappearing at random moments for variable stretches of time. Lydia still didn't know where he went when that happened, only that it frightened Jason and he didn't want to talk about it.

She reached out her senses now, feeling for the threads of his consciousness in the hope that she could bring him back. There was nothing. Just the birds and the traffic and the smell of old cooking oil and the drains.

. . .

WALKING UP THE PATH TO AUNT DAISY'S HOUSE, Lydia couldn't help but think of doing the same thing when Maddie was missing. Back when she was new to living in The Fork and still doing favours for Charlie. So much had happened since then, it gave her a queasy vertigo to think about it. If she hadn't come back to London, if she hadn't found Maddie, what might have happened? Maddie would still be alive. Probably walking up this path in Lydia's place as head of the Family. If she hadn't killed everybody, of course.

Lydia saw a shadow move behind the decorative glass panel in the front door a moment before it opened. Daisy paled when she saw Lydia.

'I'm not staying long.' Lydia walked into the house, not giving Daisy a chance to close the door in her face. She turned right, into the front room, and stood by the fireplace. A row of framed photographs, family snaps of Maddie and Daisy and John, and a couple of studio portraits of Maddie at different ages, lined the mantle. Lydia turned her back on them and faced Daisy.

'I don't want you here. You should leave.'

'He's not getting out,' Lydia said.

For a moment, Lydia thought Daisy was going to waste time by claiming she didn't know who Lydia was talking about.

Instead, she straightened her stance and met Lydia's gaze with narrowed eyes. 'I have more faith.'

Lydia produced her coin and spun it in the air, letting it rotate slowly. 'I know you hate me and that is completely fair. But I am the head of this Family and working against me is unacceptable. You know that. I am happy to chalk everything up to this point to grief. It has clouded your judgement and I'm willing to make allowances. But it stops now.'

Daisy winced.

The air was filled with coins, now, and the sound of beating wings. Daisy's eyes grew wide. 'I don't want to hurt you,' Lydia said. 'But my feelings don't matter. I am the head of the Crow Family, that is what matters. You can decide now. Are you going to restate your loyalty to this Family, to me? If not, you are free to leave London. You and John can get in your BMW and go anywhere you like beyond the M25. You can never return, though, and must cut all communication with the Family.'

'You're banishing us?' There were two spots of colour on Daisy's cheeks and her eyes were filled with hatred mixed with a growing fear. 'You can't do that.'

'I am giving you a choice,' Lydia corrected her. 'You can renew your loyalty and stay in Camberwell or you can leave forever.'

Daisy opened her mouth to speak, but Lydia kept on going. 'Before you decide, you need to speak to John. This is a decision for you both.'

Daisy closed her mouth and nodded.

'And one last thing,' Lydia gathered the coins in a swirling storm above her own head. 'If you choose to stay there will be no second chances. If you are disloyal to me again, you will both follow your daughter.'

CHAPTER SEVEN

Back at the flat, Lydia had downed a pint of water and splashed cold water onto her neck and wrists. She couldn't remember the weather ever being so relentlessly hot and dry in London. Jason wandered into the room, seeming at a loose end, so she updated him on her visit with Daisy.

'Do you think she will listen?' He drifted over to her desk.

'I don't know. I hope so.' She didn't want to think about what she would have to do if Daisy didn't heed the warning.

'What's this?' Jason picked up the small key from the magpie.

'A gift from a magpie.'

Lydia had chucked the key onto her desk with the intention of examining it further but, in truth, had forgotten about it. Jason picked it up and peered at it. He took a photo using Lydia's phone and did an image search. 'Looks like a cabinet key.'

'That's what I thought,' Lydia replied. 'But without the cabinet, it's useless.'

'Do you get a feeling from it?'

'Not so far,' Lydia said. 'Hand it over.'

The key lay in her palm. Innocuous and inert. She closed her eyes, reaching out her senses for a Family vibe or a spook. 'It's not haunted, as far as I can tell.'

'Why did a magpie bring it to you? And why are they doing little favours?'

'Magpies do like to collect things,' Lydia said. 'And corvids have always hung around me. For obvious reasons.'

Jason shook his head. 'Obvious to you, maybe. Not to normal people.'

'Says the ghost.' Lydia nudged him with her hip, feeling the cold spread over her skin. Something occurred to her. 'You disappeared before. When we were in the alley.'

'Yeah,' Jason didn't meet her gaze. 'I was upset. That can trigger it.'

'I know,' Lydia said. 'But it hadn't happened for ages. I hoped it maybe... Wasn't a thing anymore.'

'You hoped I'd grown out of it?'

'I wouldn't put it like that. But, yeah.'

'I don't want to talk about it. I don't want it to happen again and I can't—'

Jason was beginning to vibrate, the outline of his body shimmering. Not a good sign. 'That's okay,' Lydia said, putting her hand on his arm.

'May I?' Jason held his hand out for the key.

As she passed it to Jason, Lydia felt a flash of...

something. A faint sunshine gleam. Jason was holding the key and he began wandering around the flat, holding it out.

'What are you doing?'

'An experiment, I thought I felt...' He had been walking toward Lydia's bedroom, but now he stopped and rotated slowly. Then walked a few paces toward the front window. Stopped and rotated again before walking in the direction of the hall.

'I think it's leading me,' he said over his shoulder. 'I think it wants me to go this way. You try.'

With the key held out like a divining rod and only a minor sense of embarrassment, Lydia tried walking in different directions. She almost dropped the key in surprise when she felt it. When she had faced in the direction of the front door, she had felt a distinctive tug on her right arm. She looked at the key held in her right hand and stretched it out again. This time the sunshine gleam was stronger. And the key felt warmer to her touch.

'You want me to come with you?' Jason asked, as Lydia slipped her phone into her pocket and picked up a hoodie.

'That's okay, I'll check it out first.'

Jason nodded, looking slightly disappointed.

'I need you to do something for me. Only if you don't mind...'

'What do you need?'

'Can you look into Fleet's family? Online I mean. I know it's invading his privacy, but I'm on the back foot and his father is trouble. For Fleet.'

Jason was already nodding. 'I'll see what I can dig up.'

'This is just between us,' Lydia said.

'Obviously.'

LYDIA HELD THE KEY AS SHE WALKED. SHE TRIED TO be subtle about it once she joined the main street, but felt lucky that she didn't care. Plus, this was Camberwell. She would have to do something a lot weirder than this to stand out.

She could feel it warm in her hand and she tried to keep her mind relaxed, to walk on pure instinct. After several minutes, she realised that the key was leading her to Burgess Park. It was late in the evening and the park wasn't busy. The summer sky was still light, the clouds tinged with lilac and pink. She passed the play area and followed the pull of the key across the flat grass toward the centre of the park.

Perhaps it was the memories of meeting Fleet in his place so many times, but she felt the gleam of sunshine a moment before she saw what the key was pulling her toward.

Lydia saw a lone tree standing on a patch of open grass. It was hard to miss it. Partly because it was much taller than the other trees, which were neatly spaced in the plain of scrubby grass, and partly because there was a man standing underneath it, his head tilted as he gazed up through the branches.

Fleet's father turned as she approached. 'Isn't she a beauty?'

Lydia wasn't a huge fan of nature. And having almost lost her life in the Pearl court, a place of twisting tree roots and reaching branches, she had developed a healthy mistrust of trees. However, she sensed that it would be taken poorly if she voiced her opinion that it was nothing that a good chainsaw couldn't fix.

'Wych Elm. Good for boats,' he patted the trunk. 'Pliable and watertight.'

He wasn't wearing his hat, but the coat was the same soot-stained travesty. Up close, it didn't just look as if it had been patched and repaired multiple times, it looked formed from hundreds of scraps of different material. Around his neck he wore several chains in silver, gold, and a dull tarnished metal that might have been pewter. His wrists were twined with old leather strings, some of which had objects caught in knots. Small, polished bones, dull gemstones, animal teeth, feathers, and fragments of metal and china.

He took a pipe from his pocket and Lydia recognised it as an old clay one, like the ones picked up from the Thames by the mudlarkers.

'What do you want?'

'Just like that? No preamble? No chit-chat?'

'Just like that,' Lydia said. 'I am not asking because I care. I'm asking because I want to get this over with. You're in my manor and you're not invited.'

'You are very rude,' the man said. 'Some people might find that alluring.'

The not-subtle subtext was that he was not one of those people. Well, that suited Lydia, as she had no wish to charm Fleet's father.

He lit his pipe and took a puff, watching her through the smoke. 'There used to be a waterway here. The barbarians filled it in. Choked it with earth and concrete.'

'Yeah, I know. The Surrey Canal. This is my home. I told you.'

He nodded, taking another puff before offering his pipe.

Lydia ignored the offer. 'Do you always travel by water?' She had stopped a few paces from the man, but it felt too close.

'I like it,' he said, not answering her. 'You don't see many of these,' he resumed his admiration of the tree. 'The Dutch variety brought pestilence. Almost wiped the species from this island. And this,' he placed a hand back onto the tree, caressing the bark as if it was an animal, 'is lucky to be here at all.'

'Is this yours?' Lydia held up the key.

'Now, that's interesting.' He looked at her with light spilling from his eyes. 'Where did you find that?'

'I picked it up off the ground,' Lydia said, truthfully enough. There was no need to tell the man that a magpie had dropped it at her feet.

'It belongs to me,' the man said. 'And it's interesting that you felt you could steal from me. Not many would dare. Not many at all.'

'Not me,' Lydia said, spreading her hands wide, palms up. The international symbol of 'I don't want to fight'.

'And how did you find me? That's not...' He took a

step toward her. 'I'm not usually found unless I want to be. Tell me.'

Lydia held her ground. 'No.'

He stopped advancing.

'I came for my boy. I mean you no harm. You can tell me who gave you that key.'

The tone was soothing, almost musical. Lydia felt a fogginess in her mind, and the urge to lie down and take a nap. She narrowed her eyes. 'That's not very polite.' In the next moment, she held her coin in the air between them. She made it spin slowly, watching Fleet's father watch it. He didn't look surprised. Or particularly impressed.

He tilted his head. 'How long has my boy been courting you?'

'Maybe I have been courting him.'

'I can take him with me. Leave this city. You never have to see me again.'

'You cannot take him.'

He smiled, but Lydia wasn't waiting for him to speak. 'Fleet cannot be taken. He can go with you of his own free will. That is for him to decide.'

'I am his father.'

'In name, perhaps.'

Eyes narrowed. The lines on his face deepened and he suddenly looked closer to seventy than fifty. When he spoke, his voice was no longer musical. 'Be careful, Crow.'

'I wouldn't have to insult you if I knew how to address you properly.'

'I am Fleet when I am in this city.'

Well, that wasn't going to work. That name was already taken in Lydia's mind. 'Your first name? If we are to come to an agreement, we should know each other better. I am close to your son. I can be a help or I can be a hinderance.'

'Do you know the story of Spring-heeled Jack?'

'Of course,' Lydia said. She was a Londoner and she was very sick of this man telling her things she already knew. 'So, Jack, what do you want with Fleet?'

He didn't answer.

She held out the key. 'You want this? It's yours. Just leave the city. Alone.'

'You can keep that for now, Crow. A little part of me.'

Lydia pressed her lips together. That was not a pleasant image. And she was officially sick of listening to this man's riddles. She turned and began walking away.

'What about Orpheus and Eurydice? He went to the underworld to get his beloved back from the kingdom of the dead. It didn't end well.'

'I know lots of stories,' Lydia threw over her shoulder.

'Good,' he said. 'That might save your life.'

CHAPTER EIGHT

F leet was heading to the gym after work, so Lydia
went for a run. He had sounded detached and
almost robotic when they had spoken on the phone, and
she knew he had barely slept the night before. Nightmares had been replaced by a disturbing wakefulness in
which he stared at the ceiling, watching flickering
horrors unfold, unable to talk to Lydia when she reached
for him. The movement of walking helped her to think,
but she needed the exertion of running to stop the
looping thoughts for a few blessed minutes. She was
used to battling external enemies – Charlie, Maddie,
Gale – but this was something different. This was an
enemy lurking inside Fleet. It was part of what made
him Fleet, and she didn't know how to defeat the
problem without harming the man.

Training and control. These were things that
Charlie had known about. He had shown Lydia techniques to calm her mind and access her power. He had
shown her how to repeat certain patterns of thought and

movement, to practise them until they were second nature. Maybe Charlie would know how to help Fleet, but would he do it? The thought of asking Charlie for anything made her stomach lurch with anxiety. It was a ludicrous thought and she was annoyed that some part of her still thought of the man as family. He had incited a gang in Brixton to go after the Crow Family and her in particular. He wanted her dead, and the sooner she made every part of her mind accept that fact, the better.

She was due at Fleet's that evening. She showered after her run and drove over to his flat. Lydia had a key and she let herself in, expecting to find Fleet fresh from the shower and pottering around in the kitchen. Instead, the flat was empty. She did a fast walk through to make sure, which didn't take long. Her phone was already in her hand and she pressed the call button for Fleet, heart racing. Not again, not again, not again.

He picked up after a few rings.

Lydia didn't attempt to hide her concern. 'Where are you?'

A pause. She strained to hear background sounds, listening for clues in case he stopped the call abruptly.

'The Heath. Primrose Hill.'

'You went there after the gym?'

Another pause. 'I don't know.'

'Don't move,' Lydia said. 'I'm on my way.'

FLEET WAS SITTING ON A BENCH ON THE TOP OF Primrose Hill. It was almost nine o'clock but still light. The sky was palest blue shading to faint orange, and the skyline was clear and crisp. The layers of the view were so distinct and hyperreal in the intense light that it looked like the iconic London buildings were growing out of the lush greenery of the trees. Lydia sat next to Fleet and took his hand. They sat in silence and looked at the view for a while.

'Thanks for coming,' Fleet said. 'Did you want to go for a pint?'

'Why here?' Lydia asked, ignoring his attempt at deflection.

'I don't know.'

'Is something bad going to happen on the heath?'

A pause before Fleet answered. 'I haven't seen anything.'

'Is it your dad, do you think? Drawing you back?'

A shrug. Fleet didn't look at her, but he agreed it was a possibility. 'I saw him here. I told you.'

Lydia watched a man with two dogs walk past. He was sucking the life out of a roll-up and the scent of weed was thick in the air trailing behind him. She wondered what it was like to live his life. To take the dogs out at the end of the day, spliff in hand and not a care in the world. She knew that was nonsense, that nobody's life was stress-free and simple, but for a single moment she wanted to trade places. She was desperately worried about Fleet and still angry that he had been going to leave with his father. She was waiting for Charlie's next move and terrified that she had missed it.

'Maybe he's gone,' Lydia said. She knew she ought to tell Fleet that she had met his father in Camberwell, but she couldn't see how it would help him. The best thing

71

Fleet could do would be to forget his father and the last thing she wanted was him seeking him out again. 'You were going to go with him, I know, but... That changed. That might not be an option anymore.' Lydia replayed the moment in her mind; Fleet's dad had seemed to change his mind in that moment by the canal. Fleet had expected to go with him, feathers-knew where, but his father had stepped back onto his boat and motored away. Maybe, now that he had spoken to her, he was going to leave the city. It was a nice thought.

'No,' Fleet said. 'I'm still seeing him.' He tapped his temple. 'And I'm still being pulled to this place. Why else would that be?'

Memories, Lydia wanted to say. But Fleet looked so hopeful. It felt cruel. She hated to see Fleet like this. This man had been nothing to Fleet, not in his life at all, and now he had shown up and offered Fleet something he hadn't known he had been missing. He was reduced to a child, calling for his lost parent, and it cut Lydia to the bone.

'Why do you want to go with him? I thought you didn't have a relationship.' Why are you suddenly so keen to leave London, to leave me, were words Lydia kept locked up behind her lips.

'It's all I can think about,' Fleet said, not looking at her. 'I'm sorry. But it's the truth. I can't sleep. I can't stop thinking about him and about travelling on the water, about being near him. And I can't tell what's real anymore. He's like a fixed point in a landscape that keeps shifting. A mast I can cling to. I don't know why. I hate him. I hate him and I feel like I need him.' Fleet shook his head. 'It makes no sense. I told you. I'm cracked.'

'It could be magical,' Lydia said, trying to work the problem rationally. 'You have your premonitions and there is a gleam about you, but with him it's hundreds of times stronger. Maybe his mojo is messing with your head? Maybe if you got out of London while he's here, you would feel better.' Be able to think more clearly, she added silently.

'I'm not leaving you. And I can't just leave work.'

'You could take sick leave,' Lydia said and then wished she could snatch the words back.

Fleet's expression was bleak. Closed down. He stood up and began walking in the direction of the road.

Lydia followed. She hadn't told him that she had spoken to his father, had felt like it would only make things worse. He had changed his mind about taking Fleet by the canal, but seemed to have changed his mind, to want him again. Lydia didn't know for sure how Fleet would react to that news, but there was a strong chance he would go straight to the canal and step aboard Jack's boat without a backward glance.

FLEET'S PHONE WAS RINGING. HE ANSWERED IT quickly, sounding efficient and awake. Lydia was still swimming up from the depths of her dream. She rubbed her face and sat up. Fleet was on his feet, pacing the darkened room as he listened to whoever was on the other end of the call.

Lydia waited until Fleet had ended the call before asking him what was going on.

'Eleven people are in hospital.' He was holding his phone out as if he was about to call somebody. Lydia understood the impulse. He wanted to fix this.

'What happened?'

'All of them swam in the mixed bathing pond on the heath this morning.'

Lydia thought about the hot weather and wondered how many people had been in the water over the last couple of days. How many others might be affected. 'What's wrong with them?'

'Severe dehydration.'

'That's quick,' Lydia said, checking the time. 'Isn't it?'

'Apparently, they haven't stopped, um, ejecting liquid. It gets dangerous really fast.'

Lydia felt nauseous in sympathy. Then something else hit her. 'Wait, why are you getting the call? Hampstead isn't your manor.'

'Courtesy. I asked a friend to notify me of anything Heath-related.' He pulled a face. 'Don't worry, I didn't tell him I was having visions.'

'You said you hadn't seen anything happen there.'

'I saw *him* there,' Fleet countered. 'And I've had a feeling. You know I keep being drawn there, I thought... I knew there had to be a reason. I could feel it was something bad.'

That made sense. Fleet's father was freaky enough on his own, but Fleet had been attached to the heath like he was hooked to bungee cord. It kept pulling him back.

'I need to go.' Fleet pulled a t-shirt over his head.

'There isn't anything you can do,' Lydia argued. 'Come back to bed. Get some sleep.'

'I'm going to the hospital. They're in the Royal Free.'

'But why? They're being looked after. Your friend will keep you updated if there is any new information. You're exhausted and not thinking straight.'

'This is my fault.'

'Unless you poisoned the bathing pond, it absolutely isn't.'

Fleet winced.

'Please,' Lydia was out of bed now, and she wrapped her arms around Fleet. His body was tense and unyielding.

'I saw it.'

'What?' Lydia wasn't sure if she had heard him right.

'I saw people in hospital. Drips in their arms. Their skin looked blue.'

'Well, that's dreams for you. Weird.'

Fleet's face in the half-light was tortured. 'But I saw them. Eleven people.'

Hell Hawk. 'It's not your fault,' Lydia said. 'You didn't do this.'

'But I didn't stop it, either.' Fleet was shaking. 'What's the point? What's the fucking point of this?' He smacked his head suddenly and hard, surprising Lydia into letting go of him and taking a step back.

'If I can't use it, if I can't help... what's the point?'

'Come back to bed,' Lydia said, helpless to offer anything except platitudes. 'You need to get some rest. We can tackle this tomorrow.'

'They might be dead by tomorrow.'

'And if they are, you're going to be very busy, which means you'll need your strength.' Lydia was channelling the no-nonsense voice she had heard Emma use with Archie and was amazed when it worked.

Fleet got back into bed and lay stiffly, staring at the ceiling. Lydia curled around him as best she could. After a while, he relaxed and shifted, holding her back. 'I'm sorry,' he muttered into her hair.

'It's okay,' Lydia said. 'I understand.' And she did. She just had to find a way to help him.

CHAPTER NINE

The women-only and men-only bathing ponds as well as the mixed pond were all closed the next day. The Environment Agency had tested the water and found nothing untoward in the second two ponds, but they weren't taking any chances. The bacteria Salmonella typhi was found to be in dangerous quantities in the mixed pond, much to the experts' confusion.

Lydia watched a BBC report from the entrance to the heath. The serious-faced journalist explained that the risk to the public at large was minimal, but that people should avoid the area until further notice. The programme cut to an expert in pond life, who explained this phenomenon was unlikely to have happened spontaneously. It finished with the on-site journalist confirming that the police were treating it as a criminal matter and were appealing for anybody with information to come forward. The report didn't go into details about the eleven victims, just stating that they were still receiving treatment in hospital. Ten were making a good recovery, but one swimmer, a man in his fifties, had been put into an induced coma.

The flat was stifling, even with the windows open, so Lydia took her coffee out onto the roof terrace, hoping she would feel cooler. Instead, the air was thick and humid, pressing in on all sides. Lydia felt sweat break out across her skin and she pulled her hair into a pony tail to get it off her neck.

Looking over the railing into the alley, she could see Jason standing motionless. He was watching for the child, she knew, and resisted the urge to call down. His project was important to him and who was she to pull him away from it?

Straightening up, Lydia felt her tattoos moving on her skin a moment before three magpies flew down onto the terrace, their blue and green tail feathers iridescent in the sunshine.

She greeted the birds politely and waited. They weren't carrying anything, which was a relief.

The birds stood still and regarded her steadily. It was unnerving. 'What?'

The one on the left opened its beak and let out the distinctive chattering sound of a pissed-off magpie. The bird next to it joined in. It was a warning call, Lydia knew, but they had sought her out and there wasn't a cat nearby, so it had to be a message. 'Okay,' Lydia said, 'I hear you. Bad shit is coming.'

The third magpie lifted its wings in a movement that looked like frustration. It opened its beak and Lydia expected some more chattering, another voice telling her that she ought to be afraid and adding no other useful information. Instead, it let out a perfect imitation of a human voice screaming. Lydia took a step back, startled by the eerie sound. She had heard magpies imitate car alarms and human voices before, but this was on another level. The magpie did it again and this time Lydia realised what it reminded her of... People on a roller-coaster.

THE PEARLIES WORE COATS COVERED IN MOTHER-OF-pearl buttons, that's how you could tell a Pearl stall from another costermonger. That, and the fact that you'd just blown a week's wages on something you hadn't intended to buy. Pearls could sell coals to Newcastle, shoes to a duck, coffins to the cremated. Their real power, though, was that they made you feel good while they did it. They picked your pockets, but they left you smiling. Left you wanting to do it all over again.

The Pearl Family had been prolific and generous in their procreation over the years and the modern Pearls were scattered around London, England and probably much further than that. Their power, perhaps as a result, had become weaker. Diluted. When Lydia had been worrying about a clash between the four Families of London, she hadn't worried too much about the Pearls. That is, until she met the Pearl Court. Sealed under-ground by a sneaky covenant, the original members of the Pearl Family had been separated from normal time and space. They had been young and beautiful to gaze upon, but once the contract was broken and above ground time flooded in, they had crumbled to dust.

Standing outside Rafferty Hill's flat, Lydia steeled herself for the lure of the Pearl magic. It would incite desire beyond anything she had ever felt. A greater need to serve and to be near and to want than even the animal magnetism of Paul Fox or the genuine lust and love she felt for Fleet. Rafferty Hill had gone from being an average Pearl descendant when the court dispersed, blessed with above-average charisma and good looks, to something far closer to the members of the Pearl Court. In both power and personality. Lydia's theory was that the powerful energy of the Pearl King had escaped before his physical body had decayed completely, and that energy had dispersed into the nearest, or most suitable, Pearl descendants. Her hope was that that included lots of people, diluting the power to a manageable level. What she really didn't want was a new Pearl King. Especially not one who was free to roam London above.

Shuddering at the thought, Lydia pressed the buzzer for Rafferty and Amber's flat. There were noises within and then the door swung open. A stranger gazed at Lydia with a glazed expression. Music with a pulsing beat was playing somewhere in the flat, and Lydia could hear multiple voices and bursts of laughter.

'I'm here to see Rafferty.'

The stranger shook his head slowly. 'Not here.'

'Amber?'

Another painfully slow movement. 'Gone.'

Lydia left her card with the stranger. His name, apparently, was Bonehead. Either it was a mildly insulting nickname that had stuck and Bonehead had decided to embrace it, or it was the kind of obscure in-joke that made no sense to those outside of the tribe. Lydia tried, for a split second, to imagine willingly referring to herself in such a way, and came up blank.

Upstairs in the flat, Lydia sat at her desk and considered her next move. Jason floated in with his laptop. She had asked him to research Fleet's family and now felt a spurt of hope that he had been successful.

He shook his head, sitting on the sofa and opening the laptop. 'Nothing on that, yet. I've been doing some other research, though.'

'On the Foxes?'

Jason shook his head. 'On The Fork. This whole street, really. Did you know there was a bakery here before it was a café?'

'I didn't.'

'And next door? There was a grain store. Further down there was a stable.'

'How bucolic.'

'It's weird to imagine, isn't it?' Jason put the laptop onto the cushions and got up. He began pacing the room, clearly excited. 'There were animals milling about. Everything that we buy in a plastic package used to be wandering about or stacked up in bushels.'

Lydia raised an eyebrow. 'Bushels?'

'Or maybe sacks. I guess the grain would have been milled before it was brought here. What do you think?'

Lydia wanted to say she neither knew nor cared, but she understood Jason's obsessions. He still enjoyed programming and recreational maths, and read novels

81

voraciously, but he didn't sleep and had a lot of time to fill. A lot of time and no connections to the world, except for her. 'I'm sorry I haven't taken on a case recently. I know it's boring for you.'

'That's okay,' Jason said. 'You're worried about Fleet. And you have to find his father before things escalate.'

'Finding him isn't the problem,' Lydia said. 'I want him to leave. And never come back. Any ideas how I can achieve that?'

'You're the all-powerful Crow,' Jason said. 'Use that.'

If only. 'He felt strong.'

'Would more training help? Or having me on board?'

'Maybe. Or maybe I should accept that he's here, now. He is Fleet's family, after all. Maybe he will settle here and turn out to be an asset.'

Jason regarded her for a moment. He stayed steady and solid, but his face was clouded with concern. 'You don't believe that.'

'No.' Sadly, she really did not.

LYDIA LEANED BACK IN HER CHAIR. CHARLIE'S ability to get messages to Daisy from his prison was one thing but accessing his bank account was another. And was he behind the feather that Paul Fox had found in his bedroom or was that somebody else looking to stir trouble? Sinclair seemed genuinely unaware of Charlie's ability to reach beyond his confinement. Another thought occurred to Lydia. Perhaps Sinclair was allowing it. For reasons of her own.

The fact remained that somebody had accessed Paul

Fox's home, his bedroom no less. They had placed a feather onto his pillow. It wasn't exactly a horse's head, but it carried the weight of a warning. Charlie had managed to get a message to the Brixton mob to tell them that the Crows had been responsible for a murder of one of their own, almost inciting a turf war. If Lydia hadn't been able to sit down with the boss and demonstrate her ability to control every physical body in the room, not to mention broker a deal, it could have been carnage.

Since Lydia knew Daisy had been running errands for Charlie, it hit her now that she was the most obvious suspect for planting the feather in Paul's bed. She hadn't believed it possible, couldn't imagine her aunt breaking into Paul Fox's den, but no other obvious suspects had come to light. In the absence of any other leads, she realised she would have to accept that Daisy was her chief suspect.

The pearl pendant was also on her desk and it struck her, now, that if she widened the scope from Daisy and Charlie, that it could be considered the first object. She looked at the feather and the pendant, side-by-side. She had assumed the pendant was a sign from the universe that the Pearl energy had gone into Rafferty, but what if she had been wrong about that? What else could it be? She didn't want to make assumptions, not with so much at stake.

She picked up the pendant and rubbed a thumb over the yellowish pearl in the centre. It still only gave off the faintest of pearl magic, but since most people with Pearl energy were diluted descendants, weak and scattered, this wasn't surprising. It had been brought by a jackdaw, which meant it might not mean anything in particular. Maybe that jackdaw had thought it was a way to show loyalty to Lydia, like a cat bringing a gift of a dead mouse. Or perhaps it was to remind her not to underestimate the Pearl Family.

She tapped the trackpad on her laptop to wake it up and found Rafferty Hill's agency. She didn't want to keep trying his flat and hoping he would be home. She wanted a guaranteed meeting and an environment she could control.

She looked up the name of a production company. Not the one that made the period drama that had been Rafferty's big break, as there was too much risk of the agent knowing people there. Then she called Rafferty's agent with an opportunity for the actor. She read from the description of past projects for the company to get the language. A high budget series, a proven name already attached as show runner, streaming deals in place.

'He might be interested,' the agent said, not-quite hiding the excitement in his voice.

'We'll need to see him, of course. Get a reading.'

'Not an open audition?'

Lydia didn't know what that meant, but she picked up that it was bad from the tone of his voice. 'Of course not. We just need to get him in the room.' Well, that was true.

'Check the vibe.'

'Exactly.'

A hesitation. 'This week could be difficult.'

Lydia waited. Let her silence do the job.

'I think I could get him ready for Friday. Is that any good?'

'That suits,' Lydia said. She gave the address of a rehearsal space in Soho. It meant not being on home-turf, but it couldn't be helped. A Camberwell address might raise a red flag. 'And he's available for this work?' Lydia said. 'Before we go any further, there's something a little delicate I need to ask.'

'Is this about Rafferty's Instagram?'

Lydia made a mental note to check the platform. 'No. It's more a general check-in. There have been a few rumours and I wanted to hear from you. Is he ready for a job like this?'

'Of course. He's fighting fit and good to go. Rafferty's time out gave him the opportunity to centre himself. He's more professional than ever and, in my humble opinion,' a little laugh that was probably supposed to sound self-deprecating, 'whatever personal epiphany he had while he was away has taken his skills to the next level.'

Lydia finished the call. It was the agent's job to talk up his client, but Lydia still felt as if she wanted a scrub in the shower. She found Rafferty's Instagram and scrolled through the recent posts. There were a lot. Most were shots of his artwork, often with a bit of his body included in the frame. A hand or finger, mostly, but some his torso or foot. It was slightly odd, but nothing alarming. Lydia clicked on one at random to read the caption. This was weirder. As well as the standard amount of emojis and hashtags, there was a block of rambling text in which Rafferty spoke of his new eternal soul and his mission to lead the sheep from the shadow of death. The comments below ranged from the enthusiastic to the confused. And a few asking 'U ok hun?'.

Lydia clicked the next post and found a less disordered message. A short statement that the previous post was a creative piece, part of his artwork, and that posting it on Instagram was part of the 'art'. 'I aim to stimulate and spark discourse, those conversations forming part of the art, work that will be part of my forthcoming exhibition: Mastery.'

Masturbation, more like, Lydia thought. But she couldn't dismiss it with a joke. This came across as a man with grandiose ideas, possibly delusions. She was no mental health expert, but Rafferty's language and behaviour seemed disordered. The question, though, was whether this was instability caused by the sudden influx of Pearl power, or whether he had gained more than just the power. Had elements of the Pearl King's personality passed into Rafferty, too? Was that possible? The most likely explanation, having met a soul without a body on more than one occasion, was that the Pearl King's soul had entered Rafferty. The real question was this: how much of Rafferty Hill was left? And what would this new incarnation of the most powerful Pearl want?

CHAPTER TEN

Crows see well and crows see far. Crows watch carefully and learn quickly. Crows don't really do promises, but they keep the few they make. Henry Crow was whispering in one ear and Charlie in the other.

The buildings were covered in black birds. Crows, ravens, magpies, jackdaws. All the corvids of the city, it seemed, lined up along the roofs and the overhead wires, the walls and the signs. She wasn't in any part of London she recognised. It was a jumble of streets and buildings, no real place.

Lydia opened her eyes. She was in bed. She was alone. And her phone was buzzing. It was tucked underneath her pillow for easy access, and she answered it.

'There's a lot of people down here,' Aiden said. 'Waiting to see you.'

Part of running the family involved listening to the people of the community. Squabbles and thievery, disrespect and violence. Sometimes it took mediation, sometimes Lydia ended up investigating a claim of harassment or tampering. Doing her job for free in her capacity as the head of the Crows. Mostly it involved sitting at her favourite table of The Fork, drinking coffee and listening. People wanted to be heard. And Aiden said that it was good for people to see her, to know that she was closely involved. It made people think twice about causing mayhem in Camberwell. As long as it made the local men less likely to strike their partner or kids, Lydia was happy.

But she didn't have the time or the patience for it today. 'You take the meetings,' she said. 'I'm delegating.'

'People want to see you,' Aiden said.

'Don't sell yourself short,' Lydia said, closing her eyes.

When Lydia woke up next, she had a message from Fleet. He wanted her to meet Lydia at the park nearest to the Camberwell police station.

'Thanks,' he said, kissing her hello in a distracted fashion. 'I needed to get outside. The lights in there,' he jerked his head, 'they're doing my head in.'

'You okay?' Lydia asked cautiously. Fleet's skin had a greyish cast and his eyes were bloodshot. The lack of unbroken sleep was beginning to wear him down.

'I went to the hospital to see them,' he said.

Lydia knew he meant the victims from the bathing pond. 'How are they doing?'

'Not good. One man has been put into a coma. They're not sure if he will pull through. The others should recover, but some of them...' He glanced at Lydia. 'Their skin looks blue. Purplish blue.'

Lydia swallowed hard. 'Like your dream?'

He nodded tightly. 'Exactly like my dream. In hospital beds with blue skin. It's where the blood has slowed down from the dehydration.'

Lydia knew the phenomenon from corpses, knew that Fleet did, too. Not something she had ever seen in a living person, though.

'I need to tell Sinclair.'

Lydia stopped walking. 'Tell her what?'

'That I saw it. Before it happened.'

'No,' Lydia said. 'No way. She will take you into her special department and do experiments.'

'I thought you said she wasn't interested. She's not Gale.'

'I don't trust a single word that comes out of that woman's mouth. I was stupid to believe Gale and I'm not making the same mistake. Promise me you won't tell her.'

He blew out a breath. 'Fine. You're probably right.'

'We will handle this,' Lydia said. 'Together.'

'There's something else.'

'What?'

'I spoke to some of the victims. The ones that were awake, anyway.'

'And?'

'The morning when they went swimming. They said it was all the same as usual. No warning that there was anything wrong with the water, no reason not to go in. But they all mentioned seeing a man wearing an old-fashioned hat and a long brown coat hanging about at the far edge of the pond.'

LYDIA HAD HEADED TO CHARLIE'S HOUSE AFTER seeing Fleet. Partly to avoid the people who might still be hanging out at The Fork waiting for an audience with the head of the Crow Family, and partly so that she could punch something very hard for an hour or so.

She was on her way up to the training room when Paul's number flashed up on her phone and she answered straight away. His family members were scattered to the four winds, and this wasn't the time to play games. 'Any news from Jasper?'

'That's not why I'm calling,' Paul said, his voice oddly strained. 'I just had a visit.'

Lydia waited.

'A couple of big lads in suits, looking to make some trouble.'

Lydia stepped into the hallway and lowered her voice. 'At your bar?'

'The Blind Beggar. I was having a very pleasant lunch with a lady friend when they came rolling in, all puffed up and wanting to leave an impression.'

Lydia's stomach dropped. With the Fox Family scattered out of London, Paul was exposed. Unprotected. 'Are you okay?'

'As it happens, they both came down with a nasty case of broken bones, so no harm done. Thanks for asking.'

'Feathers,' Lydia swore. 'You sure you're not hurt?'

'Little Bird,' Paul's voice took on an alarmingly sexual tone. 'I didn't know you cared.'

'Oh shut up,' Lydia snapped. 'Who were they? Did you find out?'

'Naturally.'

He left a pause in which Lydia could imagine the interrogation. Her stomach rolled queasily.

'They were acting on behalf of the Silver Family. Turns out, Maria received a little gift with her morning coffee and she wanted to reciprocate.'

Hell Hawk. 'I'm on my way.'

'Appreciate it.'

WITH DENMARK HILL STATION SO CLOSE, IT WAS easier to take the overground train to Whitechapel than fight with traffic and parking. A train pulled in moments after she arrived onto the platform and twenty minutes later, she walked into the fine Victorian pub. The name The Blind Beggar had tugged at her memory and she'd Googled it on the train. It was where Ronnie Kray had shot a gang rival. Bit on the nose, but that was Maria Silver all over. No subtlety.

Having not visited the pub before, Lydia couldn't be certain that it didn't always have tipped over tables and a broken chair in the middle of the floor with fresh blood splattered across the wooden boards. Paul was sitting in a high-backed pine settle, a half-finished pint on the table in front of him.

'Where's your date?' Lydia asked, putting her hands on her hips and looking around the place. 'And everybody else?' There was nobody serving behind the mahogany bar, no punters warming the stools.

'Scarpered,' Paul said. 'Can't say I blame her. Got a bit rambunctious in here for a bit.'

'So, Maria Silver received a gift and she wasn't in a grateful mood?'

He reached down and placed a bag onto the table. 'Take a look.'

'Why did she assume you sent it,' she began, as he shook the bag out onto the table, then stopped as the object emerged. Red fur. It was a fox's tail, complete with a pointed white tip. She swallowed hard, hoping it wasn't the real deal.

'Are you getting anything?' Paul asked. He was leaning forward, staring at her intently.

She was. And she didn't like it.

'Please tell me that isn't real fur,' she said, playing for time.

'It's fur, but not a real brush. Not sure what animal it's been made from, but it's not a fox.' He showed white teeth. 'Which is why I let Maria's pals limp out of here.'

'But someone wanted it to look like a message from the Fox Family.'

'Clearly,' Paul said, his tone expressing that he knew she was stalling. 'So who sent it?'

'I can't be sure.'

Paul waited.

She touched the faux tail, stroking the fur lightly with one finger. The impressions leapt to her mind. Wings beating. Feathers in her throat. The scrape of beak against bone. Hell Hawk.

Her eyes met his. 'I will find who did this and deal with it. I swear to you.'

He sat back. 'It was a Crow, then?'

She nodded, hoping that honesty wasn't a huge mistake.

'Thank you for not lying to me,' Paul said. His voice was oddly formal. She didn't know if that was a bad sign, or just that she wasn't used to him speaking to her so sincerely.

'Someone really wants to stir up trouble,' Lydia said.

'A Crow wants to stir up trouble,' Paul corrected her. 'At a certain point, they're going to succeed.'

Feathers. 'I know. Give me time to sort this. Please.'

Paul considered. 'Since it's you, Little Bird. You can have until the solstice.'

It took Lydia a moment to work it out. 'That's in three days. I need longer.'

Paul shook his head gently. 'I shouldn't be letting you walk out of this pub.' He indicated the red and white monstrosity lying on the table. 'That's a fucking incitement and you know it.'

He was right. Paul might talk about not being a leader, of the Fox Family having no hierarchy, but that didn't mean they weren't a powerful family. It didn't mean you could insult them and walk away. You needed to fly.

She called Aiden and filled him in. 'You think of anyone stupid enough to pull a trick like this?'

'No one,' Aiden said. 'Foxes aren't exactly top priority, either. All the rumbles are about the betting shops and pubs, local stuff. No one's crossing the river looking for trouble.'

Lydia heard the unspoken 'we've got enough of our own' and she agreed. This wasn't a disgruntled Crow acting on their own. This was part of a plan. And there was only one Crow with that kind of ambition. Well, two, if she included herself. 'I'm going to try to smooth feathers.'

'You want back-up?'

'Nah, you're all right. I'm not going in person.' And even if she did, she could control Maria's body. She wasn't afraid. Out loud, she added: 'I need you to ask around. See what the Family knows. I don't want any more surprises.'

LYDIA WALKED DOWN TO THE RIVER AND FOUND A bench on the embankment. It was even busier than usual, the sunshine bringing Londoners out in force. There was plenty of skin showing and people slurped frozen drinks and ice creams. Lydia called Maria's office and waited to be put through to the woman herself. 'It wasn't the Foxes.'

'So I was informed.' Maria's voice wasn't giving anything away. She was as calm and controlled as always.

'It's the truth.'

A pause. 'And you know this how?'

Because Paul would have killed the men you sent for him, Lydia thought. 'Somebody wants trouble between us. To break the truce. I think we should meet and clear the air. Restate the truce and stop this from escalating. Nobody else has to get hurt.'

'Is that a fact? It sounds like you're making a threat, Crow.'

'No,' Lydia said quickly. 'Not a threat. A polite request. An appeal to reason.'

Maria's laugh was like a gunshot. 'Since when did a Crow resort to reason? Stick to your strengths, Crow. Go scavenge some carrion or something equally disgusting.'

'A war is bad for business,' Lydia tried. 'You have a reputation in the city, something that goes beyond the Families and our rivalry. Do you really want to divert your time and attention and money from your firm?'

Another pause, this one even more ominous than the last. 'It's fascinating that you would presume to tell me what is best for my firm and my family.'

The click signalled the end of the conversation.

'Feathers,' Lydia swore out loud. This was bad. They had never had a particularly cosy relationship, but this felt different. Lydia thought that she had seen Maria angry before, but now she realised that she hadn't had a clue. There had been a cold fury in her voice that was on another level.

A crow flew down and began pecking at a discarded takeaway box under the next bench along. It flew up to the railing opposite, a smart black iron that separated the pavement from the Thames, and was joined by three magpies and another crow. All of them managed to look disappointed in her. 'I know, I know,' she said. 'I'm working on it.'

CHAPTER ELEVEN

Lydia wasn't having Fleet's father poisoning people in London, whether they lived in her manor or not. And the more she knew about the man, the better able she would be to get him moved along. Out of her city. Out of Fleet's life and, hopefully, his head.

Jack moved around. That much was clear. So, perhaps the travelling community would have some insight. The fairground at the heath wasn't always in use, some of the larger rides were probably in storage, but most of the rides and booths were packed away on lorries and carted around Europe and beyond during London's winter, only returning when the blossom opened on the trees and there was enough warmth in the air to tempt Londoners in quantity to the heath to ride the gaudy contraptions. The rides might have changed, their decorations mutated from primary colours to neon brights, but the essential experience was the same. The thrill of danger, made all the better for the knowledge that it was temporary and slightly chaotic. In the age of safe and sanitised fun, of guardrails and warning signs and hours spent in rooms tasting danger via virtual reality, there was something piquant about boarding a bolted-together metal beast, tended by a scowling youngster with a cigarette attached to their lower lip.

Lydia had asked around and discovered that there was a caravan site for fairground show people to stay in all year round, right next to Hampstead Heath. It was something of a miracle that this prime real estate was still being used this way and Lydia assumed there had been many failed attempts to build luxury flats on the land. When Lydia had mentioned it to Jason, he had informed her that the area had been used by the fairground workers to set up, test equipment, and live for over a hundred years. This area used to be marshland, but was drained to form a pond, one of three, to supply clean drinking water for the city back in the seventeen hundreds. 'You're really getting into your history,' Lydia had said, which had earned her a 'well, duh' kind of a look from Jason. 'History is my people.' By which, Lydia guessed, he meant dead folk.

The March Madness event had been and gone, but the Summer Family Fun Fair was fast-approaching. Lydia and Aiden skirted the Vale of Heath to the fairground site inside the heath proper and not far from the ill-fated mixed bathing pond. The fairground was in the process of being set-up and there was an air of industry about the place. The site itself was hard-packed ground with a scattering of gravel, scrubby grass, and the imprinted odour of fried food. The last was definitely real and not ghostly, because Aiden could smell it, too.

And it had made him hungry. He lifted his chin. 'Are the food trucks open, yet?'

'No idea.' She was looking around, watching the fairground folk as they worked. A man of indeterminate age with a shaved head and a neck tattoo unbuckled straps holding down tarp shutters and began rolling them up to reveal a side show booth. It had yellow plastic ducks and a blue-painted backdrop with the words 'hook a prize' painted in bubble writing. He disappeared for a moment, reappearing inside the tent. He had two netting tubes filled with gaudy stuffed toys which he hung from a hidden hook so that they acted as curtains to the booth and then peeled away the netting. The toys were large and bright and there were familiar characters from films and TV. Lydia knew from experience that the prizes handed out would come from a different netting bag, hidden beneath the counter of the booth and those items would be smaller, cheaper, tattier.

'I'm looking for someone,' Lydia said.

'That so?' The man gave her a long look. 'You a cop?'

'No. I'm a Crow.'

The man nodded, but his expression didn't change. Lydia didn't know if that meant he hadn't heard of her Family or that he didn't care. It must be different for the travellers, Lydia supposed. They could always move on if there was trouble. They weren't stuck trying to sort things out. Ignoring the stab of envy, Lydia asked if there was anybody she should speak to. 'Who knows everything about everything?'

His face split into a smile. 'The three sisters. Top of field.'

'Thank you,' Lydia said.

'Behind the ghost house,' he called as she moved away.

They walked past many more side shows, food stands, and the classic rides. The dodgems, waltzers, and flying chairoplane. A more modern invention towered above the others, some kind of 'take you up high, drop you suddenly' ride. Feathers, no, Lydia thought. Who on earth would pay for that?

The rides for the littlies, the teacups and the carousel, gave her a powerful blast of nostalgia. Uncle Charlie had brought her and the rest of the young ones here for a summer treat. Her mum had sometimes come, too, but never her dad. Lydia didn't know, now, whether that would have contravened his strict rules of separation, or whether he just couldn't stand all the noise and flashing lights and the screaming kids. She paused by the silent and still teacup ride and wondered whether she should suggest to Emma that they bring Archie and Maisie. She had bloody loved the teacups when she was little.

A gigantic inflatable slide in rainbow colours was being blown up by a noisy generator, but the fun house was already constructed. It towered above them as they walked past. The grinning clowns even more sinister than usual as the track lights were running, but there was no music yet. It was only half-alive and that was, somehow, the worst.

At the top of the field, as promised, they found the ghost house. All of the Halloween staples were there, gravestones rising from the fenced ground in front, numerous grinning skeletons, some with glowing LED eyes and, at the top window of the grey-painted mock-Victorian mansion, an animatronic half-rotted skeleton with scraps of clothing and flaps of fake skin, a few strands of grey hair clinging to the skull.

'That's pretty good,' Aiden said, shading his eyes from the sun as peered up at it.

Lydia had seen dead people. She had seen ghosts and seemingly immortal people below the earth. She had seen trees and roots twisting and moving and a boy tied to a chair, chomping through a glass like it was an apple, blood running down his lips and chin. It kind of took the edge off the fairground version.

Skirting the low wooden fence that bordered the ghost house, a small purple tent became visible. It was probably about the same size as the other side show tents, but it had an entirely different feel. Instead of bright yellow or red tarp, it had many folds and layers of purple, lilac and navy velvet and a thick gold-coloured fringe which ran above the doorway. The doorway was shut, too. Not in the not-open-yet way of the other tents, but as if this was how the tent always appeared. A sign, painted with gold stars, pointed to the closed curtains of the entrance. The Three Sisters. Futures Told. Fortunes Made.

'Wait outside,' she told Aiden. 'Don't let anybody in.'

Aiden nodded. He folded his hands and assumed his 'waiting muscle' pose. He wasn't a thickly built man, but he was strong and a main bloodline Crow, so the effect was pretty good.

The curtains parted easily and Lydia pushed

through into the dim interior. The light inside came from candles with colourful glass shades, and a multitude of tiny warm fairy lights. A couple of large metal lanterns were placed on either side of the doorway, and the floor was covered in a variety of Afghan and Persian rugs. As soon as the folds of fabric fell back into place, cutting out the light from behind Lydia, it became difficult to see the edges of the tent. It seemed bigger inside than it ought to be and the air was thick with the scent of incense.

What Lydia had thought was just a pile of velvet cushions and fabric in the centre of the tent shifted and revealed a reclined figure, stretched out underneath a beaded quilt and, presumably, taking a mid-afternoon nap.

'Hello?' Lydia said, stepping closer.

The woman was sitting up now, and stretching luxuriously, as if Lydia wasn't even there. She had white hair pulled back in a messy bun, stuck all over with elaborate hair combs, and was wearing denim dungarees with a striped Breton underneath. She looked clear-eyed and her skin was lined, but glowing with inner health. She rose to her feet, shedding the quilt in one easy movement. All in all, she was a wonderful advert for the benefits of daytime sleeping. Her long feet were bare, and she stared appraisingly at Lydia with a direct fearlessness. 'Hello, Crow. What brings you to our tent today?'

'I know you're not open, yet,' Lydia said, by way of apology.

The woman made a dismissive gesture with one hand. 'You have a question?'

Lydia had been about to say 'several questions' but something about the woman's phrasing stopped her. She had the feeling that she had stepped into a fairy tale and, like those stories, there would be rules. If the sister said 'a question' that might mean she would be permitted one only.

The woman moved further back into the tent and Lydia followed. There was a small round table covered in a black cloth with simple wooden chairs on either side. She tapped a laminated piece of paper and sat down.

Lydia took the chair opposite. There was a deck of cards wrapped in black silk, what Lydia assumed was a crystal ball covered in purple velvet, and the laminated price list. 'Cross my palm with silver = £2' was the first item. The costs increased the further down the list you went, finishing with 'Fortune Maker = £66'. The symbols for credit cards ran across the bottom, along with the words 'no cheques or promise notes, valuables accepted, please enquire for alternative payments'.

The space inside the tent seemed to have increased, but Lydia realised it was just that mirrors were set up around the table. Far enough back to be discreet and draped in more thick velvet and silk, they were the reason she had found it difficult to locate the edges of the tent. Just an illusion. Just stagecraft. The lights flickered in the mottled surfaces, multiplied and distorted. In the mirror directly to the side, Lydia saw her own reflection. She looked worried, so she made an effort to control her face, to smooth her expression to something blank. She dug in her pocket for cash. She didn't have a two-pound coin, but she found a five-pound note and put that on the table instead.

The woman pushed it back toward Lydia. 'I don't want your money, Crow. You carry better prizes.'

Lydia's coin appeared in her hand and she closed her fingers around it protectively.

'I wouldn't ask for that. Not for a simple question,' the woman said, glancing at her closed fist. 'I wouldn't be so bold.'

'Or so unwise,' Lydia returned.

She smiled. 'Quite.'

'What do you want?' Lydia could have kicked herself. A question. She would get charged for that, no doubt.

'A favour owed from the head of the Crow Family would be payment enough.'

'That is a very high price.'

'But you have a question, yes? And you want our very best answer?'

Lydia looked around. It was a tent of gimmicks and cheap fabric. She could smell the fried doughnuts beneath the incense and the grass beneath the antique rugs. She was being hustled. Fairground folk were supreme hustlers. No doubt plenty of Pearls had found their way to this world. Especially those with wander-lust, those who wanted to go beyond London. The sister wasn't Pearl, though. Lydia would have laid money that she hadn't a drop of Family blood. In fact, now that Lydia thought about it, she realised she couldn't sense any sort of gleam from the woman at all. Yes. She was being hustled.

'Not a favour,' Lydia said, leaning back. 'I have more cash and will pay you well.' She crossed her hands in her lap and waited. Take it or leave it.

The sister leaned back, too. There was movement in the mirror to her left and Lydia's gaze was drawn. The woman in the mirror looked like the sister sitting opposite her, except her hair was mostly black, threaded with silver strands. She was middle-aged at most. And she wasn't behaving the way a mirror image should. The sister opposite glanced at the mirror and smiled. The mirror image did not smile.

Lydia's breath was in her throat. She knew there was a mirror to the right of the woman. A full-length one with an ornate metal frame and so old that patches of mercury showed through. She was gripped by the feeling that if she looked at that mirror, she would see the third sister. And by the sudden knowledge that that would be a very bad idea indeed. 'A favour,' she managed. 'Fair payment for a fair answer. And safe travels for myself and my associate, my kin, who is waiting outside.'

The sister nodded and held out her hand.

Lydia took it and they shook. She had half-expected that the woman would require a blood oath, with a sliced palm, or some spit, to seal the deal, so it was quite a relief that a simple handshake appeared to be enough.

'There is a man with sunlight in his eyes,' the woman said. 'You want to ask about him, so go ahead.' She reached for the silk-wrapped cards and placed them in front of Lydia.

'There are two men who match that description,'

Lydia said, picking up the deck and unwrapping the silk. 'I want to know about the older one. Ignatius Fleet's father. I need to know how to get rid of him.'

'Shuffle the cards, handle them as much as you like. Think of your question and place three face down in the centre of the table.'

Lydia had assumed that the fortune teller was the one who laid out the cards, but she did as she was told.

The woman stared at the backs of the cards, frowning. She held a hand over the left card but didn't touch it. Her frown turned to something else. A grimace of fear.

'This is a very dangerous question,' she said.

'That is why I am willing to pay with a favour,' Lydia said. 'A deal we have already shaken on.'

The woman raised her eyes to meet Lydia's. Then she nodded quickly. 'True.' She flipped the cards quickly and then reared back from the table as if expecting an explosion.

More stagecraft, Lydia thought, trying to keep her rational brain online. The truth was, the woman with the different reflection didn't feel right. She didn't feel like Crow or Fox or Pearl or Silver. But the absence of those Family signatures wasn't a comfort. It was a disturbing blankness. A space that felt like something snipped out of the world. A hole in a piece of cloth, the gap between the train and the platform, a crevasse in a mountainside. Something you could fall into if you weren't exceedingly careful.

The cards were a standard tarot deck. Lydia recognised the fool, the six of swords and the tower. Emma had been through a tarot phase and had practised on Lydia. She felt a stab of disappointment, but waited politely for the woman to tell her about a journey, a change, a decision. The tarot was excellent at helping you to divine what you already knew, to tease out thoughts and feelings from your subconscious and to even help with making decisions, but it wasn't, in Lydia's experience, capable of telling the future with any accuracy. Besides, she didn't need the future; she needed information. Then she would take care of her own fortune, thank you very much.

'Ask the cards your question and they will answer.'

Feathers. Lydia was itching to leave now, but she dutifully looked at the cards and asked her question. 'How do I make Fleet's father leave in peace?' She added the 'in peace' in the hopes that would encompass her wish for her Family's safety and for Fleet to stay. She didn't want to specify 'without Fleet' to leave that option open in case it was what Fleet truly desired. She had tried to use her power once, to control him, and the impulse had terrified and shamed her. Fleet had to make his own decisions, be captain of his own fate. She wouldn't be like the Pearl King, keeping people against their will or manipulating to believe in whatever she wanted. She wouldn't be like Charlie, using people to her own ends without hesitation.

'To answer that question, you need to know who he is,' the sister said. Her voice had a strange quality, now. It reverberated as if echoing, or as if there was more than one person speaking.

Lydia felt an itching sensation and she wanted to

look into the mirrors on either side of the fortune teller, but she didn't quite dare.

'The father of the sunshine man is not a man. He is The Collector.' She reached out her hand and tapped the first card, the fool, with one finger. 'You are wise to seek knowledge. The fool will not prevail.' She flipped the card and, instead of the blank back, it was the image of a skeleton with a scythe. Death.

The cards had definitely had the standard patterned backing and were not double-sided. Lydia's brain scrambled to explain the illusion. Had the woman done some sneaky sleight-of-hand? But she hadn't laid out the cards, Lydia had. She gripped her coin and kept her eyes on the cards.

The woman tapped the middle card, the six of swords. 'This will show you how to best your foe. Swords will not pierce him.' She flipped the card and this picture was not one from the standard tarot. It was a fox, standing beneath a tree and looking up. Its mouth was open in a smile, as if it was talking to something hidden in the tree. The sun in the corner of the card was almost hidden by clouds.

'Do you want the last card? The outcome of this path?'

'Yes,' Lydia said, not at all sure she did.

She watched the woman flip over the last card. For a moment she thought she had missed the image, that the card had been rotated back to its original position. It was still showing the tower. The structure shaking, blocks falling, lightning bolts hitting the roof, the dark sky. Chaos, destruction, change.

'This card isn't always as bad as it looks,' the sister said, her voice sounding normal again.

Lydia nodded. She felt a little nauseous.

The sister had something approaching sympathy in her grey eyes. 'We haven't dealt with The Collector ourselves, but we know of his ways. If you can, it might be easier to give him what he desires. That's the only sure way to make him leave.'

Hell Hawk. 'What's the non-certain method?'

The sister gave a half shrug. 'The cards have spoken.'

'Thank you,' Lydia kept her manners as she stood to leave.

'We know how to find you,' the woman said. 'We will see you again, Crow.'

Well, that had the ring of prophecy, Lydia thought. Feathers.

CHAPTER TWELVE

The rehearsal rooms were available on an hourly, half-day or full-day rate. Lydia chose one with a private entrance and waiting area and booked it for the afternoon. Arriving an hour before Rafferty was expected, she found a light and airy room with a sprung wooden floor like a dance studio, triple-height ceilings and white walls. A long table was set up along one end with chairs on one side, facing the body of the room. The waiting area had a small blue sofa and a table with bottled water, a stack of paper cups and a pod coffee machine. There was a basic desk with a chair behind it and Lydia set Aiden up there with his laptop and a stack of mocked-up CVs with headshots.

He slouched in the chair and Lydia decided not to correct him on it. He had the good looks and inherent confidence she associated with the acting world, and perhaps it would help to sell the lie to Rafferty. As long as he couldn't smell 'Crow' at three paces, of course. If he had that ability, they were sunk.

At the appointed time, Lydia went into the studio, leaving Aiden. She didn't close the door between them fully, and stood near it so that she could hear what was happening in the waiting area.

In the end, Rafferty was only twenty minutes late. 'Sorry, sorry,' he said as he bounded up the steps, all affable charm and excellent cheek bones.

'No problem, Mr Hill,' Aiden said, his voice just the right side of jaded deference. Lydia wondered how long Aiden would hold out before he was offering to lick the Pearl's feet. She could feel the waves of Pearl and took a slow, deep breath to calm her heart. Her coin was in her hand and she squeezed it, using feather and claw to cut through the fog of desire.

'This won't take long,' Aiden said.

'No worries,' another voice spoke and Lydia realised that Rafferty wasn't alone.

'I'll look after him,' Aiden said smoothly. 'This way, Mr Hill. They are ready for you.'

Lydia stepped quietly back, keeping behind the door so that Rafferty would walk in before catching sight of her.

Once he was inside, before he could turn to ask what was going on, Lydia closed the door and stepped in front of it. 'Hello, Rafferty.'

He frowned, but it had an air of performance. Like frowning was something he had learned from a YouTube video. In a second his skin smoothed and he smiled in recognition. 'You're the PI.'

'I'm Lydia Crow, head of the Crow Family, and I need to speak with you. It concerns the truce.'

'That old thing? I'm not interested in history.' He waved a hand. 'Can I just check. There is no reading? No film?'

'No. I'm sorry for the performance but this is important and I needed to be sure you would show up.' Lydia's use of the word 'performance' was very deliberate. She thought it would sound more forgivable to an actor than 'subterfuge'. A word to stop him thinking the truth of 'outright lie'.

Rafferty's eyes narrowed. 'And what part am I to play?'

'The part of noble Pearl,' Lydia said. 'Head of the Pearl Family in this city.' She had lapsed instinctively into the archaic and overblown speech of the Pearl King.

'There is no Pearl Family. Not in the sense you mean. And, even if there were, I'm not interested.' His phone was out of his pocket and he was scrolling. 'Congratulations. You've just wasted both of our time.'

Lydia resisted the urge to knock the phone from his hand. She kept her voice gentle, aiming for admiration and deference. Not her strongest suits. 'But you are the most powerful of your bloodline. That makes you the leader, whether you recognise it or not.'

He looked up from his phone and smiled, and Lydia felt her whole body go weak. Her mouth flooded and she swallowed, trying to ignore the tingling that was happening in every sensitive part of her body. Feathers. Claws tearing. Wings spread wide. Clear skies. Her coin was spinning in the air between them, and she hadn't meant for it to happen. She blinked and called it back to her hand. It didn't shift.

Rafferty was watching the coin with a new light in his eyes. 'That is perfect. What a picture.' He held his phone up.

'No,' Lydia said. She reached out and, without thinking, slipped into his consciousness and stopped the muscles of his arm and hand before he could press the screen to take the photo.

Rafferty's eyes widened as he realised he couldn't move that part of his body. Then they flared in fear and anger as Lydia made his fingers open and his phone fell, the screen cracking on impact.

'I don't have any interest in playing games with you. And I don't wish to insult or threaten.' Lydia released control of Rafferty's body, fighting her own urge to take a step back. 'This is a peaceful meeting. I want to get the Families together, to renew our combined commitment to the nineteen forty-three truce.'

Rafferty held out his arm, stretching and flexing his fingers. 'How did you do that?'

'I apologise,' Lydia said soothingly.

Rafferty's head was tilted and he was watching her with an appraising look. 'Can you do it again? On anybody?'

'Can I count on you for your support?' Lydia tried to get the conversation back on track. 'It's important that we provide a united front so that the Silvers and Foxes recommit to the truce.'

Rafferty blinked. 'What makes you think I'm the most powerful Pearl? I'm an actor. I'm not a...' he waved a hand. 'Freak.'

Charming. 'When the Pearl court disbanded, their

power was released into the world.' Lydia wasn't going to get into the details of *how* the court was destroyed. Rafferty didn't seem overly interested in his lineage, but that didn't mean he wouldn't be offended at the thought of her offing his royal ancestor. 'At the same time, you clearly underwent a change. A boost of power. I am putting the two events together.' Especially since you seem to have changed personality, and have started speaking like the dead Pearl King. More thoughts Lydia felt were better kept to herself.

'I don't know what you mean.'

'You do,' Lydia said. 'You had a breakdown, went missing for weeks.'

His beautiful face was twisted in displeasure. 'I told you before, it was a creative awakening. I found my destiny was bigger than I ever imagined. I always knew I was an artist, but I didn't realise my gift transcended my calling to the stage and screen.'

Lydia thought she might throw up if he carried on much longer, but thankfully he trailed off, staring into the distance as if seeing his destiny in technicolour, projected against the white wall of the rehearsal room. Maybe he was. 'This doesn't have to interfere with your life, your plans, your art. It might even provide depth and dimension. I mean, don't artists draw on adversity?'

Rafferty smiled coldly. 'I think you are mocking me.'

'I'm not,' Lydia said, truthfully. 'I don't understand art. Or being an actor. Or any of this,' she waved a hand to encompass the white studio. 'And I'm terrified that I won't be able to convince you to join the truce.'

'Why?'

'You know about the original truce?'

He nodded. 'Of course.'

'It's shaky and needs to be restated.' She wondered how to summarise Charlie's thirst for revenge, Maria's desire for power, and the new threat in the city.

'I will join it,' he waved a hand. 'Why not? I told you it doesn't mean anything, that I don't lead the Pearl Family, but I'm happy to say it. If it means you will leave me alone.'

'Would you say that in front of the other Families? The leaders, I mean?'

'Sure,' Rafferty said. 'If you hadn't broken my phone, I would offer to call them this instant.' Petulant now.

She was losing him, she could feel it. He was shifting his weight and soon would walk from the room. She could stop his body, of course, but that wasn't going to help. She needed his cooperation. 'If I put a dinner together. Somewhere exclusive. Really nice food and drinks, an exclusive party for the most powerful people in the city. Would you come?'

'Would there be paps?'

'No, no publicity. This is the real power. Not the stuff that's for show.'

Rafferty pouted. 'For show is real power. In my world.'

Lydia considered. 'I could leak a story to the press about it. Afterward. I can't have cameras turn up, but after I could plant a story about Rafferty Hill's connections. It would give you an edge. Think about all the publicity your disappearance got. This would keep the mystery going, keep you in the public eye, add hype to your next project.'

'And we're talking one party? Nothing else?'

'One evening. You would need to attend, speak to the heads of the Families, tell them you're in support of the truce. It'll take an hour tops.'

A pause while Rafferty considered. Lydia squeezed her coin to stop herself from fidgeting.

Eventually, he inclined his head. A king giving his assent. 'I think I could help you with your project.'

'Thank you. Before you go,' Lydia held up the pearl pendant. 'Do you recognise this?'

He raised a perfect eyebrow. 'Should I?'

'I am investigating challenges to the truce.'

Rafferty shrugged. 'I told you. I have no interest in Family politics. I'm an artist. Everything I do is in service of my higher calling.'

Lydia nodded, pocketing the pendant.

'Looks real, though, you should get it valued.'

'Thank you,' Lydia said. 'I'll be in touch about that meeting.'

'Can I just check?' Rafferty paused by the door. 'There's definitely no movie?'

LYDIA HAD AN HOUR BEFORE FLEET WAS DUE TO arrive. She had a long shower, trying to wash away the Pearl arrogance, which seemed to cling to her skin. It wasn't Rafferty Hill's fault, she knew. He had been filled with a burst of Pearl energy, possibly remnants of the Pearl King's personality had joined him along with his spirit. If the only effect was making him an insufferable conversationalist and a narcissistic fame hound, she – and London – had got off extremely lightly.

Towelling off in the bedroom, Lydia tried to remind herself of this fact. Tried to feel grateful. A light knock on the door jolted her from her ruminations. 'Hang on.' She quickly pulled on underwear, jeans and a black vest top with thin straps. 'Come in.'

Jason opened the door. His eyes roved the room, taking in the clothes on the floor, the bedside table over-flowing with empty coke cans, water bottles and choco-late bar wrappers. 'You live like an animal.'

'Just because you're a neat-freak,' Lydia said. 'And I've been busy.'

'Uh-huh,' Jason said, his lips pursed.

'Did you want something?'

Jason drifted to the unmade bed and perched on the end. 'Just to talk. You haven't called that insurance woman back. Or that guy with the missing nana.'

'I'm guessing they will have gone elsewhere by now,' Lydia said. 'Or their problems will have resolved them-selves. That happens.'

'You haven't taken a case in weeks.' Jason said. He held up a hand before she could respond. 'You've been busy, I know. There's been... A lot. Family stuff. Fleet. I know.'

'I'm more worried about Charlie right now,' Lydia said. 'And then there's Paul. He thinks a Crow left a feather for him, that's enough to sour things between us and the Foxes. Not to mention how pissed off the Foxes are with the Silvers and vice versa.'

'I've been thinking about that,' Jason said. 'Doesn't Maria have CCTV in her offices? Can't she use that to see who left the tail?'

'Her clients are big on privacy and confidentiality,' Lydia said. 'No cameras.'

He pushed the loose sleeves of his jacket up to his elbows, a reflex action that made him appear reassuringly alive. Or, at least, less ghostly. 'It's probably for the best.'

'Yeah,' Lydia agreed, thinking of the hit of 'Crow' she had got from the tail. 'We dodged a bullet, there.'

'So, you're sure? That it was one of us?'

Lydia loved that Jason counted himself as part of the family. It warmed her inside.

'Who would do it, though? And why?'

'My best guess is Daisy, acting on Charlie's orders. I don't think the pendant is part of it. Or, at least, Rafferty has nothing to do with it. So that's something.'

'You asked him about it?'

'Yeah. He couldn't have been less interested.'

'He is an actor.'

Lydia nodded her acceptance of this fact. 'But he's not *that* good.'

CHAPTER THIRTEEN

Lydia was dreaming. She knew it was a dream because her dead cousin was there. She hadn't visited her in this way since she had died, and Lydia wondered what had prompted her to do so now. Maddie wasn't speaking. Wasn't near enough for Lydia to hear even if she was. Lydia was on the street outside The Fork and had just caught a glimpse of her cousin rounding the corner ahead. One moment she had been there, her distinctive stride in heeled leather boots and a red swishy dress, glossy hair tumbling down her back. The next, she was around the corner and away. Out of sight.

Dream Lydia wondered what it meant, this glimpse of her dead kin. She turned back to the cafe, but instead of the familiar windows and doorway of The Fork, she found she was outside Charlie's house in Denmark Hill. Crows sat sentry on either side of his front door. And then, in the staccato nature of dreams, she was in the kitchen. The French doors looked out onto a wintery garden, thick snow that hardly ever happened in London covered the patio and lawn. The trees and shrubs were black stumps, each providing a perch for a crow, a raven, a magpie. Charlie was making an espresso, his back to Lydia.

'You made it,' he said, turning to greet her. Charlie looked young, the man from the photographs of her father and grandfather. But his expression wasn't young or hopeful or kind. His lips twitched up into a dead eye smile. His shark smile.

She woke up, heart racing.

Fleet was asleep, his breathing deep and steady. She lay still, taking quiet slow breaths through her nose, willing her heartbeat to slow. The fragments of the dream persisted and she could see Charlie's face clearly. The flatness of his gaze. The cold smile.

She wanted to call home, to hear her parents' voices. She wanted to curl against Fleet and wake him up so that he could distract her. She wanted to get out of the flat and run until she was exhausted and her mind was blank.

She produced her coin and made it hang a few inches from her face. Then she added coins until the air above the bed was filled with gold discs, each spinning in different directions and at different angles. Then she sent them flying in formation, dipping and swirling like a murmuration of starlings.

Fleet shifted, turning over so that he was lying on his side, facing toward Lydia. She sent the coins back to wherever they came from and turned to face Fleet.

He blinked sleepily and she watched the consciousness return behind his eyes.

'I had a bad dream,' she said.

Fleet put an arm over her body, pulled her close. She closed her eyes and breathed in. Fleet. Safety.

His body stiffened.

Lydia moved back to look into his eyes again. Now they were wide open and glazed, staring at something she couldn't see.

It didn't last long, just a few seconds, and then Fleet was back. She had gone rigid with tension and before she could unglue her mouth to ask, he spoke in a rush.

'Charlie's free.'

Lydia's mouth went dry. 'You saw him?'

Fleet nodded. 'He was outside The Fork. Standing in the street.'

'Could have been in the past. Might not mean he's out now...'

At that moment her phone rang. Lydia rolled over and grabbed her mobile, sitting up to take the call. It was Aiden, sounding shaken. 'John and Daisy have called a meeting. They said not to tell you.'

Feathers. 'Okay. Good.'

'Good?' Aiden sounded freaked out. Young.

'It's okay,' Lydia said, putting as much strength and reassurance into her voice as she could. 'Thank you for telling me. You go along to it and report back after. When is it?'

'This afternoon. At their house.'

Something occurred to her. 'Why would they tell you about it? Doesn't everybody know you work for me?'

Aiden's throat convulsed as he swallowed. 'I've been complaining... Sort of. Putting it about that I'm not happy. Just as a strategy, like. So that people will be open around me. I thought it would be a good way of keeping an eye on things, you know. I don't mean any of it.'

Lydia could hear the fear in his voice. He was frightened of her. That was good, of course, but it still hurt. She wasn't a monster.

'That was smart,' she said. 'It's good to keep people guessing.'

'That's what I thought...' Aiden trailed off. 'People open up when they think I agree with them.'

'Good work. You go,' she repeated. 'Just go along and suss it out. We'll work out what to do when we know what we're dealing with.'

'What if everyone is there?'

'Then we'll know that what we're dealing with is big,' Lydia said.

Fleet was watching her carefully. 'There's a Crow meeting?'

'A secret one, yeah. Daisy called it.'

'What are you going to do?'

Lydia gave him a long look in the half-darkness of the bedroom. She willed him not to ask again.

'Lyds,' Fleet said. 'You can't kill her.'

'That's what you're worried about?'

'Well, yes... I know she has gone against you, that this is plotting or whatever, but...'

'I'm not going to kill my aunt,' Lydia said crisply.

'And I can't believe you think I would.'

Fleet opened his mouth. If he said anything other than 'sorry' she was going to lose her mind.

'I'm sorry.' He gathered her in for a hug and she let it happen, leaning into his body and inhaling the mix of pheromones and clean sweat somehow warmed by sunshine, that meant 'Fleet'.

'I'm just worried about you. You have done so much for your family, and this is how they repay you. I'm angry so I know you must be.'

That made Lydia straighten up in surprise. She realised that she wasn't. She felt irritated, sure. A touch of frustration that there was yet another fire to put out, but she wasn't angry with Daisy or the Crows who might show up to the meeting to have a moan. She was the leader, and that meant being alone at the top. If she couldn't handle that, she shouldn't be doing the job. And people had every right to moan. She would learn from their grievances and do better. She wasn't Charlie, subduing everyone with fear and hate. And if she was going to continue to steer the Family into solidly legal and ethical business models, she was going to have to keep them onside with something other than old fears and the traditional power dynamic.

'And I didn't mean to say that... I don't think you would...'

He trailed off, maybe realising that Lydia had, in fact, killed a member of her family before. 'For you,' she wanted to say, but that wasn't the whole story, of course. Maddie had been psychotic. A danger to all and her threatening Fleet was just one of many reasons Lydia had counted before throwing them both off a roof together. A one-sided suicide pact.

'I'm not offended that you think I'm capable of it, just that you think I would make such a poor decision. Why would you jump to that?' As soon as the words were out of her mouth, Lydia saw a darkness cross Fleet's face. Guilt. And something else, something hard to identify. Was it fear? The truth struck her. 'You saw it.'

'I'm seeing all kinds of things. The same events, happening in multiple ways. Nightmares. Visions. Things happening over and over in a loop. Then starting again but with everyone in different clothes. I'm seeing everything and it's bleeding into how I feel about... How I judge... I don't even know what is going on right now, let alone what is going to happen. I told you.'

'I know,' Lydia reached out to him. 'I know. I'm sorry. I'm not trying to pick a fight or make you feel bad. I know you're scared.'

'I'm fucking terrified,' Fleet said, passing a hand over his face. 'I don't know how much longer I can hold on.'

AIDEN SLOUCHED INTO THE FORK. HE HAD SWAPPED his usual floppy knitted beanie for a flat cap, the brim pulled down low. He slid into the seat opposite Lydia and began drumming his fingers on the table. Lydia looked at his hands pointedly until he stopped. One knee was still bouncing, but Lydia didn't have the heart to make him stop that as well. Aiden was clearly in no fit state to sit still.

'Just tell me,' Lydia said. 'How was it?'

The café was almost empty and nobody was sitting near to them, but Aiden still glanced around before he hunched forward and began speaking. 'John and Daisy were there, obviously.'

Not obvious, Lydia thought. She hadn't been sure how much was just Daisy and how much John was complicit. That sealed things. 'Who else?'

Aiden reeled off the names of three cousins, a couple of managers from the betting shops, and a name Lydia didn't recognise. 'Who is Garth?'

'Yeah, I didn't know him. He's a second or third cousin, I think. He said his dad was out of the Family, not involved, but that he had wanted to know more about his heritage.' Aiden shook his head. 'He chose one hell of a time to get curious.'

Lydia felt the sting of rejection. 'Why hasn't he sought me out?'

Aiden shrugged and resumed tapping the table. 'I really don't think he knows anything. He teaches P.E. at a comprehensive in Clapham.'

'That's no excuse,' Lydia began, not really sure why she was fixating on Garth and his lack of manners and knowledge.

'Yeah. I set him straight. He knows about this place now.' Aiden indicated the café. 'I wouldn't be surprised to see him here soon.'

'Unless the meeting scared him off. How bad was it?'

Aiden's leg jiggled more violently. 'Not too bad, as it goes.'

'Aiden,' Lydia said, trying to stay patient. 'Just tell

me.' She could feel her coin in her hand and she slipped it into her jeans pocket.

Aiden was staring at her arms, his eyes wide, and she glanced down. Her tattoo was moving. The crow wings beating up and down and the falling feathers ruffling in invisible wind.

'Daisy was talking shit about you, saying you weren't fit to lead the Family.' Aiden's words came out in a rush and he kept his gaze lowered to the table.

'I warned her,' Lydia said, shaking her head. Hell Hawk. She would have to follow through. 'What else?'

'Nothing solid, like. No big plan. Just bitching about you and saying how much better it was in the old days.'

'When Charlie was in charge.' A cold hollow opened up in Lydia's stomach.

Aiden tucked his head even lower. 'Kind of. Yeah.'

'Who else was talking?'

Aiden seemed to notice that his fingers were tapping and he stopped himself, clasping his hands together so tightly the knuckles shone white. 'I don't feel... I dunno.'

'Aiden,' Lydia said. 'You went to the meeting specifically so that you could report back. All I want is information so I can work out how to calm everything down, bring the family together.'

Aiden was staring at his clasped hands. 'What will happen to them?'

'Daisy and John were warned. This isn't their first strike.'

'Yeah, fair dos. But what about the others? I know it's not good that they were there, but...'

'They'll get warnings. That's all. Maybe not even

that. You know me. We've worked together for a while now, and I would hope you'd know this isn't some power trip for me. I just want to keep the family safe and working together. But I don't need everyone to like me or to be sitting around singing my praises all day, every day.'

Aiden snorted, some of the tension leaving his body. 'That's good.'

'All right,' Lydia said, smiling. 'So, tell me about it.'

Aiden raised his chin from the table and looked Lydia in the eyes. 'They weren't joining in. Though the guy who runs the shop on Church Street, he was a bit mouthy. Bitching about his profits and protection and the shops getting turned over that time.'

Lydia nodded to show she wasn't surprised. 'Anything else?'

'Daisy was pushing for more, but there wasn't the appetite. I could tell it was too much too soon, you know? The others just wanted a bit of a moan.'

'I think you're trying to play it down,' Lydia said after a moment.

'Yeah,' Aiden ducked his head back down so that the words emanated from his stomach and all she could see was the top of his bowed head. 'I don't want a bloodbath.'

CHAPTER FOURTEEN

Jason's internet sleuthing had come up empty. 'He doesn't have a father named on his birth certificate and his mother basically didn't have an internet presence. It must have been difficult, even back then, but clearly it was possible.'

'Not like now,' Lydia said. These days you had to plan ahead and work extremely hard not to have a virtual footprint.

Having asked Jason to investigate her lover, it shouldn't have been that big a leap to visit Auntie behind Fleet's back. But it felt worse. Much worse. She knew she could have tried harder to speak to Fleet about his father, but things had felt so fraught between them recently it was easier to go elsewhere for answers.

Lydia's tattoos were moving as she approached Auntie's flat, but she didn't know if that was a supernatural warning or just her guilt making her uncomfortable.

A woman Lydia didn't recognise answered the door, but Auntie was on her way to the living room with a cotton bag and she had a clear line of sight to the front entrance. Lydia directed her words to Auntie. 'I need to speak to you.'

Auntie nodded. She turned to the young woman who had opened the door, but she was already moving. 'Tea. I know. Don't worry, I'll put my headphones in. Won't hear a thing.'

'Good girl,' Auntie said.

She motioned for Lydia to follow her into the cramped living room. It didn't seem possible, but somehow there seemed to be even more furniture than last time. Lydia sat on the small flowery couch, waiting until Auntie got settled in her armchair. She put the cotton bag, which appeared to be full of yarn, onto the floor by her feet.

With a quick glance to the doorway, Lydia leaned forward, her arms resting on her knees. 'I need to know everything you know about Fleet's father.'

Auntie's face creased in displeasure. 'Why? What is the point in raking up that bad penny?'

'Because he's here. In London.'

Auntie shook her head once. A sharp denial.

'I have met him. Twice, in fact.'

'No.'

This was the closest Lydia had seen to Auntie flustered. Even when Fleet was missing, she hadn't appeared as disturbed. If she had been looking for extra signs that this man was bad news, she had one now. 'What do you know about him?'

The young woman walked in with a tray and offered it to Auntie first. On it were two cups of tea, complete with saucers. 'I didn't know if you wanted cake...'

'Nothing to eat,' Auntie said. 'Our guest isn't staying.'

The woman nodded and left the room.

Lydia took a sip of her tea to be polite and then put the cup and saucer onto a spindly side table with a hexagonal top.

Auntie was watching her with clear affront. It was like Lydia had walked in and mooned the woman. She drank her tea in a determined way, finally placing the cup and saucer onto yet another small table.

'I wouldn't ask if it wasn't important,' Lydia said. 'Please.'

'I won't have this... You need to leave.'

'I can't,' Lydia said. 'I don't mean any disrespect, but I need answers. He is here and he is interested in Fleet. He won't talk about it, Fleet, I mean. You know he went missing? I found him following his dad like a lost puppy. I need to know how to help Fleet. Ignatius.'

'You mustn't speak of this with him,' Auntie snapped. 'He needs to forget about this man.'

'Then you must help me.'

Auntie glared at Lydia with renewed vigour.

Lydia picked up her teacup and sipped it, signalling that she wasn't about to leave. There was a short silence. The only sound was a mantle clock ticking loudly.

When Auntie spoke, it was as if the words were being dragged out of her throat. 'He's not a man.'

'I don't want riddles,' Lydia said. The skin was prickling and the muscles of her back and shoulders tensed.

'He travels the world. He won't stay in London for long. You just keep out of his way.'

Lydia swallowed her irritation and kept her mouth shut. Auntie was looking down at her lap. Her fingers plucked at the material of her flowery skirt and Lydia realised something: she was scared.

'I know he's The Collector,' Lydia said gently. 'I know that's a title. A label for something hard to name. I'm not trying to make trouble for your family. I only want to help Fleet.'

Eventually, Auntie spoke. 'Our beautiful girl met a traveller on a moonlit night. It didn't matter that she knew better, that she knew all the stories. He was so handsome and so charming that she forgot them all. She didn't come home for seven days. Her mother and I were beside ourselves with worry. The police were looking, our neighbours formed a search party, they sent scuba men into the river to look for her body.' Auntie shook her head, her eyes glistening with remembered pain. 'I could feel that she was alive, but my faith was beginning to shake. I was beginning to think that it was hope clouding my intuition. That's when she walked in the door. That door.' Auntie waved in the direction of the front of the flat.

'I saw in an instant. She had been taken by The River Man. Her eyes were yellow with reflected sunlight. Her step was so light it almost didn't touch the ground. I kissed my girl and I thanked the moon and the stars that she hadn't stayed another day.'

'What would have happened if she had stayed with him for eight days?'

Auntie's lips folded so tight they disappeared. She shook her head sharply. 'I will not speak of it. I will not give the words form and air.'

'And she came home pregnant? With Fleet?'

A sharp look. 'Yes.'

Lydia tried to formulate another question, something that would tell her what she needed to know. 'That must have been hard. For her, I mean.'

'She loved Ignatius,' Auntie said. 'She was a good mother.'

'I'm sure she was.'

'Even as she pined for his father, even as she came to realise that he was never coming back for her. Even when she realised what he was.'

'What was he?'

Auntie shook her head. 'When Ignatius was a baby, his eyes were the colour of sunflowers. He never cried. He babbled to people we couldn't see. He was always so warm, like he was burning from the inside.'

Lydia swallowed. Fleet's sunshine smile. 'What did you do?'

'We loved him,' Auntie said, a touch of sharpness in her tone. 'His mama put salt on the windowsill and doorway of the bedroom they shared and she prayed every night. It all faded as he grew, but she never stopped being vigilant. The heat inside her baby banked down, but her memories of the traveller stayed sharp.'

'She was frightened that his father would return?'

Auntie tilted her hand from side to side, indicating uncertainty. 'She wanted him, desperately. And she was frightened of him. She kept the name that he had given

135

her child. Like she wanted to do his bidding.' A note of bitterness crept into her tone. 'A man like that,' a firm head shake. 'I'm sure you know. A man like that can ruin the brightest and the best.'

Lydia hoped that Fleet's mother hadn't been ruined, that she had lived a happy life despite the lasting effects of an encounter with the travelling man. She thanked Auntie and made her way home, unable to shake the image of a young woman putting salt on the windowsills, of a baby with strangely yellow eyes babbling to invisible friends.

CHAPTER FIFTEEN

L ydia went to the barbershop in Whitechapel that
housed the concealed entrance to the Fox Family
hub. She didn't know where Paul slept at night, but this
was the closest thing to his home that she knew about.

There was a man sitting in one of the barber chairs.
He had an immaculate hair style, smooth-looking skin
and a short beard with razor-sharp edges – the kind of
look which advertised his skills and his willingness to
spend time grooming. He waved a hand. 'I'm fully
booked.'

'I'm not here for you,' Lydia said, walking past him to
the hidden entrance to the Foxes' bar.

A muffled curse from behind. And one word clearly
audible. 'Crow.'

Lydia stopped. She turned slowly and looked
directly into the barber's eyes.

After a moment, he looked down. 'No offence.'

Lydia turned away and headed down the flight of
stairs in the back corner. She pushed through the hidden

doorway behind the Elvis poster and into the low-lit private bar.

She found Paul sitting at a table at the back of the room. He was alone apart from a man behind the gleaming bar who nodded at Lydia. There was an empty pint glass and Paul had been reading a paperback. He turned down the corner of his page before putting it down. 'Little Bird. To what do I owe the honour?'

Lydia turned to the barman and asked for a whisky.

'She'll have the Laphroaig cask strength.'

The barman nodded at Paul and reached underneath the bar for a green bottle.

He was treating her to the expensive stuff. 'It'll be wasted on me,' Lydia said, taking the drink. 'Cheers.' She drained half of the measure with one swallow.

'Is this a social call?'

'I'm not staying,' Lydia said. She didn't move to sit down, either, but took a couple of steps to be a little closer to Paul's table. 'I'm here to give you an update.'

'You've got another day until the solstice. Is this you working for extra credit?' Paul's voice was full of warmth and it was dangerously alluring.

'This is me trying to keep the peace,' Lydia said briskly. 'Don't twist things to mean more than they do.'

He sat back in his chair, a small smile playing on his lips. 'I'm listening.'

'The stranger in town. The reason your family has left London. I assume you would be interested in knowing his identity?'

Paul sat forward. 'I gave you three days to find out who left a feather in my bed and the tail for Maria

Silver. Are they connected, or is this you trying to distract me?'

'Not distract,' Lydia said. 'Appease.'

'I like that, too.'

'I thought you would.' Lydia finished the rest of the whisky. Being nice to Paul Fox took sustenance. 'It started with a gift.'

'You were left one, too? Or was it brought by your little henchman?'

'Sort of.' Paul had been deeply amused that a jackdaw had brought Lydia a pearl pendant, and it seemed it wasn't a joke he was going to let go of anytime soon. She decided not to share with him that a magpie had brought her the key. He would probably die laughing. 'The important part is that I found the stranger.'

'I can't stand the suspense.'

'It is Fleet's father. He's the new man in town. The stranger that's unsettling everybody and everything. I'm willing to bet he's the reason the Foxes have scattered.'

'So I should be scared of your future father-in-law?'

Lydia shuddered. It hadn't occurred to her that she would be forever connected to the man with the light eyes and the ragged coat. Not a pleasant thought. But still, she wouldn't blame Fleet for his family. Feathers knew you couldn't choose them.

Paul was watching her, assessing. 'This is the truth?'

'Yes.'

He pulled a face.

'What?'

'Well,' Paul spread his hands. 'You know blood. I'm not sweating Fleet so it's hard to get worked up about his

139

old man.' He eyed Lydia. 'Unless you know something you're not telling me.'

Lydia shook her head. 'Nothing concrete, yet. Just bad feelings.' She didn't want to send Paul after Fleet's father, so she wasn't going to give him any more detail. Like the fact that she thought he had poisoned the mixed bathing pond on the heath. 'And I've got news about the other objects, too.'

'Let's have it.'

'I'm not certain, but I think it was my aunt.' Lydia wasn't going to tell Paul that Daisy was acting on Charlie's orders. That wasn't information she wanted out in the world. 'I'm dealing with it.'

Paul had gone very still. 'There's only one way to make this right. I don't say it lightly, but...'

'I'm going to deal with it. I promise you.'

Lydia had visited the Spaniards before, when she had been looking for Fleet. A barmaid had remembered him and had thought that he had been meeting somebody. Lydia assumed, now, that the person had been Fleet's father. Something else to confirm with Fleet. Her investigative mind instinctively wanted to check every fact, to make sure that she wasn't missing any details or filling in blanks incorrectly. She didn't need to follow the case of the missing Fleet. He was there, waiting in the traditional pub bar of the Spaniards Inn. He was ordering drinks when she arrived and he greeted her with a kiss and smile, as if this was a normal evening. A normal date.

She waited until they were seated in a corner, and taken their first sips of their drinks. Fleet had a pint of orange juice and lemonade and she had gone for a lime and soda. Both wanted to keep their heads completely clear, it seemed.

The barmaid that Lydia had spoken to on her previous visit walked over with a couple of menus and put them on the table. She smiled at Fleet, trying to catch his eye. Lydia watched Fleet fail to notice and the barmaid's slight disappointment. She had nothing against the woman, so she made her own thanks extra warm.

Once they had ordered, Lydia regarded Fleet and wondered when he was going to stop pretending they were in a pub in Hampstead under normal circumstances.

'How was your day?' He asked, not-quite-looking into her eyes.

'Fleet.' Lydia reached across the table and put her hand onto his, curling her fingers into his palm.

He looked away, but she felt his fingers wrap around her hand in an answering gesture.

'Did you mean to come to the heath?' Or did you just find yourself here, the unspoken part of the question. He had called her five minutes after she was expecting him at her flat, suggesting that they meet near the heath for dinner, instead of their planned takeaway on the sofa.

The shrug was so small it was barely there. A twitch.

'Do you remember how you got here?'

'My car is on Hampstead Lane.'

Which wasn't an answer. Lydia wondered how often Fleet was driving with no memory of it after. Presumably he was alert in the moment. She hoped he was alert in the moment. Or that he would see sense and stop getting behind the wheel. 'Did you see something? Something that made you want to come here?'

Another proto-shrug. 'I keep dreaming about a clearing on the heath. The sky is red and the earth is black. The buildings aren't normal. There is something wrong with the skyline. It doesn't look right, but I can't tell you why. It's a dream. Just a dream.' He broke off as the server appeared with their food.

Lydia was just working out a way to approach her towering burger when Fleet spoke again. 'I'm going to get a handle on it. I'm not going to let it affect me. So, I'm having wild dreams and the occasional premonition.' He lowered his voice for this last bit. Then he flashed her an imitation of his usual smile. 'I'm fine. I'm going to be fine. You don't have to worry.'

Before Lydia could work out how to respond to this wall of denial, Fleet dropped his fork with a clatter. He was staring at Lydia but in a way that was clear he wasn't seeing her. It was the thousand-yard stare that Archie had got when he was a tired toddler, moments before he sparked out on the sofa with his comfort blankie.

She waited until he blinked and focused on her, the dazed look fading. 'All right?'

'Yeah, yeah.' Fleet looked down. 'I'm fine. It's nothing. Just... Thinking about those people. The swimmers. Most of them are out of hospital, so that's good. That one guy. He's still...'

Lydia let Fleet talk on, trying to cover up the fact that he'd had a vision and he didn't want to talk about it. He looked lost.

'Let's go home,' she said. She went up to the bar and asked the woman to box up their food to takeaway.

'I'm driving,' Lydia said, in a tone that wasn't open for discussion. 'I'll send someone to fetch your car.'

Once they were back at the flat, she put the food into the fridge. She wasn't hungry and Fleet was sitting on the sofa, staring into space.

'I talked to Auntie.'

Fleet had been motionless, but somehow he stilled further. 'Is that right?'

'She said your father is a traveller. She called him some other things, too.'

'I'll bet.'

The frustration broke through. 'You think I won't understand? I'm Lydia Crow. My Family is one of only four magical Families in London.'

'That you know of.'

That stopped her. 'Yes. I was always told there were four. You know how it goes with stories.'

A small nod. Fleet's jaw was still clenched, but he looked at Lydia, at least.

'I know what it is to grow up with unusual heritage. To want to be normal, while knowing in my bones that I am not and never will be. And I know what it's like to be brought up separate from the stories, away from their source, but still feel the pull of them. All that mystery, all that confusion. My mum didn't want me to grow up a Crow. You know that. She didn't want me to be part of that world, so I know.' Lydia leaned forward, the words pouring out in her attempt to make him understand. To trust her. To know that he couldn't shock or surprise or disgust her. 'I know what it's like.'

Fleet closed his eyes. The tension was still written on his face, his shoulders. She took his hand and towed him to the sofa, pushing him to sit and then straddling his lap so that she could wrap herself around him. She hugged him as tightly as possible, trying to convey with her body what her words could not. After a few seconds, she felt his arms encircle her and he hugged her back, burying his head in her neck. A tremor ran through his body and Lydia rubbed his back in soothing circles. When they broke the embrace, her neck was wet and Fleet wiped his eyes.

'What did your mum tell you about your dad?'

'He's not my 'dad'. That's too homely a word. That's a role. He's my father, technically speaking, that's it.'

It was Lydia's turn to nod. No wonder he was angry. Fleet's fury she understood. What she didn't get was his fascination. His desire to leave with his father. He was an adult now. Not a lost child, keening for an absent parent.

'She told me I was her miracle. Her blessing. She didn't like to speak of the man, so we didn't. I didn't ask and she didn't volunteer. You've got to understand, nobody mentioned him. Not once.'

'That must have been confusing.'

'Not until my teens. I just accepted it until then. It seemed fine. And it wasn't like I was the only kid without a dad.' Fleet passed a hand over his face. 'Then I started wondering. I was clearly my mother's son, but I wanted to know about the other half. Was he from the same place? Was he angry, like me?'

'You were angry?'

'I was fourteen,' Fleet said, as an explanation.

'So you asked.'

'Yeah.' He pinched the bridge of his nose like he had a headache. Then looked Lydia in the eye. 'She told me he was a travelling man. That he was known to her as The Collector, but some people called him The River Man. She had called him something else, something private that was just for her and she wouldn't reveal. She told me that she didn't regret the time she spent with him, even though it took her many years to get over his loss. She said it was because she got me, but I think it was also because it was just that good. Some memories are worth the pain, kind of thing.'

Lydia's coin was in her palm and she squeezed it to stop herself from speaking. Fleet was looking at her, but not really seeing, and she didn't want to break his flow.

'I didn't ask again. I didn't want any more stories. Not ones like that. My best friend, his dad split up with his mum when we were in primary school, but he knew where he was. His dad fixed boxing matches in Manchester. He was called Tony and every few months, he would show up and take my friend to the cinema or bowling.'

Lydia understood the desire to be normal. That had been the story of her school days, too. She shoved her coin into the pocket of her jeans and reached for Fleet's hand. 'Did she tell you anything else?'

He shrugged. 'Only that he gave me my name.'

'Ignatius?'

'No, that was mum. It means 'fiery' and apparently I was a very warm baby.' A quick smile, vanishing as soon as it appeared. 'He left me with 'Fleet'. God knows why mum kept it, but she did and it stuck.'

He didn't look particularly happy about this, and Lydia understood. She knew what it was like to carry a last name that was heavy with meaning. To feel a sense of ambivalence about it. It gave you something to belong to, told other people something important, gave you meaning, but it felt like a life sentence, too.

CHAPTER SIXTEEN

F leet was in a bad way. He was confused and tired and scared, but he was still Fleet. Which meant he had a core of stubborn strength and the strongest sense of duty that she had ever encountered. He wouldn't leave London without a fight, so Lydia decided to play dirty.

Organising a trip to Auntie was simple enough. Having pretended to go to Coventry, Fleet was due to visit and he hadn't objected to Lydia tagging along.

Once the tea had been poured and Auntie had finished grilling Fleet about his disappearance, leaving him with a slightly stunned look on his face. It was now or never.

'There's something we wanted your opinion on,' Lydia began, fixing her gaze on Auntie's brown eyes.

Fleet shot her a warning look which she ignored.

'You know why Fleet went AWOL?'

Auntie nodded. She placed her cup back onto the saucer. A sign of full attention.

'He's been having episodes...'

'We don't need to talk about this,' Fleet broke in. 'There's no cause for concern.'

'You need to get a hold of this,' Lydia said, looking at him, willing him to understand.

Fleet's expression hardened. 'I am aware of that.'

'I think you need training. It's a raw talent, like mine was, and you need to learn how to control it. Otherwise you are going to go—'

'Mad. Yes, I know. Thanks for that.' Fleet's hand, holding the flowered china cup, was shaking and the cup clattered in the saucer when he put it down. He looked at Auntie. 'I'm sorry about this.'

'I'm not,' Auntie said calmly. 'And she is not wrong. I'm sorry, Ignatius,' she continued, holding up a hand when Fleet opened his mouth to argue, 'listen to her words. You are deep in the middle of the river and she is offering you a branch.'

Fleet's mouth shut. He looked at Lydia and she saw frustration and resistance there. And fear.

'I can't train you. I don't understand your power, but I have found people who can help. They don't belong to the other Families, so there is no politics, no reason for them to play games.'

At that, Fleet's shoulders went down a notch. For the first time in the conversation, curiosity seemed to overtake his defensiveness. 'Who?'

'There's a catch, but I think it's actually a benefit in disguise.' Lydia leaned forward, putting her elbows on her knees and looking Fleet straight in the eyes. 'You'll have to leave London to get the training. These people are travellers. They are moving on tomorrow and you need to go with them.'

Fleet went still. 'Travellers like my father?'

'Nothing like your father, child,' Auntie broke in. 'Use the sense you were born with.'

'Fairground folk,' Lydia said. 'From the heath.'

It was a sign of how far Fleet had accepted Lydia's world when he asked without sarcasm. 'Ghosts?'

'No, they're alive. But they have precognition. They can help you.'

'Will they help?' Auntie looked at Lydia. 'You have settled this?'

Lydia nodded. 'I will. And, like I said, they are not of London. They have no dog in our fight.'

'Speaking of which,' Fleet said. 'I'm not leaving you. Not with Charlie rattling his cage.'

Lydia hesitated. She wanted to tell him that he was no help to her in his present state, that her worrying about him was draining her mental resources and that she needed him to get strong again before he could truly help.

'You want to protect her? You need to do this,' Auntie said. 'You are no use in this state.'

Fleet was still resistant, but Auntie bulldozed over his disagreements. 'If one of your officers turned up with broken legs and severe concussion, would you send them to the hospital or put them to work?'

'I can walk. I'm not completely useless.' Fleet was still arguing. 'And I won't leave Lydia.'

'Enough,' Auntie said. 'You know this is the only thing that makes sense. This is your pride yapping.'

'Please,' Lydia said.

Fleet's eyes met hers and, after a beat, he nodded.

'Good.' Auntie stood from her chair. 'Wait here.'

Once she left the room, Lydia reached for Fleet's hand. 'Are you okay?'

'Apparently not,' he said, but there was a twist of his lips and a hint of his usual dry humour.

'It won't be for long,' she said, hoping it was the truth.

'You will keep me fully informed. And I do mean fully. Everything, every day, or I will come straight back.'

'Fair enough.' Lydia squeezed his hand. 'You, too.'

He squeezed her hand back. 'I hate this.'

Auntie walked back in, holding two small cloth pouches, about an inch high and tied at the top with yarn. 'Keep these with you.'

Fleet got to his feet to take the gift and nodded solemnly. 'Thank you.'

'Come back safely,' Auntie said, and she stepped into Fleet's arms.

Lydia looked away while they embraced, suddenly aware that she was witnessing something very private.

'You too, child,' Auntie said, and Lydia found herself wrapped in a firm hug. Auntie's voice quiet in her ear. 'Come back.'

OUTSIDE THE FLAT, WITH THE SOUND OF THE LOCAL kids playing football on the concrete below and the muggy London air filled with the scent of fried food and decaying rubbish, Lydia raised a questioning eyebrow.

'They are for protection,' Fleet said, his voice completely serious. 'Keep it with you at all times. You can tie the yarn around your neck or put it in a pocket and under your pillow at night, but don't lose it.' He squashed the pouch until it was almost flat and slipped it into the inside pocket of his suit jacket.

Lydia looped the yarn around her neck and tied a knot. She flattened the pouch and tucked it underneath her t-shirt. It stuck out a little, but it was small enough to wedge in her cleavage so that it was more effectively hidden. 'What's inside it?'

'Herbs. A chicken bone, I think.'

Lydia thought it sounded like the start of a soup recipe, but she didn't say so out loud. If it made Fleet happy enough to leave her in London, then she would wear it. Not to mention that she was a little frightened of disobeying Auntie.

The next day, Fleet got up early. Lydia watched from his bed as he dressed. He had packed a duffel bag the night before, so now he just added his toothbrush and he was ready to leave.

The ones that move around had a careless attitude to those connected to place. The ones who stay still, anchoring their lives to a patch of ground with a boundary, look upon the travellers with distrust. For those whose sense of self is connected to their sense of place, how can you ever know a person who keeps moving? Regardless, Lydia didn't have a choice. The fortune teller was the one person who would understand Fleet's gift and be able to help him. Well, the second person if you counted his father, which Lydia absolutely did not. The Collector was not interested in Fleet's wellbeing, of that she was certain.

The sky was red at the horizon, the glow turning to pink clouds with pale blue between, the promise of a fine summer's day, and the grass of the heath was thick with dew. There was traffic on the road, but it was sparse and hardly anyone was leaning on their car horn. In the city, it counted as quiet.

'I'm still not sure about this. I don't want to leave you alone.'

'I'm not alone,' Lydia said. 'And I can look after myself.'

Fleet pulled a face that Lydia could clearly read. It said 'I don't want to argue with you right now'. Since she agreed, she pulled Fleet into a hug, wrapping her hands behind his neck and pulling his face close to hers.

He kissed her thoroughly and she kissed him back. Their physical connection saying all the things that neither of them was particularly good at articulating.

Walking to the fairground area, hand in hand, they were soon surrounded by bustling activity. Trucks bearing the brightly coloured names of the attractions were pulling out onto the main road. The fully functioning fair was all packed away, lights and fun hidden behind firmly buckled tarps and the metal sidings of lorries.

Lydia felt the presence of the fortune teller before she saw her, that same eerie blankness.

'This is your man?'

The woman's white hair was in two thick plaits today, but she was wearing the same denim dungarees. Her long feet were hidden by thick-soled white sneakers, and her expression was openly admiring as she took a long look at Fleet.

Lydia didn't consider herself a possessive woman, but she felt her feathers stand on end. The woman must have been in her sixties, at the very least, but she had a girlish figure and the kind of bone structure that was beautiful at any age.

'I'm Ignatius,' Fleet said, holding out his hand to offer a polite handshake.

She took his hand, flipping it over and casting a professional look at his palm. 'Right, then.' To Lydia she said, 'I can see why you want to hide this one away.'

'You will help him?'

The fortune teller let go of Fleet's hand and held her own hand out to Lydia. 'We will.'

Lydia shook the woman's hand. 'I owe you a favour for the answer I received in your tent. What is the price for this?'

The fortune teller smiled. 'A feather.'

Lydia opened her mouth to say that she didn't have one to give, but caught herself in time. She pulled a hair from her head and held it out.

'Cute,' the woman said. She seemed to be weighing something up. After a moment's thought, her head turned as if listening to something. 'We will enjoy this and it is only fair to weigh that as part of the deal. With this in mind, we will accept your hair-feather as payment. Along with a promise.'

'Is that the same as a favour?'

'The promise is this...' The woman seemed to listen again. She nodded before speaking. 'You promise to come when you are called.'

'That's it? You want the power to summon me to your location?'

She nodded, eyes gleaming in the dawn light.

Lydia thought for a moment before replying. 'On one occasion, Lydia Crow may be summoned by the three sisters and she will attend that meeting, if it is in her power to do so.'

The gleam seemed to grow in intensity, and Lydia wondered why she looked so pleased. What loophole or hidden meaning had she missed in her attempt to clarify the terms of her promise?

'It's done,' the woman said. 'Come on, we don't want to miss our ride.'

Fleet turned to Lydia, putting his hands onto her shoulders. 'Call me if you need me. Stay in touch. If I don't hear from you every day...'

'You'll come back, I know.' Lydia went on tiptoes to kiss him. 'Good luck. And I'll see you in two weeks.'

He smiled gently. 'You have a lot of faith in my ability to be trained.'

'That,' Lydia replied. 'And I know the fair is going to be in Epping in two weeks' time and I reckon you'll visit.'

He brightened and Lydia felt the warm sunshine glow of his true self.

'I don't even have your name,' Lydia said to the

fortune teller, who was politely looking away as they said their goodbyes.

A slight hesitation. 'You can call me Bee.'

'Thank you, Bee,' Lydia said. 'I will see you in two weeks at Epping Forest. Hopefully, your part of our deal will be concluded.'

Bee nodded her understanding. She raised a hand. 'Until next time.'

Lydia watched Fleet and Bee walk away. One tall man, with broad shoulders and an easy loping gait, and a white-haired woman who moved like a twenty-year-old.

She watched until they disappeared behind a crepe van, closed and ready for travel, and then she turned back toward Camberwell and home.

Jason was sitting cross-legged on the sofa with his laptop open. He looked up when Lydia walked into the flat, feeling bone-weary and in need of food. For once she would have welcomed a cooking spree from her ghostly flat-mate, but he was immersed in whatever was on his screen.

There were cans of cola in the fridge and she popped the tab, drinking while she looked through the cupboards. Crisps. Bread. Cheese and a bag of apples, courtesy of Fleet, in the fridge. She stared at the fruit for a few moments, willing herself to cry. She felt wound up. The release of a few tears would surely help.

It was still early and part of Lydia wanted to head through to the dark cave of her bedroom, pull the duvet over her head and go back to sleep. But she knew that wouldn't work. She didn't need Fleet's gift to see herself lying wide awake before giving up and getting up again.

Grabbing a packet of crisps and an apple, she went to her desk instead. Work. Perhaps she would take a new case. Maybe Aiden or the accountant would have sent her an annoying email with something boring and administrative to manage.

'Please tell me that's not your breakfast.'

Lydia looked at her cola and crisps. 'I'm having fruit. That's very healthy.'

Jason sighed and put his laptop onto the seat. 'I'll make you something proper. Eggs.'

'We don't have any.'

'There's a café downstairs,' Jason pointed out, not unreasonably.

'Angel won't be happy if she sees eggs levitating out of her kitchen.'

'So I won't let her see. You need to eat.'

Lydia opened the crisps and popped one into her mouth.

Jason shook his head. Then he went still. 'It's early. Did you come from the heath?'

'Mmm-m,' Lydia nodded, crunching away. She took a swig from the can. Salt. Sugar. Caffeine. All would be well.

'Has Fleet gone then?'

Lydia nodded again, not trusting herself to speak.

'And this woman, she's going to show him how to control his visions? How long is that going to take?'

She put the can down and looked Jason squarely in the eye. 'Two weeks.'

'Is that long enough?'

It would have to be. Fleet wouldn't agree to stay away any longer. 'I hope so.'

'And you think she can help him?'

'Yes.' Lydia leaned back in her chair. 'But even if she can't, it gets him out of the city for a couple of weeks. Gives me time to deal with his father.'

Jason frowned. 'And how are you going to do that?'

Bee, the fortune teller, had told her that the sure way to get rid of The Collector was to give him what he wanted. Well, she wasn't going to give him Fleet. 'I don't know.'

'Is there anything I can do?'

'Maybe. I don't know.' There they were. The tears prickling her eyes. She concentrated on her crisps and didn't look at Jason.

A cold draught let her know that Jason had approached her side of the desk. A moment later, she felt his hand on her shoulder.

'We'll figure it out.'

Lydia leaned against Jason, feeling the cool smoothness of his suit jacket against her cheek. 'Everyone is scared of him. How do I defeat a myth?'

'By remembering that everyone is scared of you, too.'

CHAPTER SEVENTEEN

Lydia wasn't going to hurt Daisy and John. She had made big with the threats. That was part of her job. She was going to pay them a visit and make sure they left London for good. Banishment. Some Crows would consider that a fate worse than death, but Lydia knew they were the kinds of people who hadn't seen enough death to understand how wrong they were.

Still, they wouldn't go easy. They were main bloodline Crows and Camberwell the only home they had ever known. Aiden had said he would do it, but she knew that would be disrespectful and, as leader, she had to carry out sentencing. She would walk them out of London herself. Not literally, of course. She had booked a taxi.

She wasn't too worried about them physically fighting her, though. Daisy might do a shit-ton of Pilates, but Lydia would bet she had never been in a brawl. And John was the cerebral sort. She didn't see him throwing a punch. Of course, if he tried, she could just reach into his consciousness and remove control of his limbs. She kept forgetting that she had that ability. After living most of her life without being able to control people like puppets, it wasn't the first thing she thought of doing. It did make life easier, though, and much as she hated to admit it, she could understand why Charlie had been so keen to avail himself of Maddie's powers.

Walking up the front path to Daisy's house, Lydia greeted the magpies that were sitting on the overhanging porch roof. She knew that she wasn't going to follow through on her threat to kill them for their disloyalty, but she also knew that they had to believe otherwise. It was the only way to make a banishment stick. And the way things were at the moment, she couldn't have her authority openly challenged. If Daisy and John were seen swanning around Camberwell like nothing had happened, it would fan the flames of rebellion. She had to exert her authority and punish the disloyal in a public way.

Wanting to make an entrance, Lydia hesitated before pressing the doorbell. The decorative panel of swirled glass in the middle of the door was just too inviting. She pulled the sleeve of her sweatshirt down so that it covered her hand and picked up a rock from the front garden. The glass resisted the first blow, a crack appearing but the panel remaining intact. The second one did it, though, and she knocked the shards away from the frame and reached through to unlatch the door.

As she pushed the door open, Lydia felt the wrongness immediately. She didn't know what it was, for a moment, but just knew that her tattoos were moving and that an icy line was running from her skull to the base of her spine.

She forced herself to walk down the hallway to the kitchen-diner at the back of the house. The sun was pouring through the French doors and bursts of light bounced off the shiny appliances. There was a blue vase of white stocks in the middle of the table and a string bag of oranges on the counter. Two cups of coffee on the side, half full and cold to the touch. One of the cups had traces of pale pink lipstick.

That was it. Lydia couldn't put it off any longer. She had to focus on the two figures slumped in chairs around the table.

John's neck was broken. Lydia's first glance had told her that this was not a 'call an ambulance' situation. The Crow sense in the room was dimmed to almost nothing, which had been her first clue that something wasn't right in the house. But, more pertinently, she could see that her uncle John's head was at a very bad angle and his eyes were wide open and filmed.

Daisy was face down, but the skin of her arms and the back of her neck was mottled. Lydia had seen enough corpses to recognise that particular pattern. It happened when the blood stopped moving. And didn't appear for at least half an hour. No heroics required here. Just clean up.

There was a sticky pool of liquid on the table underneath Daisy's head. There might have been blood involved, but not just blood. There was a sweet smell she couldn't identify. Poison perhaps?

Lydia had taken in the scene, noted the details, and

had time to send thanks to the sky that Fleet had already left London. She would never have got him to go if this had happened yesterday. Now, she checked her watch. She had been inside the house for less than two minutes. She needed to get out.

She had covered her hand to smash the glass and open the door, mainly to protect it, but hopefully it had been enough not to leave fingerprints and she hadn't touched anything else except for the floor. Looking back along the hall, Lydia couldn't see footprints. And she wasn't convinced they would work as evidence, anyway. This was her uncle and aunt's house. She had been here many times and would not deny that fact under questioning.

For a moment, Lydia considered that she could call the police. Explain that she had been worried enough about them to break the door when they didn't answer. That she had found them dead.

Of course, all of that was the kind of thing an average citizen could afford to do. She was the head of the infamous Crow Family and two Crows were dead in their own kitchen. Unpleasant and disrespectful though it felt, she had to leave their bodies where they sat, and get herself far from the scene.

Intending to take one last look, Lydia saw something that made her return to the table. Something was clutched in Daisy's hand. Her fingers were curled tightly, but Lydia could see the end of a quill. Snapping on a pair of latex gloves, she pinched the end and pulled. A small, dark grey feather slid out of Daisy's grip. She was getting Crow from it. Both the bird and the Family.

She could taste feathers in her throat and feel her tattoos moving.

She took another look at the other body. John's hands were half-open, one on the table and one hanging by his side, and Lydia couldn't see anything obvious. She wanted more time to examine the scene, but she could hear a siren. It might be going elsewhere, but Denmark Hill was the nicest part of Camberwell. The most well-to-do. There was a strong chance that a neighbour had spotted her breaking into the front door and had called the authorities.

Weighing the odds, Lydia left by the front door. There was no back gate and she would have been forced to go through gardens which might have drawn more attention than simply strolling down the public street.

As she walked down the path, the magpies were still sitting on the porch. They reminded Lydia of PCs guarding the scene. She nodded to them. At the pavement, Lydia remembered leaving this house back when Maddie was missing, back when she was newly returned to Camberwell and doing a favour for her Uncle Charlie. Her heart squeezed with the thought of everything that had happened since, of the person she had been then and the person she was now.

Lydia walked back to The Fork as fast as she could without running. Running would draw attention. When she turned into her street, the harsh cawing of a crow was joined by the distinctive chattering sound of an unhappy magpie. Warning calls. At that moment Lydia saw a familiar figure standing in the middle of the street.

He was far enough ahead to make it difficult to read

his expression, but it was unmistakably Charlie Crow. He raised an arm in greeting or warning, and then turned away and walked in the opposite direction.

Lydia's feet were rooted to the ground and she watched him walk away. Charlie was out. Fleet's vision had been bang-on. She knew she would be able to control his body, that she had nothing to fear, but that knowledge made no difference, she could not make her legs move. She watched him turn the corner and disappear from view. The man who was supposed to be locked up for the rest of his life. The man who, Lydia was certain, had just murdered Daisy and John.

CHAPTER EIGHTEEN

Back at The Fork, she forced herself to greet Angel as if there was nothing wrong. There were a few punters in the café and she made a show of normality for their benefit. She didn't know how long it would be before the news got around Camberwell.

Upstairs, in the privacy of the flat, Lydia placed a call and asked for an appointment for a manicure. Less than ten minutes later, Sinclair called back.

'Daisy and John are dead.' Lydia wasn't wasting time playing games.

A pause. 'I was expecting this call.'

The breath went out of Lydia. She had been holding onto the hope that maybe she had been hallucinating. Or her eyes had played tricks, showing her the figure she feared rather than some other random person in the street. 'He's out, isn't he? You should have contacted me straight away. I told you—'

'I have orders,' Sinclair said. 'I can't just run operations the way I would like. There are rules.'

'I don't give a flying...' Lydia stopped herself from speaking and took a breath instead. There was no point losing her temper with Sinclair. She was the scorpion, just acting according to her nature. It wasn't personal. 'Is this part of an operation, then? A plan?'

Another hesitation.

Cold up Lydia's spine. The urge to spread her wings and fly. 'You have no idea, do you? Did you just open the door and let him walk out?'

'Of course not.'

Lydia squeezed her coin for comfort and control. 'When did you lose him?'

'That's not what...' A pause. A breath.

This was as close to rattled as Lydia had ever heard Sinclair. And it could still be part of her act.

'The man who was guarding him. He has disappeared, too.'

Not a plan, then. A mistake. 'You'll find his body in the Thames in a few months. You should tell his family he is dead.'

'You sound very sure.'

'I know my uncle. He isn't the forgiving type. Just because the man helped him to escape, doesn't mean he will forget the imprisonment. That man guarded his door, supervised his meals, exerted control. He won't let that go.'

'You think he had something to do with the murders of your relatives? Daisy and John?'

'Nobody else would have done this.'

'Do you know where he is now?'

'Camberwell, I believe. Don't know for how long.'

'Will you tell me if you make contact with him?'

'You will hear about it,' Lydia said, which wasn't quite the same thing. And it was as diplomatic as Lydia felt like being in this moment.

'There's something else,' Sinclair said. 'One of my sources has seen a strange man in a long brown coat near Highgate. He seemed to think it was a ghost. Thought it was your area.'

'I'm not doing you any favours,' Lydia said.

'This isn't for my benefit. When we interviewed the victims of the bathing pond poisoning, they all mentioned a man matching the same description. If there is going to be another issue with water contamination, we need to know about it fast. I need to ask if you know anything about it.'

'You really aren't in a position to make demands of me right now,' Lydia said. 'But I have no more interest in Londoners being poisoned than you do.'

LYDIA TRIED AIDEN'S PHONE BUT HE DIDN'T answer. She had a regular meeting with him at Charlie's house and there was a chance that he was on his way there right at this moment. It wasn't likely that Charlie would go to his own home, he had to know that would be a fast way to get picked up by the secret service, but on the other hand he had just murdered his loyal acolyte, so who knew what he was going to do next?

She texted Aiden and tried to ring again. This time, he picked up. 'Come to The Fork,' she said.

When he arrived, they went upstairs. This was definitely not a conversation to have in public, even in the safety of the café. She didn't relish breaking the news about Daisy and John, but he needed to hear it from her.

Aiden was standing unusually straight. Their meetings were usually fairly relaxed, having got used to working together over the months. Aiden still called her 'boss' and was deferential, but they had developed a rapport. Now, the air was filled with a crackling energy that Lydia felt as beating wings and Aiden seemed to feel too, whether he could name it or not.

His hands were clenched by his sides. 'You had a beef with Daisy.'

'I did,' Lydia said, not bothering to lie.

A muscle twitched in his jaw and his grim expression made him look older than usual.

'Ask your question.' Lydia kept her hands visible, palms upturned. She breathed deeply and tried to relax her stance.

'You went to see her before. You were... You went to threaten her. After that business with Charlie.'

Lydia's voice was gentle. 'Ask your question, Aiden.'

He took a breath. 'Did you kill them?'

'No.'

He hesitated, eyes searching her face. Then he nodded. 'Okay.'

'Good.' Lydia moved to her desk.

'We need to find out who did.'

'I have an idea about that.'

'Say the word. I'll get a crew together, we'll...'

'Charlie.'

'No.' Aiden was shaking his head. 'He's locked up.'

'He's out. I just confirmed with my contact.'

'That's not... That's not possible.'

'I can call my contact in the secret service and put them on speakerphone if you want to hear for yourself. But I saw him, too. And my word should be enough.'

Aiden had enough wits left to notice when he was insulting the head of the Crow Family and he muttered something about believing her. 'How did he get out?'

Lydia sat in her chair and leaned back. 'He's Charlie Crow. And we know he had blackmailed at least one of his guards.'

'So why come back to Camberwell? Why not disappear?'

'At the risk of repeating myself,' Lydia said tiredly. 'He's Charlie Crow. Camberwell is his home.'

'But, Daisy... And John. It doesn't make sense.' Aiden was still having difficulty with the idea. 'Why would he do that? You said Daisy was doing his bidding. She was loyal to him. Why would he kill her?'

'This way, everyone will think I did it. You did.'

'Still...' Aiden crossed his arms. Still unwilling to accept the truth.

'He wanted to implicate me. He wanted to turn the entire Family against me and that was worth sacrificing one loyal soldier. Haven't you learned, yet? Charlie is extremely comfortable with collateral damage.'

Aiden was white. He swallowed hard.

'I'm not,' Lydia said, 'but I do require loyalty. Which means I need you to tell me what is going on.'

'What do you mean? I didn't have anything to do with Daisy and John. I swear...'

169

'Not them. What's going on with you?'

She watched as Aiden's skin went chalky with terror and hoped it wasn't as bad as she feared.

'I don't... I don't know...' He swallowed hard.

'Just tell me,' Lydia said. 'Did you know about Charlie?' Lydia had been watching his face carefully when she'd told him and he had seemed genuinely shocked, but she had been wrong about people before.

'No,' Aiden was shaking his head. 'I don't know if I believe it now. I mean. That woman. Who is she, anyway? Just a voice. Maybe she's messing with you. It's MI6. They don't just lose prisoners...'

'Okay,' Lydia said. She flipped her coin into the air and let it rotate slowly. 'I believe you aren't working for Charlie.'

Aiden's eyes widened and he took a step back. 'I'm not. I swear.'

'But there is something wrong.' Lydia watched her coin spin faster. It seemed to be agreeing with her gut instinct. 'Whatever it is, we can work it out.' She hoped that was true.

He straightened up and looked her in the eye. 'I want to marry my girlfriend.' The words came out scratchy and quiet, but he held her gaze.

'Okay,' Lydia said, nonplussed. 'What else?'

Confusion crossed his face. 'That's it. Jess isn't a Crow.'

'That's it?' Lydia frowned. She recalled her coin and slipped it into her pocket.

'She isn't full blood Family, at all,' Aiden said, looking utterly miserable. 'I think her great-grandmother might have been a Fox, but she took her husband's name when she married and Jess isn't sure if it's just a family rumour.'

'Wait.' Lydia held up her hands against the tide of panicked speech. 'Why is this such a big deal?' What she meant was, 'why are you telling me about your love life? We don't have that kind of relationship.'

Aiden stopped and stared. 'You are the head of the Family. I need your permission to marry.'

'Do you?'

'I'm main bloodline, so yeah. I thought so.'

Lydia punched Aiden's arm. 'You idiot. I've been so bloody worried. I thought you were plotting against me or that you had some kind of horrible disease.'

Aiden looked cautiously relieved, but he was still hesitant. 'But she isn't a Crow. And there might be some Fox connection...'

'Will you stop,' Lydia said. 'I'm not Charlie. Actually, I don't even know if Charlie would care. And I'm definitely not my grandfather. I'm happy for you.'

When Aiden finally smiled, the worry chased from his face, he looked both older and younger all at once. He put his hand out and they shook, awkwardly. Then Lydia put aside her usual reserve and hugged him. 'Congratulations.'

'Shall I bring her round to meet you?'

Lydia was going to say 'don't worry about it' but she stopped herself in time. His face was filled with hope and longing, and she didn't want to squash his enthusiasm. And, it seemed, whether she felt she needed to give her blessing or not was irrelevant.

Aiden clearly wanted it. 'You better had,' she said with mock severity.

WITH DAISY AND JOHN DEAD IN THEIR KITCHEN, Lydia didn't know how long she had before the police came around asking questions. And with Fleet out of town, she didn't have access to any insider knowledge. She could only hope that she wasn't going to be considered a suspect. Her finger hovered over the call button on her phone, as the desire to talk things over with Fleet warred with the knowledge that he would come back to London to help her, abandoning whatever help he was getting from Bee. Instead, she tapped out her daily 'I'm fine' message and hit send.

While she still had her freedom, she decided to visit the heath. Sinclair had been asking about the sightings of Jack, and it was only a matter of time before she discovered the connection between him and Fleet. Plus, Sinclair had been right when she had said that Lydia cared about the risk to life. Annoyingly, she couldn't shake the fear that Fleet had been drawn to the heath because he had known something bad was going to happen there, and that the contaminated water of the mixed bathing pond was just the start of it. Even as half of her brain argued that she had enough problems without looking for more and that the heath wasn't part of her manor, she knew that she was going to drive across the river and tramp around the heath for an hour or two. Stupid sense of duty.

CHAPTER NINETEEN

As it turned out, Lydia didn't need to walk around the park for long. The mixed bathing pond was still closed, so she headed to the ladies' pond on the Highgate side of the park to see how things looked. The Environment Agency had tested the water several times and the pond was open once again. Lydia expected it to be deserted, but Londoners showed their usual indefatigable spirit and determination to enjoy the short summer months, turning up with their swimming costumes and towels. It was late in the day and Lydia marvelled that these women would prefer to take a dip with the ducks in the chilly twilight, rather than sit in a cosy pub or cinema, or swim in a heated, disinfected indoor pool.

Sitting on the cool grass as the sun dipped below the horizon, Lydia watched the area empty as the clock crept toward closing time. She had to admit, the women leaving the pond in groups and singles had an unmistakable glow of happiness. She was just wondering if she ought to try it one day, when she caught sight of a familiar figure walking on the path that led past the entrance to the pond. It was a man in a long brown coat and an old-fashioned hat. A man who slipped into the shadows as she watched, disappearing from view.

Lydia was on her feet and following before her brain had fully caught up. She could feel her tattoos moving and the muscles of her back tensing with the urge to spread her wings and fly. This man was wrong. This man should not be here. Every instinct in her body was screaming that he was a threat, even as the sunshine signature promised warmth and light.

Lydia exited the park and caught sight of Jack moving away up Millfield Lane, further from her than she would have expected. She followed, noting that he was moving in the direction of Highgate, and that his form was increasingly difficult to make out. It was if her brain and eyes kept on insisting that he wasn't really there, but her Crow senses were screaming otherwise. He cut between houses and Lydia discovered she was on a footpath between large, detached period properties. She couldn't see Jack, but he couldn't have gone anywhere else so she continued.

The path opened onto Swain's Lane, a narrow road, bounded by the high wall of Highgate cemetery on one side and hedges, high fences and stretches of wall on the other. It was the steep route used by the herders in the fourteenth century, taking their pigs from the pastoral land above Highgate to Smithfield Market.

Lydia refused to call him Fleet. That name belonged to Ignatius. Jack, The River Man, whatever, stepped from the gate that led to the cemetery and onto Swain's

Lane. There had been reports as long ago as the eighteen hundreds of ghost sightings on this lane. A tall man with a hat and a dark coat. She wondered, now, whether any of these sightings had been Fleet's father. He had been in London before, that was certain. Had been every-where, by all accounts.

The iron clanged as he drew the bolt on the gate. There was a moment when Lydia thought that he might not see her in the half-light. She was standing in the dark between lamps and could, perhaps, be mistaken for a shadow. She stayed still, not even breathing, and told herself this was entirely her own choice. And not that suddenly, she could not move. Whether through fear or some compulsion from the River Man, she didn't care to examine.

He turned, then, and smiled. A glow seemed to emanate from his body, illuminating the lines of his face and his expression. Happy. He looked like Swain's Lane at ten o'clock on a summer's night was exactly where he wanted to be. He raised a hand in greeting.

Lydia tried to send messages from her brain to her limbs. She tensed her muscles and hoped they would obey her if she needed to run. 'I just want to talk.'

Then the River Man sank to the ground, knees splaying so that he sat cross-legged on the tarmac. 'I agree to a parley.'

'Okay then. Good.' She looked up the lane stretching behind the seated man and wondered if they would both be shortly killed by some kids joyriding in a stolen four-by-four. This was a quiet thoroughfare by London standards, particularly at this time on a

Wednesday night, but still. The narrowness and steepness of Swain's Lane made it a popular run for thrill-seeking lawbreakers. And sitting in the middle of a road was never a good idea.

'Come along, then. Sit.'

A full breath and, thankfully, her legs obeyed her command to move forward. A few slow steps, her body still trying to rebel against her command to move closer to the man that wasn't a man.

There wasn't any traffic sound, she realised. She could hear birds twittering and the leaves of the trees rustling. It was so quiet that the click of her knees as she emulated his position sounded loud and clear. She told her brain to listen out for engine noise and turned the rest of her attention to the man-shaped figure sitting an arm's span away. 'Why now?' What she didn't voice was the question she really wanted to ask, which was 'why Fleet?'.

'You know about my children?' The head tilt. Like a puppet pretending to be human. 'All the long years, I have sown seeds around the world. Some wilt early, taken by their first harsh winter, and some grow crooked and strange. A sparse few are strong and true.'

Lydia felt her coin in her palm and she squeezed it, feeling the edges to stop herself from speaking. Light spilled from Jack, and she had to focus on a point on his forehead, above those unnerving eyes, to avoid her own eyes watering from the unnatural brightness. Her peripheral vision told her that beyond that light the shadows had deepened. They were sitting in a bowl of light and beyond that the night was blacker than before. The birds had stopped singing and, never mind engine noise, she couldn't hear anything else at all. Just her own breath, her own heart pounding in her chest.

'You might think me an uncaring father,' Jack said. 'But it is for the best. The weak are safer beyond my attention and the strong will find their own way. And I only choose the finest mothers. A strong mother can conquer all, don't you agree?'

Lydia didn't nod and didn't speak. She squeezed her coin, concentrated on breathing and tried to stop her own heart from galloping her into cardiac arrest.

'In answer to your question, though. I saw it was time. The paths we walk are the threads and I can see them all, if I care to look.' He unwound a leather string from his wrist and placed it onto the ground between them. A small bone, polished white and gleaming, was knotted in the centre. He pulled on the ends of the string and it unravelled, releasing the bone. The string disappeared inside his coat and Lydia watched Jack watch the bone. She had the feeling of a magic trick. The type that depended on lies and misdirection.

'Watch,' he said and her gaze was drawn unwillingly to the object. It was a small animal bone. It wasn't hollow so she knew it didn't belong to a bird.

Jack moved suddenly and fast, bringing down his closed fist to thump the bone. When he moved his hand, it revealed a yellow-white dust where the bone had sat. Even with full force, a blow like that shouldn't have disintegrated the bone so thoroughly. Perhaps it was a sleight-of-hand trick, replacing the bone with dust in one

177

smooth movement. Although, Lydia thought as she leaned in for a closer look, perhaps not.

The dust wasn't just lying there, it was in a shape. Lydia could see something very familiar. The shape of a crow in flight. She glanced up and saw Jack watching her. 'That's a good trick.'

'I can see all the threads. I can't see where they start or where they end, that's beyond me, but everything in between I see. That's what makes me The Navigator.'

Lydia opened her mouth to say 'I thought you were The Collector?' but she caught the words just in time.

'You see this,' he indicated the bone dust crow. 'It led me to Camberwell. I thought it was leading me to Fleet, my London Child, but I was mistaken.'

The Navigator, mistaken, Lydia thought. At least he's capable of some humility.

'It was leading me to you.'

Hell Hawk.

LYDIA'S PHONE WAS RINGING. JACK WAS TAPPING out the contents of his pipe onto the pavement. 'Are you going to answer that?'

His tone was mild and the words innocuous. As if he hadn't just threatened her.

Lydia glanced at the screen. It was Aiden.

'Don't mind me,' Jack said.

Lydia answered the call. 'Now's not a good time.'

'There's been a killing.'

'What?' Lydia's eyes were on The Collector.

'Four bodies were found in a hotel room in Camden.

178

I just had a visit from the cops, wanting to know where I was last night. A Crow, a Pearl, a Fox and a Silver.'

Lydia felt her stomach lurch in fear and she scrambled to her feet. 'Who?'

'Garth Crow,' Aiden said, like he was ripping off a plaster. Then he listed three names that Lydia didn't recognise. 'They all had their throats cut. They're all dead,' Aiden said, unnecessarily. 'They were found in a pile, the cops said. Grim.'

Hell Hawk. 'I'm on my way.'

'I'm heading to The Fork. I'll meet you there.'

Lydia ended the call, keeping her eyes on The Collector. 'Was this you?'

'What?'

'Four people dead. A Crow, a Pearl, a Fox and a Silver. They were found in a hotel room in Camden. The canal goes through Camden, doesn't it?'

'Were the bodies blue?'

'I don't think so.'

He smiled. 'Then it wasn't me.'

Back in Camberwell, Lydia called a meeting at The Fork. Aiden was already there and he and Lydia sat opposite each other and failed to eat the food that Angel put in front of them.

'Four dead. Bodies piled into a heap like they were trash.' Aiden couldn't seem to stop saying the words. It was clearly his way of processing, so Lydia didn't ask him to stop. 'And something weird.'

Weirder than a mass killing? Lydia wondered,

feeling light-headed. With gun crime not being common in the UK, mass killings were less common than they were in the US. It was just harder to kill lots of people with a knife or a car, not that some determined individuals hadn't managed it.

'The cop I spoke to said their bodies were decorated with fragments of china, old coins, buttons, stuff like that.'

Lydia felt an odd sensation. A shiver that ran through her body and made her insides liquid and her skin prickle. 'Did they show you a picture?'

Aiden shook his head. 'Nah. They was just trying to get a reaction. Might not even be true.'

The description reminded her of something, though. A crow's hoard. In addition to Garth Crow, the victims included Luis Silver, Nate Fox, and the youngest, Becca Thomas. Maiden name, Pearl. 'Someone is really gunning for the Families.'

'Someone with a death wish,' Aiden said.

'Someone who is bored of waiting for the truce to break and has decided to smash it.'

Aiden's eyes grew wide. 'What?'

'This is it. There have been breaches before. Crows killed in jail, the feather and the tail, the Foxes beating me up... But this... This is definitive. It can't be explained as a relationship issue or one-off. It's not one family against another, it's an attack on us all.'

'That's not against the truce,' Aiden said. 'That's the point of the truce... We stand together against the threat...' He trailed off. 'What? What am I missing?'

'The detritus,' Lydia said. 'It's a tag. A calling card.

You said the cop said there were coins, buttons, bits of china. Shiny objects. It's a calling card that reads "Crow".'

'It wasn't one of us.' Aiden shook his head in outright denial. 'No chance.'

'We don't know that.' Lydia was thinking of one Crow in particular. A very pissed-off one.

'So what do we do?'

'We find out who did it, and hope it wasn't a Crow. Or any of the Families. And we get the heads together to reconfirm the truce as quickly as possible. If we declare peace, it should settle everybody down. Otherwise, who knows what will happen next?'

'You think they'll go for that?'

'Rafferty has already agreed, for what that's worth. As for the others, I have no idea. But it's worth a try. If I can get them in the same room, talk sense. If we all agree this is a random act of madness, maybe we can get the truce reinstated before any more damage is done.'

CHAPTER TWENTY

The reprisals were swift and bloody. Within twenty-four hours of the families being notified of the deaths, a Crow-owned betting shop was torched, the Pearl-run grocers on Well Street had a visit from a crew sent by the Silvers who terrorised the woman behind the till, and Maria Silver had a suspicious package delivered to her office. It was filled with white powder, which turned out not to be anthrax, but the note that accompanied it was explicit and horribly detailed. Paul didn't report anything specific for the Fox Family, but most of his close kin were out of London, scattered.

Now that Lydia could reach out and pluck the consciousness of any person, taking over their body and making them do things as easily as if their bodies were an extension of her own, she felt very little fear. She walked into the Silver offices, past the security guards and into the lift. She punched the number for

Maria's floor and gazed at her reflection in the mirrored doors as she ascended.

'You can't...' Maria's assistant, Milo, stood up quickly from behind his desk.

'I'll have a coffee. Black, no sugar.' Lydia opened the closed door to Maria's office and found the woman entangled with a man mountain in a black suit. It seemed her security detail had extra duties. Not that he looked like he minded. His pupils were dilated and he had the slightly dazed look of a man whose blood had headed south.

Maria adjusted her silk blouse and pencil skirt and gave Lydia a cold smile. 'It's extremely rude to enter a private office without knocking.'

'I apologise,' Lydia said, employing her own social smile. 'But you must have been expecting me.'

'Not really. These are serious times. It's not the sort of crisis that requires Nancy Drew.'

Lydia swapped her social smile for the shark smile she had learned from Uncle Charlie. She could feel the tattoos on her arms moving and she saw Maria's gaze flicking to them with a momentary flash of fear. Good.

'Get out,' Lydia said to the man mountain. 'And send Milo in with my coffee.'

'So dramatic,' Maria said, taking her seat. 'I'm sorry you've had a wasted trip. I've nothing to say to you, so you can flap away home. Unless you're here to apologise for killing poor Luis.'

The man mountain was waiting, indecision clear on his face. Maria waved a hand at him and he moved to the door.

'You know so many things,' Lydia said. 'But you are so very stupid.'

'Pardon?'

'To think that I would kill four people at random. I take murder far more seriously than that.'

'It wasn't at random, though, was it? Four people. One from each Family.'

'A child can see that it's meant to destabilise the truce. I'm here to argue that we keep it. Restate it. Why would I be doing that if I was the killer?'

'It was a Crow. Everybody knows that.'

'That has yet to be proved, and I would choose my words more carefully if I were you.' Lydia's coin was spinning in the air and the room was filled with the sound of beating wings.

Maria's skin paled, but her expression remained calm, the small social smile firmly in place. However much Lydia hated Maria Silver, and that was a great deal, she had to give the woman her due. She was extremely calm under pressure. And a worthy leader of her Family.

'Things are bad, but they are going to get much worse. You know this. The reprisals will continue on all sides until nobody can remember what they're even for. If full war breaks out, we all lose. At the very least, your firm will get some bad publicity and you'll lose clients. But we can just decide to continue our alliance. No hard feelings. I'll even forget that you worked with Charlie against me.'

Maria didn't move for a full minute, then she slid open the top drawer of her desk.

Lydia was tensed, ready to take over the woman's body if necessary, but instead of a weapon Maria produced two shot glasses.

'There's a decanter on the side.'

Lydia didn't move. She wasn't Maria's staff and she wouldn't fetch anything.

'What makes you think I'm working with Charlie?' Maria said. 'I have no idea where the man is. Frankly, I assumed he was dead, so this is an interesting development.'

'The tail. You acted as if you thought the Foxes had left it, but I know they didn't. It occurred to me that perhaps nobody did. Maybe Charlie gave it to you to use as an excuse to attack the Fox Family.' Lydia watched Maria's face carefully, but her expression didn't give anything away.

'Why would I work with Charlie Crow?'

'I don't know,' Lydia said honestly. 'We're the new generation. I thought we would be better looking to the future, not the past.'

'That's a good line.' Maria's mouth twisted in a sardonic smile. 'Did you practise it?'

'I know you don't like me, but you don't have to. I'm being straight with you. I'm not sneaking around leaving objects and I'm not killing random members of your family to send a message. Whatever else you might think, you know I'm a simple woman. Direct. When I want to leave a warning, I don't leave a feather. Or a bag of white powder. I walk into your office, demand a cup of coffee, and make it in person. Eye to eye.'

Maria nodded her understanding. 'You really didn't kill Luis.'

'But somebody wants everyone to think it was a Crow. I would ask if you've made any enemies recently, but we both know that wouldn't narrow the suspect list by much. How many murderers have you kept on the streets at this point? You must be so proud.'

Maria smiled. 'I do so enjoy our chats. It would be a shame for them to come to an abrupt end.'

'Is that an agreement to continue our alliance? To stop this escalating further?'

Another pause. Then Maria nodded.

'Good.'

The door opened and Milo brought in a tray with a small coffee cup, an almond biscuit balanced on the saucer, and a folded piece of paper. He placed the coffee in front of Lydia and handed the note to Maria. She unfolded it, glanced at the contents and nodded at Milo.

Lydia dipped the biscotti into the coffee and laid out the details.

Maria didn't object, which was very wise. Lydia could feel the Silver in the air, taste the tang, but it was a low buzz, nothing to trouble her. She knew that the Silver Family Cup was in the room. No doubt hidden in the panelled cupboard Alejandro had used. Lydia wasn't worried. Even if Maria sprang across the office and revealed it, Lydia didn't think it would have the same effect as it had done in the past. She was stronger now. So much stronger. Besides, she could reach out and stop Maria's movements with the barest flex of her mind.

Maria would never make it to the Silver Cup, would walk herself off her balcony instead.

Outside the Silver office on Chancery Lane, the sun was beating down on the pavement. A man in a suit hurried past, his face red and sweaty, and a young woman was sitting on a bench and eating an ice cream cone as if it had personally wronged her. Lydia stepped into the shade cast by the buildings. There was a coffee shop a few doors along with a wooden chalk board menu. A magpie flew down and perched on the folded edge. Its blue wing feathers iridescent in the sunlight.

She could hear wings flapping. Lydia shielded her eyes and looked up into the bright sky. Three crows swooped down as if they planned to land on top of her but, at the last moment, dropped onto the pavement behind her. They hopped from foot to foot and flapped their wings a little, as if chivvying her forward. 'I'm going,' Lydia said. She wasn't going to anger the corvids.

Once she got close enough to the magpie on the folded sign, the crows took flight. One headed for the woman with the ice cream, as if planning to snatch a taste on their way past.

'Good day,' Lydia greeted the magpie. It had something in its beak.

The magpie fluttered down and dropped the something at Lydia's feet. It was the key she had left on top of her office desk. The magpie tilted its head to one side, waiting.

'Thank you,' Lydia said, to be polite.

It opened its beak and let out an irritated chatter.

'Fine,' Lydia said, and crouched down to retrieve the key.

As soon as she touched the metal, she could feel the tugging sensation it had given before. Was this why The Collector had wanted her to keep it? So that he could use it to summon her presence? Lydia had many more pressing matters to attend to, not least organising a meeting of the Families to restate the truce, but she didn't know what Fleet's father was capable of and that scared her.

As she followed the key, holding it out like a divining rod as before, she also knew it wasn't just fear of reprisals that was leading her forward. It was curiosity. The man was Fleet's father, which was part of it, but he was a mystery, too, and Lydia was incapable of ignoring one of those.

Half an hour of walking in the midday heat and Lydia was sweaty and irritated by the time she dropped down to the side of the Regent's Canal. It was shady, at least, with trees and a bridge providing cover from the brutal sun.

Fleet's father was standing on the path, ten paces away, blazing his own sunshine signature. Lydia gestured with the key. 'I won't follow this again,' she said. 'Just so you know.'

He smiled. 'Noted.'

'What can I do for you?'

'I like to keep moving and I've been in this city for too long already.'

Lydia felt a glimmer of hope. She wondered if that

meant she had only to run out the clock. If she could evade him and keep Fleet hidden for long enough, would The Collector simply ride the river away? 'So this is goodbye? Safe travels.'

'I always get what I want,' The Collector said. He toyed with the objects tied to his wrist. 'I don't just travel by water, I have an affinity for it. All of it.'

Lydia wanted to say 'how nice for you' but it didn't seem like the time.

'All sorts of things are carried by water. It's a beautiful, versatile medium. And it gets everywhere. Given enough time, water will find its way anywhere. There isn't a secure room in the world that can keep it out.'

Lydia's coin was in her hand and she squeezed it for comfort.

The River Man shook his head, almost sadly. 'You don't want to test me. I don't think London would enjoy a cholera outbreak.'

Could he do that? Her bones and gut said 'yes'. Hell Hawk.

'London is so proud of its sanitation these days. Gone are the days of the great stink, using the poor old Thames as an open sewer, but the water remembers. The rivers and streams and tributaries, the underground lakes, they all remember. It would barely take a nudge. A few pipes broken, sewage mixing with the drinking water, a little helping hand with some fresh cholera bacillus. Or some heavy rainfall and a malfunction in the main pump house.' He clicked his fingers. 'Just like that, you've got a tide of excrement flowing over the streets, lapping at your doorways.'

He smiled. White teeth in his lined face. 'Oh, your government would fix it fast. They know it's not bad smells these days, they know the water is important. But how many would die first? A thousand? The 1848 outbreak claimed over 14,000 souls. The faulty pump in Broad Street took 616 in 1854. Somewhere in between those, I would guess. We could lay a little wager, if you're in the mood. No?'

Lydia was glad that Fleet was out of London, away from the temptation to hand himself over to his father. He would, she knew, do it in an instant. To save the lives of hundreds, maybe thousands, of Londoners.

'I could offer a small demonstration,' he continued, unwinding one of the strings from his wrist. The object knotted to it was a fragment of fired red clay. 'The bathing pond wasn't enough, I can see that. An amuse-bouche, when you want a full entrée.'

'Not necessary,' Lydia said quickly. 'I believe you.'

His eyes were sparkling. The bastard was enjoying every second, Lydia realised. 'You're sure, now? It's no trouble.'

'Just tell me what you want.'

'I came back for my son. My London child.'

'And I told you he is off limits.'

'I'm The Collector,' Jack said. 'I have picked up all kinds of shinies from around the world.'

'You're not collecting Ignatius,' Lydia said. Or me, she added silently.

'Salmonella typhi, that's a good one. Spreads easily in water and causes a nasty fever. You can use antibiotics, but they don't always work.'

'Something else,' Lydia said. 'There must be something you want. Not a person, but maybe a favour?'

The Collector shrugged. 'You will come with me. In place of my London son.' It wasn't a question.

'Why would I do that?'

'Because you love him.'

'I love my family, too. And London. I am not cut out for the travelling life.'

'Don't worry yourself about that. You wouldn't travel for long.'

A clear threat. Lydia took a moment to form her next words. 'And is that the same for Fleet? If he were to go with you?'

'All journeys are sacred. No matter how short.'

Bloody riddles. The man was worse than a fox. Lydia reached out and plucked at the strands of his consciousness. Instantly, her mind filled with blinding sunshine and she retreated. She blinked to clear her vision and found Jack watching her with a new interest. No, more than interest, a hunger. That was good. Hunger could sharpen a predator but it could make them foolish, too. Hungry was close to desperate. 'If I were to agree, what guarantee would I have that you would leave Fleet alone in future?'

'No such guarantee. But the knowledge that I would be satiated and would not look in this dreary part of the globe for a good long while. I travel. I move. I do not return often and never for long.'

Lydia nodded. 'How long do I have to say goodbye?'

He smiled. 'You have decided? Just like that?'

'I see no point in pretending I have a choice. I will

not allow Fleet to come to harm. I have killed my kin to ensure his continuing freedom and health. And I won't let you poison my city, either.'

'I chose well,' he said. 'You are a fine addition to my collection.'

Lydia felt her guts lurch, but she squeezed her coin for strength. 'So, how long?'

'The tide turns tomorrow night. You will meet me downstream. At the Limehouse basin. 'You will come alone and without your mobile telephone, and I swear to leave London's waterways untainted.'

'I accept your terms.'

Jason was agitated, excited. Lydia had been thinking about calling her parents, wondering if it was better or worse to attempt a last conversation. Part of her, she realised, was in denial. It wouldn't be a last conversation. She would find some way out of this. Or maybe The River Man just wanted a companion for a bit of a trip. Maybe they would take a canal boat holiday and she would be home in a couple of weeks.

Either way, she hadn't been lying to Fleet's father. She would not let him take Fleet and she would have to leave Aiden in charge of restating the truce. After all, the four Families starting a war paled into insignificance next to the threat of mass illness. There was no point her saving her own life in order to lead the Crows, if half the city died from cholera. It made you realise how fragile human beings were when you considered how microscopic organisms could kill so many so easily.

'It wasn't a girl I heard, it's a boy,' Jason was saying, and Lydia forced herself to focus.

'In the alley?'

'Yeah,' Jason was circling the room, his feet not properly touching the floor. 'He's stuck, I think. He's not here here, like I am. He's more in a limbo state. I was in the kitchen one night and he appeared and walked through the wall out into the alleyway. I spent the next night in the cafe and he did the same thing at the same time, and again last night.'

'Did you speak to him?'

'Loads,' Jason stopped circling and hovered in front of Lydia. His face twisted in anguish. 'He didn't respond, though. He isn't really here, like I said. He's like an echo or something. Like you said about those ghosts at the heath.'

Jason was vibrating, looking more ghostly than usual. That was a sign that he was upset. Lydia didn't know why this was bothering him so much and she struggled to know how to respond.

'What if he's sentient? Or what if he was? You know things have changed in the street? That historical research I did?'

'The bakery.'

'Yeah. What if the kid was sentient like me, but lost his anchor? What if he's trapped as an echo because the object he was haunting decayed? Or if he was anchored to the bakery or stable or whatever and it got knocked down to build housing?'

'At least if he's just an echo, he's not suffering,' Lydia tried.

Jason's shaking was getting worse. 'It's just so sad. And what if the echoes are sentient? What if they know they're trapped in those loops, but they can't escape?'

'What do you want me to do?' Lydia hoped she sounded appropriately supportive. It was hard to get worked up about a harmless ghost echo, however sad it was. Lydia had enough problems protecting the living of London without adding the dead, too.

'Nothing,' Jason said looking a bit hurt. 'I just wanted to tell you. To talk.'

'Right. Sorry.'

'I know you've got a lot on,' Jason said, and disappeared.

Hell Hawk.

CHAPTER TWENTY-ONE

The Limehouse basin was where the Regent's Canal ended. Another short stretch linked the marina to the Thames and with an appropriate vessel, you could follow the Thames past Greenwich and eventually out to sea.

The sun was high in a clear blue sky, its light catching the water between the rows of boats moored in the marina, breaking it into a thousand sparkles. From narrowboats and barges to yachts with sleek sides and complicated rigging, it seemed like every small-to-medium craft was represented. Not that Lydia knew anything about boats. And she wasn't in any hurry to learn.

She spotted The Collector's barge. It looked older than she remembered and she hoped it was water-worthy. Of course, if her plan worked, she wouldn't be on it for long. She may have given Fleet's father the big speech about sacrificing herself for the greater good, but she had no intention of going quietly. Just because her ability hadn't worked on the River Man before didn't mean it wouldn't in the future. All she needed was an opportune moment. Get him when he was distracted, when his guard was down. By handing herself over, she would lull him into a false sense of confidence.

An iron fence with a gateway opened onto a ramp which led down to the dockside. The water in the basin was still enough to have collected green algae on the surface, and Lydia eyed it with suspicion as she made her way to the barge. She could feel her tattoos moving and she rubbed at her arm, trying to relieve the prickling sensation. Her hand brushed the heavy bracelet. She had infused it with Crow power, intending for Jason to be able to use it to keep himself powered up when she died. It had been his idea for her to bring it, now. 'Belt and braces, right?'

Distracted for a moment by the thought of Jason's concern, and the poor way she had handled their last conversation, Lydia was surprised by a movement behind her on the narrow walkway. Then her vision went black as material was pulled over her head and strong arms wrapped around her body, lifting her from the ground as if she was a sack of potatoes. The blinding sunshine flashed through her mind and she knew who had crept up behind her, silently and undetected.

She forced her body to go limp and took steady breaths through her nose. This was the plan, she reminded herself. This was exactly what was supposed to happen. She had to go limp like a prey animal playing dead.

It turned out that was easier than she would like, as

the blinding sunshine was getting stronger and stronger. Lydia's eyes were squeezed shut and she was digging her nails into her palm as she squeezed her coin more tightly than she had ever done before. It didn't help. The light was growing more and more intense until it was nothing but pure pain. She thought her head might explode with it, burst like a ripe fruit thrown onto concrete. Instead, just when she thought she would have to slit her own wrists to stop the pain, that she couldn't bear another second, she slipped mercifully unconscious.

The cloth hood was pulled from her head and Lydia saw that she was inside a wood-panelled space. The pain had gone as quickly as it had come, sweat cooling on her skin. The echo of it was there, though. A memory. A warning?

She had already smelled the coal and smoke and felt the gentle movement, so she wasn't surprised to see that she was inside Jack's boat. The man himself was folding the cloth hood, tucking it away in a drawer, one of many in an antique wall unit. Above the rows of drawers there were cabinet doors with key holes, familiar keys poking out from all but one. The ceiling was gently curved wooden boards, and the walls panelled in lacquered oak. Light and fresh air poured in from an open skylight, giving a tantalising reminder of the world outside.

Lydia was tied to an upright chair, could feel her ankles pulled firmly against the legs. There was a small kitchen ahead, everything slightly smaller than usual like in a caravan. A collection of pans hung above the cooker and a small enamel saucepan sat on the hob, and it was this homely touch which made Lydia's fear twist inside like a snake.

Jack was watching her look around. He was wearing his pieced-together coat but had hung his hat on one of the many hooks. 'I've got nothing against you, child. I like you.'

That wasn't good. That sounded like the words of a psycho who was about to slit her throat. Lydia didn't know what to say to delay the inevitable, so she didn't say anything.

'This won't take long,' he said, voice gentle. 'It's not as merciful as some ends, but better than you were expecting.'

Lydia found her voice. 'How do you know what I'm expecting?'

'You are a leader.' Jack regarded her for a moment. 'And you're not stupid. You know leaders don't die easy in their beds.'

'Some do,' Lydia said, baring her teeth.

'But not us,' Jack said, almost sadly.

Lydia's hands were bound in front of her. She had learned how to break zip ties from this position, but Jack had used thin rope. It smelled of hemp and diesel and took the top layer of her skin when she attempted a twisting movement. Another rope was around her upper arms and body, meaning she couldn't lift her arms either. She knew she no longer needed to produce her coin, could conjure a sky full of shining gold, but her head felt thick and she couldn't hold onto the thought. She reached out, anyway, trying to feel the threads of his consciousness. If she could grab them, she could control him. Maybe not enough to make him untie her, but enough to walk him into the wall or to climb above and step off the boat and into the black water. Her plan, she remembered. She had her bracelet and her tattoos and she was the head of the Crow Family. She had her power and Maddie's and she could reach out and pluck the strings which connected brain to body.

There was nothing there. Nothing except the awful burning brightness. A golden light that was like the sun blazing on a summer's day, if you were stupid enough to stare right into its fiery heart.

'You can stop that,' Jack said. 'I can feel you,' he tapped the side of his head. 'Scrabbling at the door.'

'Why did you leave Ignatius and his mother?' Lydia's tattoos were writhing on her arms. She could feel them trace patterns in her skin and it burned.

'I have left a thousand women and a thousand sons. That's not the most important question.'

Lydia was still trying to find a way in. She thought that if she could distract him with conversation, he might let down whatever guard he held up against her abilities. All she needed was to catch hold of one little thread. Just one thread she could pull, then wind and twist. 'I'll bite,' she said. 'What's the most important question?'

He smiled gently, the sunshine light intensifying. 'A story for another time.'

'I don't think there will be another time.'

'No. Well, it doesn't matter now. You're here in his place. And I am sailing in a matter of minutes.'

'And you'll keep your promise?'

'I will,' Jack said. 'I will not return to London for many years. So many that my Fleet will have returned to the earth.'

'This won't take a moment,' Jack said. He moved behind Lydia and returned with a grey plastic basin. The kind you put in the sink to do the washing up.

Lydia shook her head, trying to clear it. The River Man had filled her mind with fogginess again.

He placed the basin onto the floor and Lydia could see it was filled almost to the brim with black water. No, thicker than water. Oil? A moment of terror as she imagined him dumping oil over her and lighting a match. No. That was fear talking, skipping from horror to horror. He wouldn't light a fire in his boat. That would kill them both.

The Collector put his hands into the basin and closed his eyes. When he lifted them out, the liquid fell from his hands like water and it looked clear. Lydia felt relief that it wasn't oil. It just looked weirdly dark in the basin. It had to be a trick of the light.

He wiped his hands on his coat, head tilted as he regarded her closely. Then he darted forward and pulled at the neck of her t-shirt. She was horribly trapped and powerless to stop him from revealing the pouch from Auntie. He brought out a knife and cut the cord, pulling it away. 'How sweet.'

He moved around her chair, out of her vision. There wasn't time to worry about what he was doing, as she felt the chair tip forward. The muscles in her arms fired, as if she could catch herself, but of course she couldn't move. She was bound to the chair and her body tipped forward with it. She pushed away the panic, trying to find a calm centre, find a place to gather her power. That was her only hope of getting out of this.

As the water in the basin got closer, she realised what The Collector intended and pure fear washed through her, freezing her mind in blank terror. She stopped reaching for the threads of his consciousness, she stopped trying to focus her power, to feel for wings beating. He was going to drown her. In a kitchen basin. You could drown in an inch of water, after all, and she was going to die in the belly of this old boat. Facedown in a plastic basin her murderer had probably bought in the home goods aisle of a supermarket.

Why would he kill her, she reasoned, trying to get a hold of her fear. This was a ritual. A weird, creepy ritual. He would dunk her and then lift her out. She just had to close her eyes and hold her breath.

She was over the basin now, the water an inch from her nose. If she kept her neck rigid and pulled back, she could keep her face out of the water. A hand on the back of her head and then she was pushed firmly down, her head in the liquid.

She kept her eyes closed and began counting. It would last twenty counts, she decided, arbitrarily, then he would let her up. This wasn't how her life ended.

She got to eighteen before losing count. The fear was too great, the water had gone up her nose the moment she had been submerged and it burned. She was struggling against the ropes and the sense impressions from The Collector. The sunlight was mocking her. Fleet's sunlight. Fleet's smile. The thought came to her. If she just took a breath, she would see him again. As soon as she thought it, she wondered why she had been afraid. She could breathe water. It was as easy and natural as breathing air. All she had to do was relax. The water would do the rest. No. That wasn't right. Her mind was clouded. It was a false calm. From the oxygen deprivation. Her synapses were sluggish. Her lungs were burning with the effort of not inhaling, screaming out for air. She could start counting again, a small voice suggested, but numbers slipped away before she could order them. She could hear hearts beating. Her own and thousands of others. They were far away, though. Crows would take a bath in a puddle, but they didn't dive under water. They couldn't follow her here. There was a kind of peace to that. If she just gave in, she could fall asleep. No more fear. No more pain. She breathed in and let the water take her.

LYDIA WOKE UP WITH THE SENSATION OF BEING soaking wet. Her face felt cold, but then something rough and wet and unpleasantly warm hit her skin. She yelped and tried to open her eyes. Either it was still dark with smoke or she had gone blind. Either way, she couldn't see anything except a greyish swirl. The swirl went darker for a moment and the warm, damp licking recommenced. Along with the smell that could only belong to a dog's mouth. Small mercies, she told herself. Although, wasn't it true that a dog's mouth had more bacteria than a toilet? Or was she thinking about how toilets were actually cleaner than most kitchen worktops? She had definitely heard something like that once. The blackness lightened to dark swirling grey as the licking sensation stopped. The air cool on her damp skin.

Lydia thought she had yelped. That meant she could vocalise. She cleared her throat and tried to speak. A stream of liquid came out and she felt her body arch with convulsions as she coughed and hacked.

'Don't speak,' a voice said, alarmingly close. The grey light altered, again, and Lydia assumed that whoever had spoken was blocking the light. Or had moved the dog that had been licking her and blocking the light. Suddenly, she wasn't at all sure if the world had become lighter or darker. Things looked different. She knew that.

'You're going to be okay,' the voice said. 'Help is on its way. You're going to be fine. I've called an ambulance.'

She didn't want an ambulance. Ambulance meant hospital. Meant medicine and white coats and gowns which didn't close at the back. It meant lying in bed and making everybody she loved worry. It meant being trapped. Never mind that it would be for her 'own good'. She wouldn't be caged. Not ever again. 'Nnnnnn.' Well, that was embarrassing. Come on, Lyds, she told herself firmly. You can do better than that. You are head of the Crows. You can speak.

'It's okay, it's okay.' Her good Samaritan was almost chanting the words. She didn't recognise his voice. Wondered what he was seeing. Had she fallen? Was she spread on the pavement, her wings broken?

No. That was before. She had fallen from the

hospital roof, pulling Maddie with her. She had expected to die, had accepted that she would die, but had ended up in a hospital bed with a broken arm. Arm. That's right. She didn't have wings.

Where had she been? Somewhere smoky and dark. Not a nightclub. Not a cave. But like a cave. Her mind strained to remember. Then she heard the sound of a motor, ropes creaking, the slap of water against the side of a boat, and it rushed back. Jack Fleet. Maybe he was nearby. Had she escaped? Was this the middle of a chase? Perhaps he was stalking her now, perhaps the boat she could hear was his, sliding toward her as she lay helpless on the ground with this kind-hearted stranger muttering that all was well. He would slit the stranger's throat. She had to warn him. She had to get away. She focused her mind on her own body. She had to move. Her throat was burning with vomit, her lungs and nasal passages were on fire and hurt more with every breath, but she was alive. She tried to marshal her fragmented thoughts and sit up.

Pain exploded and the world went pitch black.

CHAPTER TWENTY-TWO

Waking up with what felt like a steel pick being driven into her temples, a dry mouth, and the kind of bone-deep ache that she associated with the day after extreme exertion, Lydia concluded that she wouldn't recommend it. If she never woke up in pain and confusion, again, it would be too soon. Opening her eyes to the painful light, she discovered a welcome fact; she wasn't in hospital.

The fact that she didn't recognise the bedroom should have been deeply alarming, but as she struggled to sit upright, she could feel the unmistakable impression of Fox. That she found this comforting, and that she could discern that it was Paul who was hovering outside the door in the moment before he opened it, probably should have alarmed her for other reasons, but in that moment all Lydia felt was relief. She was safe. She wasn't in hospital. She was alive.

'Painkillers,' Paul said, putting a packet onto the nightstand along with a glass of water.

'Coffee?' Lydia said, wincing at the scratchiness of her throat. She felt as if she had been burned by some hot food, but she didn't remember eating. Maybe the strange black water had been corrosive. Or this was just what it felt like to drown. Not a pleasant thought.

'Water,' Paul said. 'Let's see if you keep that down first.'

'I don't feel sick,' Lydia whispered. She hated that it made her sound weak, but it hurt less than trying to speak normally.

In response, Paul picked up the water glass and handed it to Lydia.

She managed a couple of sips, and then popped two tablets.

'You should rest,' Paul said, turning to leave.

'Don't go,' Lydia said. 'Tell me what happened.'

'You were found on the dockside path at the Limehouse basin.'

'I remember someone being there. A civilian.'

'Yeah, he had put his jacket under your head and called an ambo, but I moved you before it turned up.'

'Thank you,' Lydia said sincerely.

He nodded in acknowledgement. 'It seemed like the right thing to do.'

'How did you get me here?'

'I carried you,' Paul said, as if it was obvious. Perhaps it was. Lydia wasn't sure her cognitive function was back to normal. Before she could ask where, exactly, 'here' was, Paul spoke again. 'Do you remember what happened? Who did this?'

Lydia wasn't going to answer that, not yet. She shook

her head and the pain stabbed through her skull. Bad move. There was something very wrong, she knew, but she couldn't bear to examine it. Not yet.

Paul's hands moved to his hips and he blew out an exasperated breath. 'I figured hospital would be too dangerous. The way things are with the Families at the moment, who knows who might take advantage. Same with The Fork or the DCI's place. You'll be safe here for now. Nobody would think to look for you here.'

Suddenly Lydia wanted to cry. She felt her eyes sting and blinked rapidly. Luckily, Paul seemed to have reached his own limit and he muttered something about leaving her to sleep. He closed the door gently and Lydia let her eyes close. The bad thoughts were circling, but she pushed them down deep. There was a truth she had to face, but she could lock it away for another minute. And then another. She didn't intend to fall asleep but she did.

When she next woke, she wasn't alone. Paul was dozing on the floor, his back against the door. He moved as soon as she shifted. Maybe not dozing, after all. She sat up and drained the glass of water. Her head felt better. Not perfect, but well enough that she could think. 'Are you guarding the door?'

'Yes,' Paul said. 'I didn't know what to expect.'

'I think the danger has passed,' Lydia said. There was a digital alarm clock on the side table showing that it was almost five. 'It left on the tide at midnight.'

'Poetic,' Paul said. He looked completely alert and

Lydia found that comforting. Every part of her was soft and useless, like a bundle of rags that had been left out in the rain.

'I suppose.' Her body was aching and she felt hollowed out. She was too soft and too weak to keep the bad thoughts down any longer. They rose up. She felt like she hadn't eaten for a week. Like she had launched from a branch but found her wings didn't work. Like the sky was filled with her friends, but she couldn't join in. Like the end of a love affair.

'Little Bird?'

She opened her eyes and checked the time. Half past five. She had drifted off, again.

'You ready to eat?'

'Yes.' Her stomach turned over. 'No. I don't know.'

He got to his feet in an easy manoeuvre and Lydia caught a flash of red fur, the scent of good earth after rain. So that was still with her. She could still sense the Fox from Paul, would presumably still detect Pearl and Crow and Silver, too.

The sudden lump in her throat made it hard to swallow. She blinked quickly, trying to stop the prickling sensation before it turned to tears. She would not cry in front of Paul Fox. She was still the head of the Crow Family. She still had a job to do.

PAUL WASN'T GONE FOR LONG AND HE BROUGHT A bowl of soup and a ham sandwich on a tray.

'I can get up,' Lydia said.

'Eat first.'

Feeling the hollow deep inside, the way she was carved out, Lydia decided not to argue. She propped herself with pillows and ate. The soup was spiced root vegetables and the ham was salted and thick. Proper stuff and not rubbery slices. She hadn't pegged Paul Fox as a cook, but wonders never ceased.

'We have a housekeeper,' he said, watching her devour the food from his position by the wall. 'She cooks for the pack. Saves arguments.'

Lydia stiffened, wondering how many Foxes were in the building at this very moment.

'You are safe,' Paul said, noticing. He didn't move to sit on the bed, perhaps feeling it was too close. Lydia appreciated his sensitivity.

Lydia scraped up the last spoonful of soup and then cleaned the bowl with the crust of her sandwich. She didn't know why Paul was looking after her, but she knew she needed it. That wasn't weakness, that was good sense. And she ached all over. Her muscles felt as sore and quivery as if she had run a marathon.

'Better?' Paul said.

Lydia pushed the tray down the bed, but Paul didn't make a move to retrieve it. 'Yes. Thank you.' She wanted to ask why he was helping her, but was frightened to break the peace. She still wasn't sure how things stood between them.

Something else occurred to her, something that should have hit her earlier. 'How did you know I was at the dock?'

'I've been following you,' Paul said.

'Not possible. I would have known.'

A quick smile. 'Not me personally. I know about your senses, so I enlisted non-Family surveillance. You told me your boyfriend's father was the stranger causing consternation and that didn't sound like something you would lie about. But I didn't know what it meant and needed eyes on the situation.'

Lydia digested this. 'And you wanted to make sure that I dealt with Daisy?'

'You gave me your word that you would.'

That was diplomatic. He was watching her and Lydia could smell fur and earth, feel the tingling desire that accompanied his presence. That meant she must be getting her strength back, at least. She deliberately didn't think about what was missing. She had felt its absence even as she had been surfacing from deep unconsciousness. As clearly as if a wing had been amputated. She went to flex the missing limb, to feel her coin in her hand, but it wasn't there. Forcing herself to look at the tattoos on her forearm she could see they were static. Dull. Ink on skin and nothing else.

'I still care for you,' Paul said, his voice rough.

Lydia opened her mouth in surprise, tearing her gaze from the useless images on her arm. Paul didn't do raw honesty. He did sly teasing and innuendo.

He moved from leaning against the wall in one fluid motion and paused by the door, eyes filled with emotion as he looked at Lydia. 'Get some sleep.'

After the door closed behind him, Lydia got up and turned the key in the lock. Her legs were weak and she felt sick in her heart, but the core of self-preservation that had kept her alive this far was running on auto-pilot.

She looked out of the window, recognising the street as in the centre of Whitechapel. The barber shop which had the hidden bar in the basement was almost opposite. She was deep in Fox territory and she felt nothing but relief. The River Man would have left, she was almost certain, but she was grateful to be hidden nonetheless.

When Lydia next awoke, it was almost noon. She had slept away the morning and felt significantly better for it. She got up and pulled on her jeans. There was an ensuite bathroom, luckily enough, so she could take care of business and wash her hands and face before unlocking the door and venturing into Paul's house.

It was a warren of passageways, doorways, and stairs. A massive old terrace that had been made into several dwellings, she passed an empty kitchenette and four bathrooms, as well as numerous bedrooms and a room with a massive TV facing a leather sofa. Finding it empty of Foxes was a massive relief. She felt a little bit guilty at that thought, remembering that Paul was probably worried about his family's mass exodus from Whitechapel.

She was still reeling from her lack of power, though, and the strange, hollowed-out feeling. Like The River Man had scooped out her insides when he drowned her. She supposed she ought to be grateful that he hadn't killed her, but that job would no doubt be finished by Charlie the moment he discovered she was powerless.

With that cheerful thought, she followed the scent of coffee to find another kitchen. Paul Fox was sitting at a breakfast bar, his phone on the counter next to a mug and an empty plate.

'You're up.'

'Coffee,' Lydia said. 'Please.'

'And you're feeling better. Making demands as usual.' The words had no heat and Lydia was grateful that Paul was back to using his habitual confident tone. Perhaps they would be able to pretend that the moment of emotion hadn't happened. If he felt embarrassed by it in any way, Lydia was concerned he might react badly. She really couldn't handle losing her alliance with the Foxes on top of everything else.

He moved from the stool and around to the coffee maker. It was so strange to be in a domestic setting with Paul. She suddenly felt self-conscious.

He put a mug onto the counter and she took a long sip.

Paul was watching her. 'You ready to tell me what happened? Who did this?'

Lydia looked down at herself, wondering how wrecked she looked. She had avoided her reflection in the bathroom, all of her energy directed inward, looking for the power that had been curled up inside her for so long and was now absent. She felt a lurch of nausea as she contemplated the yawning gap, the terrible emptiness.

Paul was next to her, now, his fingertips on her chin, tilting her face up. She looked at him in surprise at the contact. The jolt of desire was welcome, for once. The impressions of red fur and good earth a reminder that she wasn't completely dead, that The Collector hadn't taken everything. She was still a Crow. 'It was Fleet's father,' she said, suddenly wanting to be honest with this man. Her sometime enemy who had scooped her up in the street and brought her to his den for safe-keeping.

'Is that right?'

'He took my power,' Lydia said. She felt transgressive and terrified. That was not smart information to share. And, worse still, saying it made it real. She couldn't stop the tears and Paul ran his thumbs under her eyes, wiping them away.

His hand was on her neck, then it moved to cup the base of her skull. Lydia tilted her head up and looked into his eyes. For a moment she wondered what it would be like to give in to their animal natures. She craved the blankness of that connection, the way it would wipe her looping thoughts and hold back the terror, for a few minutes at least.

Paul was staring into her eyes, his pupils wide and black and his expression a mix of tenderness and desire. In that moment he looked naked. Honest. Then he shook his head gently, letting his hand fall away. 'You're not in the same place, are you?'

'I care about you,' Lydia said carefully, truthfully.

'But you love him.' Paul stepped back, the shutters going down over his expression. The leader of the Fox clan was back.

'Yes.'

Paul nodded, accepting. 'It is such a waste. We could have ruled this city.'

'But you don't want to rule anything or anyone.'

'True.' The Fox showed white teeth. 'But I would have done it for you.'

Lydia wanted to say that she had no interest in ruling, but she wasn't going to lie. It was an attractive proposition, especially now. Without the power she had taken from Maddie, how would she control the Family and keep war at bay? How would she defeat Charlie when she didn't know where he was and who he had enlisted? 'I wish I felt differently,' she said, and it was partly true.

Paul's phone began ringing and it reminded her of something. She hadn't checked in with Fleet. If she didn't, he would return to London, whether he was ready or not.

Before she asked to borrow his phone, she wanted reassurance that things were still on a friendly basis with Paul. They had shared an awkward, raw moment. Lydia knew that some people reacted to being made to feel vulnerable with violence.

'Will you restate the truce?' Lydia kept eye contact, willing Paul to agree.

'For you, Little Bird. Of course.'

LYDIA DIDN'T HAVE HER MOBILE. SHE HAD LEFT IT at The Fork on the orders of The Collector. She asked to use Paul's phone, grateful that she had memorised Fleet's mobile number in case of emergency. He answered almost immediately, sounding guarded.

'It's me,' she said. 'Sorry I'm late...'

'Lydia, thank God!'

'I'm okay, everything's okay.'

'I'm in a cab, just passing Finchley. I'll be there in less than an hour.'

'No, don't leave. You need to stay and finish...'

'You're not okay,' Fleet said. 'I saw it. I'm on my way. Where are you? Why aren't you using your phone?'

Lydia didn't want to tell Fleet, but she was done lying to him. Having been on the other side of the coin, she knew it wasn't a real option anymore. 'I'm with Paul. I had to leave my phone at home, so I'm using his.'

A short silence. 'As long as you're safe.'

'I'm going home,' Lydia said. 'I'll meet you there.'

'I'm not...' Fleet's voice cut out as his mobile reception went out.

After a few seconds of shouting 'hello?' into the phone, Lydia gave up and ended the call.

'I NEED TO GO HOME,' LYDIA SAID. SHE KNEW THAT Fleet would come to Whitechapel if she wasn't waiting at The Fork, safe and sound. He would probably bring an armed team of police and that would not help her alliance with the Foxes.

Paul was still being careful with her, borderline formal. 'You might be in danger, still.'

'I don't think so. Fleet's father left on the tide.'

'So he said. Maybe he didn't, maybe he's waiting to finish what he started.'

She shook her head. 'He got what he wanted.' She felt a wave of sickness at her vulnerability, and couldn't quite believe she had told Paul Fox outright. Now she could only hope he wouldn't use it against her. She felt a wild urge to laugh. Why would he want to hurt her? It wasn't as if she had just rejected him for the second time.

'You all right?' Paul was looking at her questioningly, and Lydia realised that her lips were turned upward.

She rearranged her expression. 'Fine. I'm just relieved I'm still breathing. Thanks to you. I won't forget it.' She knew she ought to add 'the Crows won't forget it' but it felt like she would be slapping him with protocol, when he had done a very human, very personal thing.

'I'll drive you,' he said.

Lydia realised she had never seen Paul in a car, hadn't even been sure that he could drive. 'You don't have to...'

'There's no point saving the head of the Crow Family if I let her get killed immediately after. Spoils my leverage.'

So, Paul was back in control and acting as if nothing had happened. Fine. She knew she would be safer with Paul driving her to Camberwell at this point in time. Until she was certain that Fleet's father had left the city. Better the devil you knew and all that.

THE SMOKE HUNG OVER CAMBERWELL IN A THICK black cloud. It was solid, like a creature was crouching over their part of London. Lydia made Paul stop the car in the middle of the street so that she could get out. Up ahead, the police were cordoning the road and traffic chaos was building as vehicles attempted three point turns to go back the way they had come. The air was filled with a cacophony of sirens, horns, engine noise and shouting. As soon as she stepped from the car, she could taste something acrid.

'Wait,' Paul said from behind her.

'You can't leave the car. I'll go on.'

A few steps and Paul had caught up. The car sat with the driver side door still open. An irate man was getting out of his vehicle, shouting obscenities at them.

'I can't wait,' Lydia said, speeding up.

Paul shot the shouting man a look that made the words die in his throat. He abandoned his car and stayed with Lydia. He shouldered through the people on the pavement, and she stepped in his wake. She knew the source of the smoke. She knew it. The certainty didn't help, was nothing compared to the slamming shock of seeing the street. The road with The Fork, her road, was a mass of emergency vehicles, flashing lights and people in uniforms and high vis.

There was a fire engine, but it wasn't spewing water or foam. The crew were standing in the road, talking to police. There were more people here, pressing up to the cordon and taking photos. Uniforms were telling them to move back, that it wasn't safe.

Lydia and Paul stepped up to the tape. A uniform began his spiel. 'That's my home,' Lydia said. 'Let me through.'

Whether due to police policy or Crow whammy it didn't matter, the man lifted the tape for Lydia and Paul to duck underneath.

The last steps felt as if she was walking through

thick mud. There was the pavement. There was a police car, its blue lights flashing. There was the sky. A slice of grey London normality. And there was The Fork. Her home.

Only it wasn't.

There was a yawning gap in the row of buildings.

There was a pile of rubble.

CHAPTER TWENTY-THREE

Lydia pulled away from Paul. Until that moment, she hadn't been aware that he was holding onto her, stopping her from approaching the site.

'Wait,' he said. 'There could be more. It's not safe.'

'More what?'

Paul leaned down to speak quietly into her ear. 'There could be another bomb.'

'This wasn't a bomb,' Lydia said, her voice at normal volume.

Paul flinched and looked at the nearest uniform.

She couldn't look away. Her eyes were stinging from whatever was in the air and her heart was squeezing painfully, but she couldn't even blink. 'This is demolition. Look. It's a lovely piece of work. Someone really knew what they were doing.' She couldn't tear her gaze from the exposed wall of the building next door to The Fork. The blackened bricks.

'We need to get out of here,' Paul was tugging on her

arm. 'Unless you want to end up in an interview room for the rest of the week.'

'No,' Lydia said. 'I need to see...' She couldn't finish the sentence. She needed to see if there had been any survivors.

Her desk and laptop. Her home. Her sofa. Her terrace where the birds liked to visit. Those were small losses. Tiny pricks of feeling that would fade as quickly as the sun rising.

'We really can't,' Paul was saying. 'Little Bird. Lydia. We have to go.'

'I need to check. I need to see...'

'You can't,' Paul said. 'I'm sorry, we have to go.'

'What happened? Who could do this?' She knew, though. She knew there was one man who would be able to get a demolition crew to work in the middle of the night, a man who could pay off councillors and planners and police, a man who had the cash and the clout to pull off something like this. Charlie Crow.

'Let's get out of here,' Paul was saying. He still had his arm wrapped around her and Lydia allowed herself to lean against him, just a little. Her whole body felt weak with shock.

Who had been in The Fork? Surely Charlie would have cleared it first? Stupid. She realised she was being stupid. Charlie had planned this to take her out. If she hadn't been detained by Fleet's father, she would have been asleep in the flat when the first explosives went off.

Jason was anchored to The Fork. Lydia could hear his voice, clear in her mind. 'This is my home.' She had to find him. She had to see for herself.

'This way,' Paul was still walking Lydia away from the site. She stopped moving, rooting her feet to the ground so that Paul had to stop, too. 'I've got to go back.'

Before he could answer, a familiar figure appeared in the crowd of onlookers ahead. Fleet pushed his way through until he reached them. Lydia felt a rush of relief and fear. The sunlight signature was tied up in pain and fear and the loss of her powers. She blinked and focused on him, reminding herself that this was Fleet, the man she loved.

'Copper,' Paul said, tightening his arm around Lydia.

She pulled away, feeling self-conscious about how their cosy stance would look to Fleet.

'The Fork has been destroyed,' Lydia said, hoping to distract Fleet from Paul's presence, and to get him up to speed in the shortest time possible. 'The whole building. It's all gone.'

Fleet tore his gaze from Paul Fox and focused on her. 'Anyone hurt?'

'I don't know, we just got here.' Another stab of fear. What if Angel hadn't got out in time? 'I need to find out...'

'I'll help,' Fleet said, stepping past Paul.

If Lydia had any emotion to spare, she might have felt irritation or amusement at the macho posturing between Fox and Fleet, but she didn't have the bandwidth for anything except fear and exhaustion.

'You can get your car back,' she said to Paul. 'Thank you for everything.'

'Yeah, run along,' Fleet said. Which wasn't helpful.

Paul hesitated, as if debating whether this was worth

a fight. Then his shoulders moved with the smallest of shrugs and he turned away, melting back into the crowd without a backward glance.

THE SITE WAS STILL BEING GUARDED BY A COUPLE OF uniforms. There were arc lights set up, presumably to discourage skulking in the shadows and make it easier for the guards to spot anybody trying to get too close to the rubble.

'I need to be closer,' Lydia said quietly. 'And can I use your phone? I left mine at home...' She trailed off, realising that was a phrase she wouldn't be using for a while. She had no home. It was a terrifying pile of rubble and dust.

He gave her his mobile without a word.

Lydia didn't know Angel's number by heart, but she had memorised Aiden's. She called it and waited for him to answer, missing the reassuring presence of her coin in her hand. She kept clenching her fist, expecting to find it there, and its absence was a punch in the gut every time.

'Who this?'

'It's me,' Lydia said. 'Using Fleet's phone.'

'Boss, I've been trying to get you. Where are you?'

'I'm okay,' Lydia said. It was pure habit not to volunteer any other information, but it struck her that it could be a good instinct. She had built up trust with Aiden, but he had been Charlie's right-hand man originally. Perhaps his loyalty to her would disappear now that Charlie was back on the scene.

'Angel's been calling. She said The Fork has been knocked down, but that doesn't make any sense.'

'Is Angel okay?'

'Yeah, she's fine,' Aiden sounded both impatient and upset, as if Lydia were being deliberately obtuse. 'But what do you mean? It's The Fork. Who would dare?'

'Charlie,' Lydia said, closing her eyes.

'No, no, no. That's not right. He's...'

'Don't say locked up. I told you. He killed Daisy and John. He's out and he's cutting a path through the family. Obviously thought he could get me in my sleep.'

'Have you heard anything?'

'No, nothing. Just from Angel. She's freaked, man. You're gonna have to call her.'

'I will. Just hold the fort for the next couple of days. I might need...' She had been about to say 'recovery time' but she stopped herself. She didn't need Aiden to know she wasn't at full strength. She had to be the leader. 'I'll be in touch,' she said, and finished the call.

While she was speaking to Aiden, Fleet had walked to the nearest uniform and struck up a conversation. Lydia watched him do his thing, grateful that he seemed so much more himself than when she had last seen him. After a couple of minutes' chat and a thorough inspection of Fleet's warrant card by the uniformed officer, he turned back and made a 'come on over' gesture with his head.

Her feet didn't want to move. She had been desperate to get closer, to see, but now her feet seemed to be nailed to the ground. 'Come on,' she whispered to herself. 'For Jason.'

The pile of debris was largely grey, covered in thick dust which still choked the air. There were the distinctive London bricks, buried among plaster, wood, concrete and tiles. The side wall which attached to the building next door was largely intact, painted plaster still visible in places. On the ground floor, both Angel's beloved range cooker and the industrial-size fridge hadn't moved. The metal splashback behind the cooker was still attached to the wall and, if you didn't look at the devastation around it, you could almost see Angel stepping over to fry hash browns. The relief that Angel hadn't been in the building, that she was safe at home with her wife, washed over Lydia.

There was an acrid smell and, within a minute of stepping closer to the rubble, the inside of Lydia's nose and mouth was coated with a stinging dust. She took off her shirt and wrapped it around the lower part of her face, tying it behind her head. Picking over the uneven ground, she got as close to the centre of the site as she could. Looking up, where she should have seen the ceiling of the café, knowing that directly above had been her flat and her bedroom and her office with her notebooks and laptop and her Sherlock Holmes mug, she saw only sky. It was bright blue with just a few wispy clouds, but from this vantage point it was filtered through smoke and dust, and looked grey. She stood still and reached out her senses. She knew her power had been taken, but she had still got the hit of Fox from Paul and the sunshine from Fleet. Surely that meant that she would still be able to find Jason's signature. If he was still here.

Jason?

Nothing. No answering voice, no brush of cold air, no glimpse of baggy eighties suit. Nothing. She swallowed. She was not going to cry.

Jason? I'm here. You can come out.

She waited again, each empty second crawling by as she stood on high alert. Clearing her throat, she spoke out loud, no longer caring if the nearby crew heard her. She called his name, first quietly and then more loudly. Finally, she yelled it.

A man in a high-vis jacket shouted at her to clear the area, and she ignored him.

'Jason! I'm here. Hop on. Time to go. Let's go, Jason.'

Lydia didn't know how long she had been shouting, but when Fleet's arms circled her waist and lifted her over debris and away, her throat was raw and her eyes were streaming.

At the edge of the site, Fleet lowered her to the ground, keeping a firm hold as she immediately tried to run back. 'Stop, Lyds. You need to stay off the site. It's not safe. We're being told to leave, we need to—'

Lydia twisted in his grip, trying to free herself. 'No, no, no. I need to find him.'

'We need to clear the area,' a man's voice said.

Lydia didn't see who, didn't look. She was staring at the space where The Fork should be. Looking for a glimpse of Jason. He had to be there. This was his home. Still his home. Maybe there was the psychic imprint of the café and her flat, just as Jason himself was some kind of imprint from the flesh-and-blood man he had been.

'Jason,' she whispered, her throat scratchy and painful. 'Come with me. I won't leave without you.'

Fleet's arms tightened around Lydia as the strength left her muscles. She sagged against him and felt his arms holding her up. 'I'm sorry, Lyds,' Fleet said quietly, pulling her against his chest. 'He's gone.'

CHAPTER TWENTY-FOUR

F leet drove to his flat, but Lydia wasn't able to take anything in. Later, she would barely be able to recall the journey. She was numb with shock. Her laptop was gone. And her phone. That didn't matter, not next to the loss of her home and her friend, but these were the things she could fix on, the things that were bearable to contemplate. She kept up a stream of 'to do' items. Most of her important stuff was stored in the cloud, but there was the nagging feeling that there might have been something on the hard drive. She had wiped her old laptop before giving it to Jason, of course. Jason. Sitting on her sofa cross-legged, the laptop open and his ghostly face bathed in blue light.

'My laptop. My phone.' She said out loud, trying to shake the image of Jason. Trying to get back on track to the manageable losses.

'It's okay, you're insured. You can replace your stuff.'

Lydia didn't have loads of personal items. If you had asked her, she would have said she travelled light, but now she could picture her bookshelves stuffed with the collection she had gathered over the years. All gone. Books could be replaced. It wasn't as they were rare and valuable volumes. Just her paperbacks. Well-loved and re-read. Just her stuff.

'How did you know?' Lydia looked at Fleet's face. His visions. He had seen it. 'Oh, yeah. Stupid question. Sorry.'

'It's okay.'

He was being so gentle with her. So careful.

Lydia stared out the window at the passing buildings and people, not really seeing anything. 'I don't know how it happened. It was a big place. How can it just be gone?'

'Demo crew in the small hours. They used a small amount of explosive, but mainly an excavator and wrecking ball.'

'Who?'

'No one knows.' Fleet kept his eyes on the road. 'Well, no one's talking. Apparently, the permits have all turned up, signed and dated, so it looks legit. The people on the scene were getting orders to stand down once some fencing arrives from a building company.'

'It's my place. I own it. I'm the one who would have had to sign permissions for it to be bulldozed.'

Fleet shrugged. 'Forged. Hacked. I don't know. Whoever did this has a lot of sway with the local council, the planning people and the police.'

'It needs investigating.'

'It will be,' Fleet said. 'But I wouldn't hold your breath for an official indictment. No one was hurt which keeps it low priority, even if there are problems with the paperwork.'

'No one was hurt?' Lydia said, her voice icy.

Fleet glanced at her. 'Sorry. You know what I mean. Nobody official.'

Jason wasn't official in the eyes of the law. Of course he wasn't. But in that moment Lydia felt as if Fleet was speaking for himself. That Jason didn't count in his eyes, either. She curled her hands into fists and wished, more than anything, that she could feel the comforting weight of her coin.

Fleet parked the car outside his flat. 'I'm sorry. About Jason.'

Lydia's eyes filled with tears and she put her hands over her face. It was too much. Too raw.

'You go on up. I'll head to Tesco, get some supplies.'

He didn't have food in the flat because he'd been away. Lydia felt a dull stab of guilt. She wiped her face briskly. 'I haven't asked how you are. You came away early. I'm sorry.'

'I was ready to come home,' he said. 'I missed you.'

'I missed you, too,' Lydia said. She wasn't lying but it felt like she was talking about somebody else. Past Lydia. The woman she had been before Fleet's father had drained her power and Charlie had demolished her home. She couldn't recall how that woman had felt, not really.

'Crisps and coke, yeah?' Fleet said, getting out of the car.

'Can't hurt,' Lydia said, and pushed the door open.

. . .

Fleet was on his phone, a supermarket bag-for-life in his other hand. Lydia had been pacing his flat, trying to produce her coin and failing. She felt guilty about mourning the loss of her power, but even that was more bearable than thinking about Jason.

'Yeah, she's fine,' Fleet said, eyes flicking to Lydia.

'Appreciate it,' he said, before finishing the call and putting his phone on the kitchen counter.

'Sinclair,' he said shortly. 'Wanted me to know there wasn't going to be an investigation.' His lips twisted. 'In her world, I think it counts as being friendly.'

'Because of the permits and all that?'

'I don't know if they are part of her department covering things up. She said it wasn't terrorism and she didn't want it to incite a mass panic, so it was important to make that clear.'

Lydia wondered what classed something as terrorism. She knew who had done this and he most definitely wanted to inspire fear. 'She's fucked up and she's trying to cover it up.'

'Clear it up, yeah. Let's hope the service don't get any more involved. We don't need their attention. Unless you think we need some help...'

'No.' Lydia shook her head.

'I know this isn't the time.' Fleet had been putting groceries away, but now he crossed the room and put his arms around Lydia. 'But I know you saw him. My father.'

Lydia buried her face in Fleet's chest. Partly for comfort and partly because she didn't want him to see her face. 'You saw it?'

'Yeah. A vision. I've been much better. Bee showed me how to keep them from spiralling out of control.' She could feel the vibrations of his voice and she clung to him tightly, eyes closed, listening. Now that it was a moment of calm, she could hear the old certainty in his speech. 'We were doing a ritual. A meditation type thing and it was focused. I think I would have seen it earlier, otherwise.' A little pause. 'I'm sorry. I should have been here sooner.'

Lydia forced herself to look at him. 'It's okay. I'm glad the three sisters helped.'

'I saw you in water. Did you go swimming?'

Lydia swallowed. 'I gave The Collector something worth having. And he left on the midnight tide.'

The sunshine in Fleet's eyes dimmed a little, and Lydia understood. He was terrifying and a threat and he had most likely poisoned the bathing pond, but he was still his father. His flesh and blood.

'What did you give him?'

Lydia couldn't say the words, so instead she stepped back and opened her hands, showing Fleet her empty palms.

He shook his head. 'No.'

She shrugged. 'It's not a big deal.' She was proud of that. Breezy. Strong. Spoiled only by the cracking of her voice.

AFTER TRYING, AND FAILING, TO EAT THE FOOD Fleet had bought and cooked, Lydia had trailed to bed and fallen into a deep sleep. Haunted by nightmares she couldn't recall when she woke with a sore throat, as if she had been screaming. It was still sore from being drowned, she realised. That had happened less than twenty-four hours ago. It just felt like a month.

'You want coffee?' Fleet was getting up, but Lydia felt a weight in her limbs, and moving seemed like far too much effort to contemplate.

'Sure,' she said, when she realised, a few minutes too late, that she hadn't answered him.

An hour later, Lydia was propped up in Fleet's bed, staring blankly at the wall opposite, a full mug of cold coffee on the bedside table.

A large painting, all swirls of blue and black, and not at all restful, was centred above a chest of drawers. Lydia had never really looked at it before, had always been distracted by other matters. Now she looked into it and thought she saw loss. Or that was just what she was feeling and she was projecting that meaning onto it. Maybe if she was happy, she would see the swirls as joyous and free. If she didn't feel so empty, so miserable, she would have asked Fleet. Was that the point of this kind of art? It didn't depict anything clearly so that it could mirror your thoughts and feelings? Make you feel understood by something outside of yourself. But it was a lie. It was paint on canvas. Swirls and swoops of brush-work that couldn't talk or feel or help.

Stop moping. If Jason was here, that's what he would say. Probably followed by 'do you want some pancakes?'. Her eyes were suddenly hot and stinging. She blinked rapidly, trying to stop the tears that were gathering. Took a deep breath and another. Throwing off the covers, she got out of the bed. She had to move, had to find a distraction. This loss, this miserable emptiness, it would pass. She just had to get moving again, get busy. Jason would...

She slapped a hand over her mouth to hide the sob that had ripped from her throat. Her friend. Jason had been her constant companion. He had saved her life. He had been a sounding board and a comfort. He had been funny and kind and a friend. The tears were flowing now. He was her friend. He had been dead and he had been her friend. And now he was truly gone. Truly, utterly, dead. Gone, who knew where? She hoped it was blank nothingness, and not whatever he had feared.

Swiping her face, she straightened up and stared down the painting. All she needed was a change of perspective. Those swirls were full of energy, not paralysing sadness. She would see anger. She would take her revenge. Make those responsible pay. Somebody had destroyed her home. Destroyed Jason's home, killing him in the process. She would not cry. Jason had been dead for years, she would...

Rude.

It was Jason's voice again. So clear in her mind. Hell Hawk. *I'm sorry*, she said silently. *I will make them pay.*

Good.

She had lived with Jason, heard his voice a thousand times. She wondered how long it would stay so clear in her memory. How long it would take to lose every part of him.

You should eat something. You're always cranky when you're hungry.

Something uncurled deep in her being. In the part

235

that wasn't just her mind, the place that could only be her soul, the place that knew it could soar high in the sky, if only it had the wings. It wasn't her; it was an interloper. A passenger.

Lydia sank to the floor, her muscles suddenly unable to hold her up. She didn't dare hope. *Jason?*

Bingo. Let's make pancakes.

CHAPTER TWENTY-FIVE

L ydia knew she didn't have time to rest up. Fleet seemed stronger and steadier than before, but she still tried to get him to return to Bee, to finish his training.

'Absolutely not. And you should be resting.'

'The Collector took my power. Physically I'm fine.'

'You almost drowned,' Fleet pointed out.

'I'll rest when the truce is restated.'

Fleet had left the bedroom to make breakfast.

After Lydia had showered and dressed, she joined him. After a mug of coffee and three slices of toast, she felt almost ready to face the day.

'Let me call Sinclair,' Fleet said. 'Maybe she can provide back-up.'

'Absolutely not.'

'Ah.'

'What did you do?'

At that moment, the intercom buzzed. Lydia looked at Fleet. 'She's here?'

'Sorry,' Fleet said. 'She helped me find my father before. I thought...'

'That's something else I need to thank her for, then.'

'You had a lucky escape.' Sinclair crossed one leg over the other. 'I must say I'm glad.'

Lydia curled her fists so that her nails were digging into her palms. She wanted to feel her coin for comfort, but it wasn't there. Her head was banging with the effort of trying to produce it, an action that had always been as easy as breathing. As easy as clicking her fingers. Now, drained by The River Man, she felt cold and empty. 'No thanks to you.'

'Yes, well,' Sinclair had the good grace to look faintly embarrassed. 'We have mobilised units and distributed his likeness. He isn't going to be able to flee the country.'

Charlie leaving the country wasn't exactly Lydia's prime concern. Him leaving would be a wonderful result.

'Why would he do this?'

'To kill me.'

'There are easier ways to do that, surely.'

'You'd be surprised,' Lydia said, baring her teeth.

'Fair enough.'

'But this was also a message. For the rest of the Family. And the other Families.'

'What does it say?'

'That we are weak. Ripe for destruction.'

Sinclair shook her head. 'I don't see Charlie Crow wanting to give in that easily.'

'Oh, he doesn't,' Lydia said. 'It's a charade. He will be doing something completely different. Maybe he has consolidated an alliance with the Silvers or the Pearls. Maybe he is looking to destroy them all.'

'But why demolish his own place?'

'Because it wasn't his, it was mine. I took it from him and he's like a child. If he can't have it, he doesn't want anyone to have it. Especially me.'

'You think he's that petty?'

Lydia gave her a long look before replying. 'I think he's absolutely fucking nuts. And that was before I helped you guys put him in a cage.'

CHARLIE'S HOUSE WAS IN DENMARK HILL. IT WAS A solid town house with three bedrooms, an exercise studio, open-plan kitchen-diner, a formal dining room, living room and had the original cornicing, fireplaces and solid wood floors. In short, it was worth a fortune, and Lydia was extremely tempted to put it on the market and pocket the cash.

On the other hand, her home was now a pile of rubble. It turned out that both the deeds to The Fork and its insurance were in her name, so money was not going to be an issue for the foreseeable future. And, while she wasn't interested in upholding most of the Family traditions, there was no harm in honouring the past in small ways. As head of the Crow Family, moving into Charlie Crow's house sent a good signal.

She wasn't just looking for a new place to crash, or even a way to assert her leadership of the Crows. She had another reason for claiming Charlie's house as her new home. Now that she walked into the house, she wondered whether it would work. Jason had not been able to leave her body, despite his voice getting louder. He still went quiet for large periods, doing whatever ghosts did when they weren't fully 'there', but the periods when he was conscious were definitely getting longer. If he was haunting her now, instead of The Fork, that was a temporary solution at best. Jason had said in the past that he didn't want to live on once she was dead, but Lydia wanted to give him the option. And, in all honesty, she didn't relish the prospect of carrying Jason with her on a permanent basis.

But was it even possible for him to anchor to a new environment? That was the question. That he had managed to hang on long enough to jump into Lydia had to be a good sign, but she didn't know if she was asking for the impossible. Spirits haunted specific places or, as in the case of the button she had found at Churchill's bunker, a significant object. It could be that they could anchor to people, too, and that Jason was now linked to her, but Lydia hoped that if she explained Charlie's significance to Jason, that knowledge might be enough to produce a strong emotional response and link him to Charlie's old home instead of the place he died. Of course, Jason had always wanted to stay in the dark on the exact details of his demise, in case it was the puzzle that was somehow keeping him here. The unfinished business that people assumed kept some people's spirits trapped in this world, rather than letting them go on to the great beyond. Whatever that was. This was a gamble that might release Jason completely, might open a door to the next stage that they couldn't shut.

'You ready?' Lydia spoke out loud.

Not really.

'You were murdered. You know that, right?'

A pause. Lydia moved to Charlie's living room with its imposing fireplace and fine furniture. The row of candles on the mantlepiece were asking to be lit. There should be a sense of occasion, she decided, using the long matches which were tucked in a basket of logs. She carried the chunkiest of the candles, shielding the flame with one hand, to the low table in the middle of the seating. Kneeling beside the table, she stared into the flame, willing Jason to do the same, if he could. 'Charlie Crow was commissioned by Alejandro Silver to kill you.' She paused, listening for Jason's response. There was silence from that part of her, the part she imagined as a small compartment, which helped her to feel less weird about having another soul hitching a ride. The silence was listening, though, she was pretty sure. 'The hit was planned for your wedding day, to give Amy the maximum opportunity to change her mind. If she had jilted you, you would be alive. And so would she.'

Lydia felt a rolling sensation, like an animal was moving in her guts. It was the sort of sensation that was usually followed by projectile vomiting and she hoped that psychic vomit would be easier to clean up. Charlie's carpet was a pale silver grey.

She kept going. Pale carpet or not, this had to be said. 'The hit was a favour for Alejandro Silver. The Silver Family had other ideas about Amy's future. And her political value. Ideas that didn't go along with her marrying a non-Family no-name.' Lydia was being deliberately blunt. Having protected Jason from the unpleasant truth for so long, now she needed to use it to hurt him. Now she had to be harsh. She could feel his distress and she ignored it in order to keep on speaking her cruel litany. 'Having carried out his task, Charlie Crow found himself in the kitchen with Amy. She was distraught, fighting him. She knew something had happened and, being no fool, had a pretty good idea of where to lay the blame. Not even she realised where the order had come from and that has to be some comfort. That she died not knowing how completely she had been betrayed. But there was a struggle and Charlie pushed her. Amy fell and hit her head. She died of a haemorrhage right there on the floor of the café that Charlie Crow owned, one of many venues for his business dealings. But this house, this is where he came back to afterward, where he washed his hands and poured himself a whisky and sat in this room and watched the flames of his fire and felt nothing but pride for a job well done.'

People will tell you that anger is pointless, that it only hurts the person who feels it, that it corrodes. They are wrong. Anger is fuel. Anger is fire. And rage can bring you back from the dead.

Jason's spirit roared from Lydia, doubling her over with its violence. She tasted bile, but managed to keep the contents of her stomach where it belonged.

Jason's form, shimmering and translucent but clearly recognisable, was standing in the coffee table, surrounded by the flames from the candles. His face was a picture of rage and grief, and together with the flickering candlelight and the vibrating edges of his body, he looked like a demonic presence summoned from hell. Lydia straightened up, holding her stomach gingerly. She took deep breaths until she was sure the danger of vomiting had truly passed. 'I'm sorry,' she said.

Jason flickered, but his expression was calming. He looked around. 'I'm here?'

'Yes.'

'Was it true? Or were you just trying to make me angry?'

'It's all true. I'm so sorry.'

Jason flickered more violently and then seemed to stabilise a little.

'Where is he?'

'I'm going to kill him,' Lydia said.

'Good.'

And Jason disappeared.

CHAPTER TWENTY-SIX

Lydia didn't want to tell Aiden what had happened, but he noticed that her tattoos no longer moved and it was only a matter of time before he realised she could no longer produce her coin. Lydia had been in the habit of flipping her coin over her knuckles or spinning it in the air and she cursed her past self for being so blatant.

He took it well, although that could have been a sign that he was getting better at hiding his feelings. Aiden had grown up a lot over the past year, that was for certain. She couldn't always tell what he was thinking, though, and that was an uncomfortable feeling.

'We have to cancel,' Aiden said.

'No,' Lydia pressed the button on the coffee maker. The sun was streaming through the French windows onto Charlie's kitchen table - her kitchen table – which was covered in piles of paperwork, unopened post, and several empty cola cans.

'The whole plan relied on you being able to remote

control anyone in the room. Without that... It's too dangerous. There will be shooters. And God only knows what Rafferty can do. You said he was the new Pearl King.'

'I'm not cancelling. And he might not be... that's just a possibility. Even if he has absorbed all of the King's power, doesn't mean he's got the same personality or desires. So far, he's all about his art and his acting.'

'Yeah, but from what you told me, the original King was all about a good party. I'm not feeling particularly reassured.'

Lydia didn't disagree with Aiden's assessment, but she didn't see an alternative. If she cancelled at this point, it would be an admission of defeat. At the very least, it would show weakness and feathers knew what that would inspire. 'We don't have any other option.'

'What about Charlie? Shouldn't we focus on finding him?'

'No,' Lydia said. Perhaps now that Charlie had demolished The Fork, his need for revenge would be satiated and he would move on with his life. Maybe even leave London? 'I'm hoping he will lie low for a bit, let us get the truce back in place. Then we can face whatever he brings with the strength of the four Families.'

'Don't know if lying low is Charlie's style.' Aiden leaned back in his chair. He finished another can of coke and crushed the can.

'You in need of caffeine?'

'Late night,' Aiden said. 'Everyone wanted a word and they wanted to have it separately.'

'Makes them feel important,' Lydia said.

'Something like that,' Aiden said, and yawned so widely she could see his molars.

'You get some rest. I can check the venue.'

'Thanks, Boss,' Aiden said and he got up to leave.

Lydia listened to the front door close and the quiet of the empty house. Something had seemed off about Aiden. Something underneath his words. Maybe she had picked up on his micro-expressions. Or maybe she was being paranoid.

LYDIA'S PHONE RANG. IT WAS FLEET AND SHE KNEW she had to answer. His voice was tense but she still felt a burst of sunlight. It reminded her of Jack Fleet and she felt her stomach lurch.

'Don't do it.'

'Do what?'

'Whatever you are about to do. Please, don't do it.'

'What did you see?'

'Where are you?'

Lydia looked up at the façade of the hotel she had just left. 'Mayfair.'

'I'll meet you. We need to talk.'

'I can come to you,' Lydia argued. 'You don't need to schlep across the river.'

'Promise me you'll leave Mayfair now. Get away from buildings. Don't go inside anywhere.'

Lydia looked around at the grand houses and hotels, the shops and white stuccoed terraces. She was in central London. Avoiding buildings was going to be tricky.

'Green Park,' Fleet said. He sounded breathless and his voice was uneven. Lydia realised that he was running. 'Or St James's. Go there and stay in the open. Don't go underground.'

'Another demolition?' Lydia didn't use the word 'bomb' in case she was overheard and caused a panic. Last thing she needed was to be arrested on the street under suspicion of terrorism.

But Fleet had already gone.

Just as she wasn't going to say the word 'bomb' out loud, she wasn't going to run through the pedestrians in this part of the city. This wasn't her part of town and she was likely to get tackled by an over-zealous uniformed officer or private guard. This was the place for tourists to see royalty and the red-suited palace guards with their ridiculous hats, and the home of old institutions like the Royal Academy of Arts, the Royal Air Force Club and foreign embassies. It was, in short, covered by the police, the guards, the secret service, and more CCTV than Heathrow.

Ever-aware of the imposing buildings that lined the wide streets and the crowds of day-trippers and tourists, thronging the streets on this blazingly hot summer's day, Lydia dodged as quickly as she could toward the nearest green space. Down Piccadilly, past the Ritz and across the road. The sign for the Green Park underground station was a temptation. She wanted to get on the tube and head back to Camberwell, to home, as fast as possible, but Fleet was on his way. And he had seen something serious. She had to trust his advice and stay out in the open.

Taking the nearest entrance to Green Park, Lydia passed a fountain. People were crowded around it, filling their water bottles from the arcs of water falling from the bronze spouts. The fountain contained a female figure with a sleek hunting dog, surrounded by giant gilded flowers. It didn't seem to be an official water fountain and Lydia wondered how safe it was to drink the water.

A mounted officer and two armed police watched the crowds, reminding Lydia again of what a prime location for mayhem this was. She hoped Fleet was wrong. She hoped she wasn't bringing danger to these people by joining their sunny park afternoon.

The path from the entrance opened into a large grassy area bordered by enormous mature trees, their spreading branches providing shade. The grass was packed with people lying on towels and reclining in wooden deck chairs.

Lydia wanted to stay in sight of the entrance to catch Fleet arriving, so she made a compromise calculation of distance from buildings. She couldn't see how to stay away from the park-lovers. This wasn't the heath, and it was the hottest day of the year so far - there simply wasn't the space.

Ten minutes later, Fleet walked into the park. He was wearing a shirt and trousers, so she knew he had come straight from work. His face was sheened with sweat and he had rolled the sleeves of his shirt to the elbows.

'Thank God,' he said as soon as he saw Lydia.

'What did you see?' Lydia could feel every muscle in her body, tensed and ready for action. She was on her tiptoes, still feeling the urge to fly, even with the dead-weight feeling pinning her to the ground.

'We need to get away from people,' Fleet was looking around wildly.

'We're as far from buildings as we're going to get in this part of London.'

'I know.' He flashed her a panicked look. 'I might be overreacting. I don't know. But I don't want to be overheard.'

They walked across the grass, weaving between the lounging bodies. The air smelled of sun cream and flowers and, since this was still London, exhaust fumes and the faintest tang of rotting food.

They joined one of the wide paths and headed away from the station entrance and the deckchair-hire cabin, into the dappled shade from the tree-lined walk. Lydia was waiting for Fleet to elaborate, but there were still lots of people on the path and he was gripping her hand firmly, tension flowing through his muscles. After they passed the fourth elegant iron gas lamp, Lydia remarked to Fleet that you could tell they were in a Royal Park. Just a casual remark, something to defuse the awkward atmosphere.

He flashed a tense smile and they fell back into silence.

A slab of polished granite with three circular holes was being investigated thoroughly by a golden retriever and its owner. It wasn't until they got closer that Lydia realised it was a water fountain. Her encounter with Fleet's father would never let her unsee the vitality and importance of water in the city ever again.

'Here,' Fleet veered from the path and into the deeper shade of an ancient sycamore. Lydia would never be a nature-lover, but she was aggressively pale-skinned and appreciated the leafy canopy on this fiercely hot day.

Pulling her t-shirt away from her sweaty neck, she flopped onto the grass next to the tree trunk. 'Does this park have a lake by any chance, because I would like to get in it.'

Fleet was walking around the perimeter of the tree and he didn't answer.

When he returned, he didn't sit. He looked ready to run or fight and it almost hurt to look directly at him, as if he really was the sun.

'You need to calm down,' Lydia said. 'Take some deep breaths. What techniques did Bee show you for keeping control?'

Fleet started to answer, but Lydia couldn't focus on his words. 'Whatever it is, do it now.' Lydia had one hand shading her eyes, but it wasn't enough. She could feel the light, like a sharp object was being driven forcefully into her brain.

After a minute in which Lydia studied the grass and listened to Fleet taking noisy breaths and mumbling something to himself that might have been a mantra or a spell, she saw the green of the grass dim, as if a light had been switched off. Then she looked up at Fleet and, thank feathers, it no longer hurt.

'Why do you see it?' Fleet gestured to his face.

'Your light? The River Man took my power, but I'm still the head of the Crow Family, my father is still

Henry Crow. I might not be strong, but I've always seen powers and that isn't something he could take. I think that's with me till death. Like my impeccable fashion sense.'

Fleet didn't smile.

'That stuff, whatever you were doing, that worked. You're feeling better?'

He nodded and sat down on the grass next to her. Magpies flew in and out of the trees around them.

'I've never seen so many in London before,' Fleet said. 'Or maybe I just wasn't paying attention.'

'They've been following me,' Lydia said. 'I saw them at Daisy and John's before I found them, too. And they were waiting for me at Charlie's. And one of them brought me this.'

Lydia had been carrying the small key in her pocket. Although it had connected her to The River Man, she still felt affectionate toward it. Maybe because the magpie had delivered it and maybe because she felt it had helped her to prevent a cholera outbreak in London.

He touched the key with one finger. 'Why does it feel like that?'

'Like what?' Lydia wondered if he was getting a burst of sunshine from the key the same way she did. Maybe his blood connection to The River Man gave him the ability to sense his signature. Or the training with Bee had sharpened his power in different ways.

'Real.' Fleet shook his head. 'It feels very... Real. Solid. I can't explain it.'

'I get sunshine.'

He frowned. 'Like you get from me?'

Lydia didn't know if he would hate this connection between himself and The River Man, but she wasn't going to lie. 'Yes.'

Fleet absorbed this. 'I know I shouldn't want anything to do with him. After what he did to you, now that I know what he is.'

'It's not that simple though, is it? He's still your father.'

'Only in name,' Fleet said, a spark of his old fire igniting. He shook his head. 'I wanted to find him so badly...' He looked her in the eye. 'I wanted to go with him. I can't explain why.'

'It's okay.'

'I'm glad he's gone,' Fleet said. It still sounded as if he was trying to convince himself, saying the words he ought to say.

'It's okay,' she said again.

'Would it work as an anchor? For when you're having dreams or you aren't sure if it's a vision or reality?'

'Maybe.' Fleet had hardly stopped staring at the key. His eyes were hungry.

'Have it,' Lydia said, passing it to him.

'What about you?'

'I don't need it,' Lydia said. And it was true. What she needed was her coin back. She clenched her fist reflexively. Still empty.

Fleet turned the key in his fingers for a few moments and then put it into the hip pocket of his jeans. 'It feels like part of him. Is that stupid?'

'No,' Lydia said. 'And we take parts of our ancestors.

Doesn't mean we replicate them entirely or repeat their behaviour.'

He nodded, understanding her meaning. 'You've been thinking about that a lot, I'm going to guess.'

Lydia smiled. 'Maybe a bit.'

The magpies were swooping in and out of the branches, occasionally landing near to Lydia, as if checking in.

'Are they corvids?'

'Yeah, part of the crow family,' Lydia said. 'All crows are scavengers, but magpies especially so. They're fearless, too. They're smaller than crows, but will front up any kind of pest or predator, even when they're completely screwed. Very handy in a fight.'

'Really? With the bright colours I thought they were more ornamental.'

'Lower your voice if you're going to talk shit about them,' Lydia said as a magpie swooped dangerously low to Fleet's head.

'I take it back,' he said quickly. 'Sorry. No offence intended.'

'You were in danger,' Fleet said. 'There was glass on the floor, shouting, blood. It was definitely inside and it was dark.'

'And that's why you don't want me to go into a building? Or use the tube?' Lydia wanted to tell him that his plan wasn't very sustainable. She wasn't going to live in a tent for the rest of her life.

'It was real,' Fleet said. 'Bee showed me the difference and I know it now. I'm not in full control, I'm still seeing multiple futures, but I can feel when one has crystallised.'

'Crystallised?'

'That's what Bee called it.'

'Okay. So this was like that? Crystallised?'

'No,' Fleet said reluctantly. 'It was still changing and I saw a few different things. They were all bad, though.'

'Do you have a time scale? For when things are likely to happen?'

'You believe me?'

'Of course,' Lydia said, confused by the question.

'Even though I didn't know where I was or what I was doing last week? You believe me just like that?'

'I never stopped trusting you,' Lydia said truthfully. 'I believed you then and I believe you now.' She also wasn't sure she believed in fate. Fleet had admitted that his vision wasn't set. Crystallised, as Bee called it. But the truth was, even if it was, Lydia wasn't sure she would let that influence her plans. As far as she was concerned, even a crystallised vision could change. She wasn't going to share that, though. Fleet would think she wasn't taking him seriously, and that wasn't the case. She took the warning seriously, but she wasn't going to give into it, either. She would take the information and work out how she could use it, but she wouldn't assume it was immutable. She was Lydia Crow, head of the Crow Family, and fate could suck it.

'They're so dark,' Fleet said. 'The visions. I wish I could see more clearly. Tell you something helpful. I don't know if I'm just not controlled enough or whether it's in such a state of flux that I can't get a proper look.'

Lydia touched his arm. 'It's okay.'

'That's it? You have to call it off. You were able to protect yourself before. You could control people. It was still dangerous, but doable. Now it's suicide. You can't trust Maria or Rafferty. Or Paul. I know you think you can, but you can't. He's the head of the Fox Family first and I'm worried you can't see that.'

Lydia felt a coolness sweep over her skin, despite the warmth of the day. 'Maria and Rafferty don't know that I've lost my power. It'll be all right. And you said yourself, it's not a fixed vision. It's in my hands.'

'I could feel it. In my bones and my heart and my gut. You were in serious danger.'

Hell Hawk. Lydia's skin was prickling and she felt sick. But she couldn't let Fleet stop her. 'Did you see me in this vision?'

'No,' he shook his head. 'But I know you were there.'

'How?'

'The place was filled with feathers.'

Lydia opened her mouth to say that didn't sound too bad.

'I knew you were going to die,' Fleet said. He looked her dead in the eye. 'In every vision, I felt the loss of you.'

Lydia's mouth was dry. 'I'll be extra careful, then.'

CHAPTER TWENTY-SEVEN

Beckenham in the June sunshine was a pleasant sight. All the years she had spent dreaming of escaping suburbia, of forging an exciting life with the Crows of Camberwell or in another country, far from London and its familiarity, and now she could truly see what her parents had seen in this modest street with its plane trees and wide pavements, the neighbours tending to colourful front gardens, and the sounds of children playing.

Her mother had told her they were in the garden, so she lifted the latch on the side gate and walked down the side of the house. Henry and Susan Crow were sitting on their small patio, surrounded by pots overflowing with blooming flowers and the sound of bees buzzing in the buddleia. Henry was in a striped deckchair, his head tilted to the sun, while her mother sat at a small round table, pouring Pimm's into glasses. A large glass bowl of hulled strawberries sat next to a small chopping board and knife and a massive punnet.

'Got enough there?' Lydia asked, after kissing her parents.

'Gordon, you remember Gordon? Your father's friend from school.'

Lydia nodded automatically, although she didn't.

'He went to a pick your own. Got carried away. Had to carry three of these things back on the train with him, daft beggar.'

Lydia picked up a strawberry and popped it into her mouth. She took the glass her mother offered and faced her parents. It was best to get this over with. 'Have you got any trips planned?'

Susan put down her knife. 'Should we?'

'Maybe.'

Lydia had been avoiding spending too much time with Henry Crow, in case her ability to power-up those with innate talent caused him to get ill, again. He had spent his life denying and subduing his Crow power, and it meant her battery effect had a deleterious effect on his mental health. She supposed that was something that she wouldn't need to worry about as much anymore. A bright side to having had her power harvested by The River Man. If only she didn't feel like she had lost a couple of limbs and half her soul, maybe she could feel more grateful. 'You know about Daisy and John?'

Henry nodded seriously. Susan's lips were a tight line.

'I've got more bad news, I'm afraid. Four Family members were killed. A Fox, Pearl, Silver and Crow. All at once. There was stuff left on the bodies, stuff that was clearly meant to implicate the Crow Family in the slaughter.'

'Oh my God,' her mother's hand was at her mouth. 'Who died?'

Lydia listed the names and watched her mother's face relax.

'Did you know Garth?'

'No,' Susan said. 'Henry?'

'Eric's boy. He was a PE teacher in Lambeth. Not connected.' Henry might have been officially out of the Family business, but that didn't mean he wasn't close to the Crows. They were still his kin and he kept up to date with their lives.

'I'm sorry,' Lydia said.

'Who did this?'

'I don't know.' She was pretty certain it had been Charlie, but she didn't want to frighten her parents. Or accuse her father's baby brother without solid proof.

'You need to find a killer. Fast.'

Lydia noticed he didn't say 'the killer'. Henry was telling her that she needed to apply blame and that speed was more important than accuracy. She didn't disagree.

'There are rumblings about a stranger in town. He would do.'

'If you can sell it.'

Susan was looking between them. 'I hope you're not talking about setting somebody up? Find the real murderer or, better yet, get out of London and let the police do their job.'

'That would be ideal, I know,' Lydia said, hoping to

placate her. Problem was, if the real murderer was Charlie, as she suspected, naming him would cause more problems than it would solve.

'Don't treat me like a child,' her mother said sharply. 'I know what you're discussing and I'm telling you it's a bad idea. Putting aside the morals, it's a bad solution. The truth will come out eventually. You can find the true culprit. You're a good investigator. Don't give up without even trying.'

Lydia wanted to tell her mother that she hadn't meant that, that she had been intending to investigate and that the promise of a fit-up job had been a backstop. Or a way to halt further carnage. But she wasn't sure how much her mother knew or how much she wanted to know. Henry Crow had left the Family business in order to keep his wife and daughter out of it all and Lydia knew she had to respect his wishes. 'I won't. I promise.'

'Good,' her mother said. 'Now drink your Pimm's. It's bloody summer.'

AFTER A GLASS FILLED WITH FRUIT AND CUCUMBER, which Lydia was definitely counting as her 'salad portion' for the day, Lydia laid out the case for her parents getting out of London for a few weeks.

'We're in Beckenham,' Henry said, as if that was the same as saying 'we're on the moon'.

'Charlie is angry,' Lydia said. She shot a look at her mother, trying to gauge her reaction. 'With me. And he's no longer contained. Who knows what he will do to vent that anger?'

Henry shook his head gently. 'He's my brother. I'm not running.'

'Mum?'

Susan placed her empty glass onto the table and plucked a strawberry from the bowl. 'Don't worry about us.'

Later, when her mum had gone into the house to make Lydia a sandwich 'for the road', Lydia lowered her voice and leaned toward her father. 'It's really bad. I'm working on a solution, but I can't protect you at the same time.'

Henry shook his head, cutting his eyes to the back door to check that Susan was still out of earshot. 'You're strong. You can handle it.'

Much as Lydia appreciated the vote of confidence, Henry didn't have the whole story. She didn't know whether to tell him about the River Man taking her power or not. On one hand, she wanted him scared enough to leave London, but on the other, she didn't know if he might try harder to stop the meeting. Instead, she focused on Charlie. 'He's killed people. Crows. I don't know what he is going to do next, if he still wants to lead the Family or whether he wants to burn the lot of us to the ground.'

'They won't accept him. Not now.'

Henry sounded sure and his certainty was comforting. But it didn't solve all of Lydia's immediate problems. 'He has got to pay for what he's done. I know he's family, but he's so far out of order... But I need to reinstate the truce first. Before anybody else gets hurt.'

'You are the head of the Crows. By birth and by right. Don't back down.'

Lydia looked at Henry and saw an expression she recognised from Uncle Charlie. And the mirror. Obstinance. A touch of arrogance. And a cold, calculating certainty.

'Did you hear about The Fork?'

Henry nodded. 'I haven't told your mum yet.'

'I figured.' If Susan Crow had known that her daughter's home had been demolished with the intent to kill her in her sleep, she would have sent out a search party and then probably barricaded her in her childhood bedroom for safekeeping.

'It was Charlie,' Lydia said, watching her father carefully.

His expression hardened and he didn't speak for a moment. When he did, he seemed determined to look for the positive. Lydia wasn't sure if he was trying to convince her or himself.

'It's for the best. You've been trying to kick-start a new era for the Family. Best way to do that is to break down the old.'

Lydia opened her mouth to say something else, but Henry shot her a warning look.

'Thanks, love,' Henry said, looking over Lydia's shoulder.

She rose from her seat as her mum approached with a foil-wrapped package.

'Cheese and ham on wholemeal. I don't know if you're getting enough fibre and it's very important, you know. I read a really interesting article on the gut microbiome and apparently fibre is key.'

'Thank you,' Lydia accepted the food, hugged her mum, and waved goodbye to her dad. He raised a hand in a closed fist. Not a gesture of 'see you soon' but one of strength and 'go and kick some arse'.

Next on her list was Emma and her family. Tom was at work and Emma was in Kelsey Park with the kids. Picking up two coffees and two milkshakes, she made her way to the children's play area.

Emma was sitting on a bench while Maisie and Archie clamoured over the brightly coloured equipment. She was wearing enormous sunglasses and looked tired, grabbing the coffee like a drowning woman.

'What's on fire?'

'What do you mean?' Lydia sat next to Emma and put the cardboard tray with the cups on the floor at her feet.

'You're here,' Emma said, gesturing to the playground, the park, Beckenham.

'Nothing,' Lydia said, trying not to feel defensive. Emma wasn't being unfair, just accurate.

'Sorry,' Emma said, after taking a sip of her coffee. She tipped her head back and took a deep breath. 'I'm tired. It's making me cranky.'

'Cranky?' Lydia smiled. 'If I was looking after two small children full-time, I'd be certifiable.'

'They're really good kids,' Emma said. 'I'm really lucky.'

'I know that. But it still looks like bloody hard work. And if you're not getting enough sleep...'

Emma let out a short laugh that was more like a bark. 'Sorry,' she covered her mouth with one hand. 'I can't remember the last time I slept for more than a couple of hours in a row. Maisie needs to be lifted at midnight or she wets the bed, Archie has night terrors, and Maisie wakes up before five, ready to start her day. I put her into our bed and she usually dozes off again, but not always. And that's on a good week, when none of us is ill. Did I tell you Maisie had tonsillitis again last week? That's the third time this year.'

Lydia waited until Emma ran down. She had nothing useful to say, so just murmured her sympathy and sipped her coffee.

'Anyway. That's me.' Emma pulled a face. 'Knackered, but fine. How about you?'

'Oh, you know.' Lydia didn't want to bring her worries to Emma, didn't want to add to her friend's stress. And there was more to it than that. She didn't want to pollute the homeliness of Emma's world with her own. It felt wrong.

At that moment, Archie ran up. 'Auntie Lydia!'

Emma bent down to retrieve the tray of drinks just in time. Archie threw himself into Lydia and she hugged him back, a hit of green grass and coconut sunscreen filling her nose.

'What's your favourite dinosaur?'

Lydia glanced at Emma, who smiled serenely.

'T-Rex?'

Archie accepted this unoriginal answer with good

grace. 'I like Ankylosaurus. It's one of the biggest armoured dinosaurs and it has a tail club.'

'Is that right?' Lydia said. 'You know birds are descended from dinosaurs.'

Archie gave her a withering look. 'Theropods.'

'Not that one,' Emma suddenly shouted. 'Maisie. Come here.'

Archie didn't so much as glance away. His desire to explain to Lydia the finer points of bird evolution took precedence. Eventually she distracted him with a milkshake while Emma jumped up and retrieved Maisie from the lower reaches of a climbing frame meant for bigger kids.

Once Maisie was sitting on the bench next to her brother, slurping her milkshake through the straw, Emma turned to Lydia. 'Sorry. You were going to tell me what's up with you.'

'There's some friction between the families.'

'Uh-oh,' Emma said, cutting her eyes to the kids.

'Yeah,' Lydia said. 'Nothing I can't handle, but along with Fleet... I don't know.'

'What's going on with Fleet? You two okay?'

'I think so.'

'That's not good enough,' Emma said, kneeling down to adjust the Velcro strap on Maisie's rainbow-coloured shoe. She looked up at Lydia. 'You've got to talk to him.'

'I know.'

'No. I mean really talk to him.' Emma straightened up. 'I'm sorry I'm being blunt, but I'm too tired to filter this. I want you and Fleet to make it, and if you keep

going the way you are, you won't. Long-term relation-
ships are-'

'Hard. I know that,' Lydia said. She really didn't
want 'the talk'. She knew they involved compromise and
communication. She wasn't a complete idiot.

'Well, sort of,' Emma paused, hand on hip. 'I don't
know if I would say "hard". More, kind of, relentless.'

'Oh, sign me up,' Lydia said, sarcasm breaking
through.

Emma bumped her hip against Lydia's. 'I mean it
doesn't stop. And everything compounds. You don't talk
properly now, when things are easy, you'll find you just
can't talk properly when you really need to.'

Lydia didn't think things were particularly easy, but
she took Emma's point.

After their milkshake break, Emma herded the kids
away from the play area with the promise of feeding the
ducks.

As Archie aimed precise pieces of lettuce at his
favourite ducks and Maisie threw indiscriminate joyful
handfuls of seed, Lydia steeled herself to tackle her true
reason for visiting. 'There is something I need to tell
you.'

Emma didn't take her eyes off Maisie and Archie,
but Lydia knew she was listening intently.

'Charlie's out. The secret service let him go. Or he
escaped. It's hard to know the truth with that lot.'

Emma swore very quietly.

'He wants to run the family again,' Lydia said,
hoping that was true. 'He's not going to do anything too
terrible. He wants the family on side.' She could taste

feathers in her mouth. 'He's not a crazed killer like Maddie. You're not in any danger. But I wanted you to know. Just to stay aware, you know. And let me know if you see anything out of the ordinary, anything that worries you. I will sort it.'

Emma nodded. She glanced at Lydia. 'What about you?'

'I'm expecting him, so that helps. And I beat him before. I'm even stronger now, so I'm not worried.' The feathers were almost choking.

'That's good,' Emma said, sounding unconvinced. 'We are due a visit to the in-laws, though, and there's an inset day next week. Maybe we should take the kids out of school and go to Cornwall for a week.'

Lydia forced a casual shrug. 'If you're due a visit anyway...'

Emma nodded her understanding. 'Right-oh.'

Lydia got ready to leave, hugging Emma tightly.

She called the kids to say goodbye, but Lydia stopped her. 'Leave them, they're happy.'

'No,' Emma said. 'They need to say it.'

'Okay,' Lydia leaned down for quick, slightly sticky hugs and mumbled goodbyes from Maisie and Archie.

'Can we go back to the swings?' Archie asked immediately after.

'Maybe,' Emma said. 'Let me finish talking to Auntie Lydia and we'll discuss it.'

Archie immediately turned his attention back to the duck pond.

Lydia frowned at Emma's serious face. 'Everything's fine. I'll see you when you get back from Cornwall.'

'I heard about the café,' Emma said. 'This is Becken-ham, not Mars.'

'Right. Uh... I was going to tell you, but I didn't want you to worry.' And she had been preoccupied. As usual.

Emma's mouth twisted. 'Luckily, your dad called to let me know you weren't hurt.'

That floored her. Her dad had thought to call her best friend when she hadn't. 'I didn't think about it being in the news... Shit. I'm really sorry.'

Emma pushed her sunglasses onto the top of her head and fixed Lydia with a disappointed look that could rival Susan Crow. 'You're right, everything is going to be fine. And when I get back from Cornwall, we're going to have a big talk about keeping me in the dark. You're my best friend. I want to know these things.'

Feathers. 'I'm sorry. You're right. I'm a terrible friend...'

Emma shook her head. 'That's not what I'm saying. I just don't want to find out that you lost your home from my local Facebook group.'

'Fair enough.'

CHAPTER TWENTY-EIGHT

F leet still wasn't convinced by the plan, Lydia could tell, but he had stopped trying to talk her out of it. Now she just needed to convince him to stay away. 'I need you to do this.'

'No,' Fleet was shaking his head. 'I can get a tactical team in position around the hotel.'

'No, they will be seen. The truce will fail there and then.'

'They won't,' Fleet said, but he was losing conviction. He knew as well as she did that the four Families of London had not survived without being able to sniff out police presence. And even if they didn't, the moment the tactical team made contact, it would break the terms of the meeting and nullify any progress made between the leaders.

'I need you to watch my parents. They won't leave Beckenham, so I want you to watch the house. Protect them.' Lydia didn't add 'if this goes badly' because she knew that Fleet knew already. If she died and Charlie lived, he would come for Henry and Susan next.

'I can have a team watch your parents. I can be with you.'

'You can't,' Lydia said. 'I can't have you near. You're police. You're not Family. It breaks the terms, just the same as a tactical team. I can't risk it.'

Fleet closed his eyes. He was probably counting to ten. When he opened them, a muscle was jumping in his jaw, but he nodded.

'You'll protect my parents?'

'Yes. Of course.'

Lydia took his hands in hers and squeezed. 'Thank you.'

THE PEARL COURT, THE ORIGINAL FAMILY, HAD been more powerful than the other three put together. If Rafferty Hill decided to reform the court above ground and explore their new freedom, it could spell the end of the Crows, Foxes and Silvers. The Silvers were richer in both money and political power than ever before, and the Foxes were back in the city now that Lydia had removed the threat of The River Man. Lydia didn't know what they wanted, only that she might have insulted Paul Fox one time too many. If she didn't shift the relationship between the Crows and the Foxes onto a truce-mandated professional footing, and fast, feathers-knew what might happen. Lydia knew in her bones that she had no choice but to call a meeting and to broker a new truce. No matter how little she wanted to sit in a room with Maria Silver.

She had chosen the venue and sent out invitations. Black-edged calling cards and polite language. A formal meeting that could not be mistaken for something else.

Neutral territory was vital, as well as privacy. A private dining room in a historic and renowned European café-restaurant in Mayfair was the perfect choice. It had an impressive marble interior with arched windows, interior columns, and dark polished wood panelling. The private dining room had its own staircase to the left of the main restaurant and was filled with white flower arrangements and candlelight.

As hosts, Lydia and Aiden had arrived first. Which also gave her the chance to choose their seats. The flames were reflected in the glass light fittings and the wide expanse of the impressive windows. It was after eleven and the sky a navy London-dark, the lights of Piccadilly holding back the night.

The kitchen was officially closed and Lydia had seen the last diners in the restaurant finishing coffees and liqueurs, picking at the remains of cheese plates or making to leave. Unofficially, however, the chef and her team were ready and waiting for whatever the Families might require. Lydia had a bottle of Ardbeg single malt open, with a carafe of water and cut-glass tumblers.

She was just contemplating getting stuck into the whisky when she tasted the bright tang of Silver. Maria, a handsome bald man with a briefcase, and two large men stuffed into suits were standing in the open door. The large men came in first and looked around before Maria followed. 'Family only,' Lydia said, holding up a hand. 'Your friends can wait in the main restaurant. I have a cheeseboard and wine waiting, but they should feel free to order from the menu if they want anything else.'

A nervous-looking waiter appeared behind Maria. 'Your table is this way.'

Maria's blood-red lips curved into a smile, but her eyes stayed flat. 'I assume this rule extends to everybody?'

'Naturally,' Lydia said. 'Aiden is Family, as you know.'

'This is my cousin Sal,' Maria indicated the man with the briefcase.

Lydia could feel the waves of Silver coming from the man, so she nodded. 'The hired muscle has to wait outside, though.'

Once Maria had waved away her goons and chosen a seat, she allowed Aiden to pour her a whisky. Sal declined a seat and took up position standing behind Maria, holding tight to the briefcase as if worried someone was going to try to steal it.

'Water?' Aiden picked up the carafe.

'Just a splash.' Maria leaned forward to accept the glass from Aiden, her fingers brushing his and her eyes flicking up to meet his slightly glazed gaze.

A deep blush covered his face, and Maria smiled properly for the first time. 'Sweet boy.'

Lydia stopped herself from rolling her eyes with a supreme effort of diplomacy.

Maria looked around. 'Where is your tame copper? Trouble in paradise?'

Lydia was saved from responding immediately by the arrival of Paul and Jasper Fox. Paul was wearing his usual uniform of black t-shirt and jeans, and it was hard to tell if Lydia's physical reaction was due to the Fox Family magnetism or the undeniably pleasant set of his shoulders.

Jasper probably thought he was keeping a stony, impenetrable expression, but Lydia could practically feel the sneer. A moment later, his lips curled, and the sneer escaped. Lydia smiled brightly at him. 'Glad you could both make it. Drink?'

'No,' Paul said, taking the seat opposite. His brother remained standing, crossing his hands in front of his body like a nightclub bouncer.

'Where are the Pearls?'

'I have no idea.'

Maria stood up. 'I thought this was all the Families. We can hardly re-state the nineteen forty-three truce without all parties present.'

'We should give them more time,' Aiden said. 'They're not very late.'

'Yet,' Maria said. 'And it's a discourtesy that doesn't bode well.'

Lydia looked to Aiden, who moved to the door of the room, returning with a nervous-looking waitress carrying champagne in an ice bucket.

'That's a bit premature,' Paul said.

Lydia ignored him, motioning to the waitress to open

the bottle. Once glasses were filled, Lydia picked up a flute. 'I propose a toast.'

Paul reached across the table and took the whisky bottle. He poured a splash into a tumbler and raised it instead. Bloody Foxes.

'What are we drinking to? The Pearls aren't here. You are wasting my time.'

'You all felt the recent threat. There were rumours of a stranger,' Lydia nodded to Paul. 'You spoke to me about it.'

Maria raised an eyebrow in Paul's direction and he kept his face perfectly blank, not giving anything away. Fine, then, Lydia thought. Be like that. 'I am raising a glass in celebration of the Crows' success. The Crow Family moved that threat out of London. You're welcome.' She drank.

Paul and Maria looked unimpressed, but they both drank.

Maria, not to be outdone, held out her glass for another toast. 'The Silver Family has grown its client base by twenty per cent in this financial year. And,' she looked around the table, 'we now represent key members of the government.'

It seemed Maria was continuing Alejandro's plans for political power, but in a different way. Lydia could feel the bright tang of silver and she drained her glass of champagne to try to clear it.

'The Foxes are here,' Paul said. 'The Foxes have always been here.' He raised his whisky glass.

Lydia splashed some more champagne into her glass and raised it.

'Now the niceties are over,' Maria said, 'it's time for business.' She looked around in an exaggerated manner. 'Except we're still a Family short. I told you, the truce needs all four Families. Otherwise it's meaningless. I think we have to accept that its time is over. We can make different agreements. I have drawn up some papers,' Maria clicked her fingers and her cousin stepped forward, opening the briefcase.

Paul shoved to his feet. 'I will not be signing anything, Silver.'

'Don't worry, dog, you can just make an "x" or a paw print.'

Paul's lips curled back, revealing his teeth, and his brother stepped up to the second Silver.

Just when Lydia thought the whole endeavour would fall apart, she caught a hit of Pearl magic. Seconds later, a server opened the door and Rafferty Hill walked through it. It was a mark of the amount of Family power in the room that the whole crowd didn't get up and start fawning over Rafferty the moment he took his place at the table. Maria showed she wasn't completely immune by licking her lips, while Jasper's jaw hung open for a full twenty seconds before he got a hold of himself and closed his mouth.

Rafferty looked around. 'Have I missed anything?'

'No,' Maria said, leaning toward Rafferty and gifting that half of the table with a view of her smooth and inviting cleavage. She was wearing her signature red in a low-cut, fitted jacket over a black pencil skirt. On her feet were Manolo Blahnik stilettos, so that when she sat back down and crossed one leg over the other, it looked like the prelude to a fight.

'We were just about to toast,' Maria said, as if they hadn't just been doing exactly that. 'You're right on time.'

Rafferty accepted a glass of champagne, smiling as if his photo was being taken. In the candlelight, he looked inhumanly beautiful. Lydia just hoped that the Pearl King energy really was all being channelled into art and performance, and that Rafferty hadn't inherited anything else. She had just picked up her glass, when Maria said: 'Silly me, we're still waiting for someone.'

Lydia tasted feathers in the back of her throat as the door swung open. There was Charlie, looking sharp in a black suit with a black shirt and tie. He might have spent months in an underground cage, but he still filled the doorway. It was more than his physicality, it was the sheer energy of his presence.

Aiden's arms were around Lydia and, for a moment, she thought he was covering her, protecting her. She was going to tell him that he had her arms pinned, her brain assuming that was an accident in his haste and inexperience, but then she realised the truth. Aiden was restraining her deliberately. He had one arm pinned and the other bent up behind her back. It wasn't to the point of serious pain. Not yet.

'That's my place, I believe,' Charlie said, nodding to Aiden.

Aiden bundled Lydia away from the table and Charlie stepped in front of her seat at the head of the table. She felt a hollow open in her chest and her stomach dropped.

In the next moment, Charlie had a gun in his hand and it was pointed at Lydia, covering her almost casually. He smiled his shark smile. 'I know your tricks, Lyds, and I won't hesitate.'

Aiden's body was solid against Lydia and his grip was firm. She didn't twist or test it. She needed to conserve her energy. Besides, it was Aiden. She didn't want to fight him. When she had arranged this meeting, she had expected to be able to control every single body in the room with the power of her mind. She hadn't considered weapons or back-up. Now, as she watched helplessly, she knew that had been a mistake. Tingling in her fingers and toes as this realisation set in.

'It's good to see you all.' Charlie looked around the room, pinning every person with his gaze. 'I believe we were about to toast. How about "to old friends"?'

'Who are you?' Rafferty was regarding Charlie as if he was a waiter who had stepped out of line.

'I'm Charlie Crow. Head of the Crow Family. Who the fuck are you?'

Rafferty tilted his head back, managing to look down his nose at Charlie. Something which made Lydia feel a grudging respect, even as she winced inside. 'Head of the Pearl Family.'

'Is that a fact?' Charlie glanced at Lydia for confirmation. Old habits die hard. 'Got a name, Pearlie?'

'This is Rafferty Hill,' Aiden said quickly, trying to smooth feathers. 'And he is the de facto head of the Pearl Family, although he is attending tonight as a formality.'

'All right, then,' Charlie said.

'Maria Silver,' Maria said, standing up. 'Head of the Silver Family.' She smiled devastatingly at Charlie. 'As you well know.'

'Paul Fox,' Paul said. 'Head of the Fox Family. Are we doing this, then?'

Maria, Aiden, and Charlie nodded. Rafferty shrugged.

'So,' Paul continued. He hadn't looked in Lydia's direction. He hadn't looked at her since arriving, in fact. 'To restore the truce, we need to balance the wrongs that have been done. We need to forgive and move on, put all the uncertainty and trouble behind us. There can be no on-going tension, no further repercussions. We settle it all tonight.'

'I called this meeting,' Lydia said, hoping her voice didn't betray her fear. 'I am the head of the Crow Family.'

'Doesn't look like it,' Maria said, her red-painted lips curved in delight.

Charlie looked at her, then. 'If you're the head of the Crows, you should step up to me right now. If this is your perch,' he indicated his position at the table, 'take it back.'

Everybody waited in silence. Perhaps waiting for Lydia to struggle. Or to break free, to strike Charlie. They were waiting for a fight.

Lydia couldn't even produce her coin. She tried, wanting its reassuring presence in the palm of her hand, but even that was too much effort. She felt the skin of her tattooed arms stinging, as if the ink was no longer happy, inscribed on the pale imitation of a powerful Crow she had become. She was drained. Weak. And in big trouble.

'This is not the way,' she tried. 'I am the head of the Family. I have been working to maintain the truce. Why would you accept Charlie in my place? He is unstable. A murderer.'

'That's a big accusation,' Charlie said. 'With no proof.' He turned to face the table, the people assembled around it. This was a show for them, not a conversation. 'You killed your own cousin, Maddie. You killed her parents, Daisy and John. And you slaughtered Garth Crow, Luis Silver, Becca Pearl and Nate Fox. You left a hoard on top of their dead bodies.'

'Why would I do that?' Lydia was trying to keep the note of desperation from her voice, but she wasn't sure she was succeeding. 'I didn't kill them, but if I did, why would I implicate my own family?'

Charlie didn't look at her, he was still playing to his audience. 'To break the truce, of course. You want chaos. It's the only way you could hold onto leadership. A position you have proved you are not fit for. Ask Aiden. Ask Daisy and John. Oh,' he paused, smiling nastily. 'That's right. You can't. You killed them.'

Lydia knew there was no point denying it again. Either the people in the room believed her or they believed Charlie. Or, more likely, it didn't matter either way. The people in the room had to decide whether they wanted to reinstate the truce and, if so, who they thought was the better Crow to work with in the future. If it was personality, Lydia flattered herself that at least one person in the room would vote for her. However, it wasn't personal. It was power. Always had been, always would be. And at this moment, she was a broken bird, held in place by her subordinate.

She had just saved them all. Saved London. Countless lives and livelihoods. But she couldn't tell them. They had no reason to believe her. And it would lead to questions of 'how'. And that wasn't something she wanted to broadcast. Not that her weakness could be kept a secret. The most powerful members of the Families were in this room, right now, watching her do nothing. She was finished.

Maria watched Lydia for a moment longer. It seemed she knew enough about Lydia to wonder why she wasn't doing anything, and Lydia knew she was waiting for her to act. When Lydia didn't break free of Aiden's grip or do anything except look away, unable to meet Maria's challenging stare, she unbuttoned her fitted jacket and removed a small handgun from an inside pocket.

Charlie was carrying a Glock. Lydia recognised it as it was the weapon given to the armed officers of the Met. Maria's gun was smaller and that was all Lydia could say about it. Except that she still wasn't a fan of firearms. A memory of the first gun she had ever seen in real life flashed into her mind. The hit man, when she first arrived at The Fork. She remembered the way her insides had gone liquid with fear when he had pointed a gun at her chest. This time was easier. It was true, you truly could get used to anything. She had been prepared to die many times. Now she just felt rage. Rage at Charlie. And the Families.

Paul Fox didn't have a gun. For a moment Lydia thought that was some kind of reprieve. That she would die at Maria and Charlie's hands, only, not the man she had once been intimate with, the man she had come to consider a friend. It was short-lived, though, as Paul turned to his brother to retrieve something from inside his coat. A crossbow. An actual crossbow, just in a compact size. He fitted the bolt and raised it to point at Lydia's heart. It didn't look any less lethal for its modest dimensions.

At that moment something banged on the window. A bird flying into the pane. Its wings briefly visible, spread against the glass.

'Better hurry up,' Maria said, her eyes flicking to the smear that was left on the glass.

Another bird slammed against the glass, Lydia caught a glimpse of the black shape before it fell. A corvid, she would've laid money. Her heart squeezed in sympathy and she hoped the bird was stunned, not seriously hurt.

'I shouldn't be here for this,' Rafferty said. 'This is...'

'Don't move,' Paul said. 'This is part of the truce. We are acting together. That is the agreement.'

'I don't want to hurt anyone,' Rafferty said. He jumped as another bird hit the window. The bravado had gone from his voice and Lydia noted that she was still capable of feeling relief. Maybe Rafferty Hill really was going to be a benign presence. A little bit of good news to ease her parting from this world. Which was bollocks, of course. She didn't want to die. There was nothing easy about it, nothing comforting.

'Are we doing this?' Paul was asking the room, but his gaze was on Lydia. He looked her dead in the eye and the crossbow did not waver.

'It's necessary,' Charlie said. His voice was so filled with satisfaction that it made Lydia want to throw up. Two birds hit the glass in quick succession and the glass shuddered in its frame.

'Rafferty,' Maria said. 'Do you agree?'

'Yes. Okay. Fine. Whatever.'

The candles flickered in the room as another bird slammed against the window. And another and another. A group hit at once, creating an almighty thump, louder than anything so far. A crack appeared in the glass.

'Holy shit.' Rafferty was staring past the table at the window. 'What the...?'

At the same time, Maria fired. The gunshot was so loud.

Paul let the crossbow bolt fly.

CHAPTER TWENTY-NINE

Lydia's ears were ringing. She couldn't move. For a moment, she thought she couldn't see, but then her vision cleared. The room was filled with feathers and the candles had been blown out by the rush of night air. Shadows were shifting and merging, breaking apart and re-joining. A crazy swooping dance that wasn't meant to be contained inside a room. One of the wall lamps exploded as a bird dived into it, further dimming the light in the room.

Wings were beating, but it wasn't Lydia's power. That had gone. This was real crows, ravens and magpies. Flying around the room in panicked circles. The ringing was being replaced by the sound of harsh caws. A sign that her hearing was coming back.

Talons dug into her shoulder and she cried out in shocked pain. Which meant, she realised, that she couldn't have been shot. If she was carrying a gunshot wound, the lesser pain of talons wouldn't have registered.

Aiden was still holding her tightly, stopping her from moving, but in that instant she felt him release her. He was yelling, now, she realised. She turned to see him spin away, beating his arms above his head to fend off the crow.

Lydia wanted to tell him to stand still, to let the bird perch. That it wouldn't hurt him now that he was no longer restraining her. But when she opened her mouth, she started coughing instead.

The hotel had been well paid. The staff had agreed not to enter the room once the meeting had begun, not for any reason. Lydia had explained that there would be noise. Possibly loud noise. Sudden loud noise. The manager had nodded, merely noting that he couldn't guarantee that passers-by or neighbouring properties might be moved to telephone the authorities, in the event of sudden, loud sounds. He had been very discreet, the model of the grand old age of hotels, married with the pragmatism of the modern age. A fat stack of notes, neatly wrapped and delivered with his lunchtime super-food salad the next day, had sealed the deal.

However, he was right. Lydia didn't know how long it would be before the police were alerted that gunshots had been heard. And there was the immediate question of where that gun was now. The bird shifted on her shoulder, digging fresh wounds into her flesh. Lydia gritted her teeth against the pain and managed to say 'thank you', instead of yelping. Politeness was important. And the crows had come. She couldn't summon their wings, couldn't feel their hearts beating, couldn't send coins spinning or reach out to pluck at the strings which controlled people, but the crows had come instead. 'Thank you,' she said, again, louder this time. Then she had to cough again as a small feather flew into the back of her throat.

'Jesus, Jesus. Oh my God.' It was Rafferty, chanting a string of profanity in a shocked litany, as he crouched on the floor. His arms were over his bowed head.

'Be quiet, Rafferty,' Maria's voice sounded, clear and confident. 'Is he dead?'

The birds were settling onto the furniture and the floor. As the air cleared, the tableau was revealed. Maria was still pointing her gun, but Paul had lowered his crossbow. A moment later he handed it to his brother, who spirited it away back inside his coat.

'I'll check,' Paul said. To Maria he said, 'don't shoot me'.

Lydia moved cautiously to the side until Charlie came into view. He was on the floor, arms spread wide. The entry wound on his chest was dark and wet, the red hardly visible against his black shirt. The pool spreading from underneath his body was glistening obscenely, caught in the soft light from the remaining wall lamps.

Lydia reached into her pocket for her inspection torch and stepped toward the body. Paul glanced at her, then held his hand out for the light. 'I can do it,' he said.

For a moment, Lydia felt anger. Then she realised he was trying to save her from having to examine the body of her uncle. She shook her head. 'I need to see.'

Paul held her gaze for a moment and then nodded. He reached down and placed his fingers on Charlie's neck, feeling for a pulse.

Lydia switched on the focused beam of light and, starting at Charlie's feet, she worked her way systematically. It wasn't necessary. The two wounds were pretty obvious, but procedure and order were calming, so she leaned into them.

The chest wound was no longer bleeding freely. The pool of blood on the floor was bright red when Lydia focused the beam of torchlight onto it, but the spreading had slowed. It would form a skin soon, and the colour would alter as the blood oxidised.

Lydia pressed her tongue against the roof of her mouth, an old trick to stop herself feeling sick or tearful at crime scenes, and then let the torch light move to Charlie's face. A crossbow bolt had entered his right eye. It was a mess. She let the beam of light move away and swallowed hard to keep the contents of her stomach where it belonged.

Turning back to Maria, she offered the torch. 'Your turn.'

'No thank you,' Maria said, as if Lydia had offered her a handful of crap or a cheap white wine.

'You need to see for yourself,' Paul said. He had finished checking for a pulse and moved aside.

Maria blew out an irritated sigh, but she walked over to Charlie's body and stared down at his dead face. She clicked her fingers and Sal joined her. When he didn't read her mind, she snapped. 'I can't crouch in this skirt.'

He dipped down obediently and pressed his fingers to Charlie's neck.

After a minute, he straightened up. Shaking his head at Maria.

'Good, then,' Maria spun around. As if only just noticing the hundreds of bright black eyes, she looked around at the crows that were shifting from foot to foot and tilting their heads. 'There's no need to be so dramatic, Lydia.'

Lydia opened her mouth to explain that it wasn't her doing and then shut it. Instead, she smiled in what she hoped was an enigmatic way.

Rafferty had got to his feet and was edging toward the door. He stopped moving as Maria, Paul and Lydia all swivelled to face him. 'It's over, right?' His voice was thin and wheedling. 'We have the truce. I'm all done. Right?'

'You are the head of the Pearl Family,' Maria said. 'Any trouble and we will come to you.'

Rafferty went even paler. 'This is just ceremonial. Just a performance.' He looked pleadingly at Lydia. 'You said...'

She gestured to the dead man on the floor. 'I think we're past that, don't you think?'

Rafferty swallowed hard.

'Don't look so worried,' Paul said. 'There's not going to be any trouble.'

'Indeed,' Maria said. 'We all have our own business to manage. Speaking of which, I have an early start tomorrow...'

Lydia took one last look at Charlie. It wasn't him anymore, that was clear. His soul had flown. The windows were open so it wouldn't remain trapped. The crows were here to mark his passing, and so were his successor and second-in-command. It had been quick. As endings went, he could not have expected better.

'We should go,' Aiden said quietly. As if conjured by his words, the sound of sirens began. They were faint, but getting louder.

Maria took Rafferty's arm and smiled devastatingly into his perfect face. 'Come on, beautiful. You can walk me out.'

Paul nodded to Lydia. There wasn't anything to say and she was grateful that he didn't try.

'Boss?'

Lydia took one last look at Charlie's body. Then she bowed low to the assembled birds. 'Thank you.' The crow on her shoulder didn't seem to be in any hurry to move, so she walked out of the glass-and-feather-filled room, through the wisely empty entrance hall and down the steps of the hotel into the Mayfair night. Once outside, the crow dipped its head close, touching her cheek with its beak and then flew up to join its friends. Lydia had thought the room had been filled with the crows of London, but now she realised her mistake. Every wall, roofline, lintel and balustrade was lined with corvids.

They waited in silence as Lydia and Aiden walked away from the hotel, patient and watchful. Hundreds of hearts beating, hundreds of bright eyes. 'I didn't know you could do that,' Aiden whispered, his voice reverential.

'Neither did I,' Lydia said, smiling at him.

CHAPTER THIRTY

There were advantages to taking Charlie's house, Lydia had to admit. The front door wasn't just nice to look at, it had top-of-the-line locks and was reinforced with a steel drop bar. There was a full CCTV system which covered the house and surrounding area, and the training room with its sprung floor and equipment. Not to mention, every room had a full complement of high-end furniture and fittings.

Lydia stood in the middle of the wooden floor of the training room, watching her reflection in the wall-size mirror as she went through a workout. One with lots of punching and kicking. The hollowed-out feeling had passed and she felt almost normal, but she still needed the burn in her muscles and lungs to quiet her mind for more than a few seconds.

She still couldn't produce her coin, but the corvids were keeping an eye on her. Usually several of them, and it gave her a similar feeling of comfort. She had the sash windows open and a line of jackdaws were perched on the window sill, pecking at the seed Lydia had put out for them.

Her phone buzzed as she went through her cool-down stretches. It was Aiden, keeping her up to date in the slightly panicked manner of a man who had recently seen his old boss being shot through the eye with a cross-bow. Lydia hadn't known that Charlie was going to turn up to the meeting and she appreciated Aiden's quick wits in the moment. By pretending to side with Charlie against Lydia, he had helped to lull the man into a false sense of security. Still, it had left a slight strain between them that would take time to ease.

Another missed call caught her eye. Paul Fox. She called him back, pacing the studio and ignoring the jack-daws that were now flying around the room with her.

'Little Bird,' Paul said. 'You need my help again, already?'

'You called me,' Lydia said, hating the defensive tone in her voice. One day she would master the stupid Fox magic that clouded her mind when she spoke to Paul Fox, but apparently it was not today.

'Just wanted to let you know that the Foxes are back in Whitechapel. After I dragged Jasper back for the meeting, the others followed.'

'Why didn't you leave with them?' A question that had been at the back of Lydia's mind.

'Violence increased in Whitechapel when the Foxes left, and I didn't want it to get any worse for my commu-nity. I'm the head of the Family,' he said. 'Turns out you were right about that. I am the leader and I realised I had to act like it.'

Well, that was disarmingly honest. Lydia decided to reciprocate. 'Thank you for restating the truce. With me, I mean. For a moment there I wasn't sure...'

'There's something you should know, before you decide I'm not so bad after all,' Paul spoke quickly, mercifully heading her off. 'I got Maria onside by telling her about your little power-issue. She decided she would prefer a powerless Crow in the leadership role, rather than Charlie.'

Feathers. Maria was going to be interesting to handle now she had that bit of information. Still. It had worked and she hadn't shot Lydia, so she couldn't really be too angry with Paul. 'Why are you warning me?'

'We signed a truce, innit,' Paul said. 'Thought I'd kick things off in the spirit of goodwill and all that.'

'And because you want me distracted by what Maria might try next?'

'Couldn't say,' Paul said. 'Bye for now, Little Bird. Stay lucky.'

AFTER SHOWERING AND CHANGING, LYDIA MET Fleet downstairs for a late breakfast. He was back at work and seemed fully in control. He was still plagued by visions and premonitions, but now that he could easily tell what was vision and what was reality, he seemed to have adjusted. And Lydia wasn't going to lie, having a fit copper boyfriend who also had the powers of precognition wasn't a bad thing.

Walking into the kitchen, Fleet said her second favourite phrase in the whole world. 'I made coffee.'

She accepted the mug and sat at the table. The doors were open and a jackdaw, a crow and a magpie were lined up just outside. She nodded 'hello' and felt an answering itch in the skin of her arm. She focused on her tattoos. Had she just seen movement? Or was it hope making her eyes play tricks?

The magpie opened its beak and let out a call that sounded suspiciously like 'idiot'.

'Sorry?' She looked around, realising that Fleet had been speaking to her.

'It's okay. I was just... It's nothing.' He sat down with his own cup of coffee. 'I was just thinking about my dad.'

Lydia wasn't sure what to say. She scratched at her arm. 'You miss him?'

'No. But thinking about him has made me think about my mum. I miss her.'

'Of course,' Lydia reached out and covered Fleet's hand with her own.

'It's okay,' he said. 'Just weird thinking about all that. I always had her and Auntie, and that was enough. Now I know it was more than enough.' He flashed a sunshine smile. 'I suppose I should be grateful they met, though, or I wouldn't exist.'

'So he named you Fleet because he met your mother in London?'

'That's a delicate way of putting it, but yes. I've probably got a half-sibling in Paris called Seine and one in Vienna called Danube.'

'An Isar in Munich,' Jason's faint voice whispered next to Lydia's ear, making her jump.

'Jason?' Fleet asked.

292

'Yes.' Lydia narrowed her eyes at the wispy figure of the ghost, barely discernible in the bright daylight. 'He is having way too much fun.'

Jason spread his translucent arms in a 'what else can I do in this state?' gesture.

Despite her words, Jason didn't look like he was having fun. His expression was the same misery-soaked desperation she had seen ever since his home had gone kaboom, and the outline of his body was watery and indistinct. He was also popping in and out of existence more than ever before, so she spoke quickly before he disappeared. 'You can sit quietly and concentrate on getting powered up. I miss my hot chocolate.' Was it her imagination or did Jason become a little steadier, a little more solid with those words? If she reminded him of who he was, maybe it would help him get stronger.

She got up from the table and began opening cupboards in Charlie's kitchen. 'There is a lot of space, here. I could get all kinds of stuff. Pans. Pots. Knives.' Her cooking knowledge quickly ran out of things to tempt Jason. Fleet's forehead creased for a moment, and then he caught on. 'Waffle iron,' he said. 'Skillet.'

Jason was floating in the corner, his head tilted on one side. He wasn't moving like an alive person, wasn't solid like an alive person, but he was clearly listening.

'Popcorn maker,' Lydia continued, remembering Emma's machine.

'KitchenAid,' Jason said, his thin voice carrying.

Lydia paused, her hand on the cupboard handle. 'What's a KitchenAid?'

'Fancy mixer,' Fleet said. 'Pricey, but supposed to be

293

really good if you're into that sort of thing.'

Lydia narrowed her eyes at Jason. 'How pricey?'

Was that a smile?

Using Fleet's iPad, Lydia ordered two new laptops. One for her and one for Jason. She would think about the KitchenAid, but had to keep the faith that one day Jason would be powered up enough to use a laptop again. She curled her fingers to her palm in the instinctive gesture of holding her coin. The absence slamming into her all over again. If she was still a battery, perhaps she would power herself up, given enough time. And once she was strong enough, her coin might come back.

Fleet was sipping his coffee. 'Is he still here?'

'Jason?' Lydia looked around the room. 'No. He keeps disappearing. He's not strong enough to stay.'

'He'll get better,' Fleet said with total certainty.

Lydia decided not to ask if he had seen it in a vision or whether he was just being reassuring. She didn't want to know if it was the latter. 'I hope so. I can't lose anyone else.'

'I'm not going anywhere, I told you.'

'You were going to, though.' Lydia could see Fleet on that canal path, the resolution in his eyes. She couldn't just push it down and not think about it. She needed to air it out, to communicate, Feathers help her, her *feelings*.

'To protect you,' Fleet said, his forehead creasing. 'Yes.'

'Not just to protect me, you wanted to spend time

with that man.' She wouldn't call the River Man his father or use any of his names if she could avoid it.

'I wanted to find out more about who I am. And find a way to stay in control so that I didn't end up in an institution, but the end goal was always to be with you. And you know that means being strong enough.'

'I don't need protecting.' Lydia's face ached with the effort of not grinding her teeth.

'I know that. But I don't want you to have to protect me, either. Not all the time, anyway. It's fine for us to help each other, to look out for each other, but only when it's an equal partnership. I won't be a complete liability. I can't do it.'

Lydia couldn't argue. She knew he was right. She loved him and liked – and hoped – to think that meant in sickness and in health, but if she had been thrust into the role of caretaker, it would have changed their relationship. Not ended it, not stoppered her love for Fleet, but definitely changed their dynamic. And she couldn't blame Fleet for not wanting that to happen. Feathers, *she* didn't want it to happen. Not yet.

'We're good?' Fleet ducked his head to look into her eyes.

Almost. 'We have to make these decisions together,' Lydia tapped his chest lightly with one finger. 'What I can't handle, what can't keep happening, is you shutting me out. You tried to do this – find him, go with him – without me.'

Fleet's jaw was tense. 'I knew you would stop me.'

'And I've done the same to you. Shut you out, not been open in the moment. I know that...'

'I don't need you to change. I'm not asking—'

'But I think I have to,' Lydia broke in. 'I think I should. We're both used to operating on our own, and I'm not trying to clip anybody's wings, but big stuff like this? We have to talk to each other. Decide stuff together.'

Fleet was quiet, but his expression was no longer tense.

'Deal?'

Fleet nodded, a golden smile pulling at his lips. 'Are you ready for this?'

Lydia responded by pulling him closer for a kiss. Her Fleet. Her partner. She might not have her full Crow power, but she seemed to be powering up Jason slowly but surely. Her battery effect was still working and even if she never regained the abilities that she had stolen from Maddie, she would be okay. She had a super-smart copper boyfriend with precognition on her side and, besides, being able to take over people's bodies was creepy. Super-helpful, but creepy.

The sound of the front door opening made them break apart. Seconds later, Aiden appeared, a bag of pastries in one hand and a cardboard tray with tall coffees in the other. 'I wasn't sure if you had stocked the kitchen yet.'

'Good call,' Lydia said, reaching for the tray. As she did, she felt the slightest tingle in her hand, and she heard the faintest sound of wings beating. Then, the sight of Aiden reminded her of something she hadn't got around to telling Fleet. 'Aiden's got some good news. He's engaged.'

'Congratulations,' Fleet said. He surprised them both by shaking Aiden's hand and then pulling him into one of those quick 'bro hugs'. 'When's the big day?'

'November,' Aiden said, slightly pink in the cheeks. 'We don't want to wait.'

There was a ten-month waiting list, but Lydia had called the register office and made it happen. 'I'm not getting dressed up,' Lydia said. 'Fair warning.'

Fleet's eyes glazed over and his body stilled. Lydia recognised the signs of one of his visions and she curled her hand into a fist, reflexively searching for her coin. Was he seeing something bad? Something about Aiden's wedding day. At that moment, Jason reappeared in the corner. He was looking worried, too, and wished she could hug him or pat his arm. Some kind of contact to remind him that he wasn't alone, that he was here, and that she wouldn't let anything else terrible happen to him.

Fleet blinked, shifted his weight.

'What did you see?'

He smiled at her. 'Nothing bad.'

'Are you sure?' Lydia felt hope flutter in her chest. Maybe it was all over. Maybe she could just be for a while, enjoy Fleet and her Family and her friends and get back to Crow Investigations.

He slipped an arm around her shoulder. 'Clear skies ahead.'

THE END

THANK YOU FOR READING!

I hope you enjoyed reading about Lydia Crow and her family as much as I enjoyed writing about them!

I am busy working on my next book. If you would like to be notified when it's published (as well as take part in giveaways and receive exclusive free content), you can sign up for my FREE readers' club online:

geni.us/Thanks

If you could spare the time, I would really appreciate a review on the retailer of your choice.

Reviews make a huge difference to the visibility of the book, which make it more likely that I will reach more readers and be able to keep on writing. Thank you!

ACKNOWLEDGMENTS

The Magpie Key is the eighth Crow Investigations book – a fact that is miraculous to me. I still remember the moment the idea for the series dropped into my mind, and the electric feeling of excitement that came with it. I am so deeply grateful to the readers who have enthusiastically supported the series and enabled me to spend so much time in the world. Thank you!

As ever, it takes a team to produce a book. My sincere thanks to all involved, especially my lovely husband, Dave, Kerry Barrett, and Stuart Bache.

Thank you to my wonderful advance readers: Matthew Dashper-Hughes, Beth Farrar, David Wood, Karen Heenan, Caroline Nicklin, Judy Grivas, Paula Searle and Jenni Gudgeon.

Thank you to my brilliant friends and family for the good times, love and support. And for understanding when I disappear into my manuscript and lose track of time/reality.

And to my writing pals (especially Clodagh, Hannah, Julia, LK, and Sally) for all of the above, plus Zoom calls and writing sprints, practical help, sage advice, cheer-leading, conference fun, and more.

And a shout-out to August for telling me about Norwegian brown cheese!

Finally, massive thanks and much love to Holly and James. You are always so supportive and encouraging, and I appreciate your willingness (and ability!) to talk through plot problems and discuss publishing quandaries. You (and your dad!) are my most favourite people in the whole world and I love you more than words can ever express.

ABOUT THE AUTHOR

Sarah Painter is a bestselling author of magical fiction, including the Crow Investigations urban fantasy mystery series. She also writes non-fiction for introvert authors.

Having always been a reader and a daydreamer, she now puts those skills to good use with a strict daily schedule of faffing, thinking, reading, napping and writing. She also spends a portion of every day thanking her lucky stars for her good fortune. Sarah lives in rural Scotland, drinks too much tea, and is the proud owner of a writing shed.

Head to the website below to sign-up to the Sarah Painter readers' club. It's absolutely free and you'll get book release news, giveaways and exclusive FREE stuff!

www.sarah-painter.com

 facebook.com/SarahPainterBooks
 twitter.com/SarahRPainter
instagram.com/SarahPainterBooks

LOVE URBAN FANTASY?

Discover Sarah Painter's standalone
Edinburgh-set urban fantasy
THE LOST GIRLS

A 'dark and twisty' supernatural thriller.

Around the world girls are being hunted...

Rose must solve the puzzle of her impossible life – before it's
too late.

Made in the USA
Las Vegas, NV
22 October 2022

57986592R00182